Barry Unsworth has written ten novels, four of which are published by Phoenix in paperback (*The Hide*, *The Partnership*, *The Greeks have a Word for It* and *The Big Day*). His latest novel, *Sacred Hunger*, was winner of the 1992 Booker Prize and has been described by Tom Sutcliffe in the *Independent on Sunday* as a 'narrative in the grand style, morally ambitious and energetic in pursuit of its large goals . . . it exerts a very considerable grip.' Barry Unsworth is a Fellow of the Royal Society of Literature. He lives in Italy.

The Greeks have a Word for It

BARRY UNSWORTH

PHŒNIX

A PHOENIX PAPERBACK

First published in Great Britain in 1967
by Hutchinson & Co Ltd

This paperback edition published in 1993 by
Orion Books Limited, Orion House,
5 Upper St Martin's Lane, London WC2H 9EA

ISBN 1 85799 002 1

Photoset by Deltatype Ltd, Ellesmere Port, Cheshire

Printed and bound in Great Britain by
The Guernsey Press, Guernsey, C.I.

British cataloguing in Publishing Data available

1

At eleven o'clock in the morning the steamer entered the bay and made for the harbour. Kennedy and most of the other passengers came up on deck, to lean on the rail, acknowledge the fact of their arrival. Mrs Pouris didn't though, and Kennedy thought this strange, after her patriotic sentiments during the voyage. Perhaps she had left her packing too late. One of the sailors began to attach strings of bunting to the mast, the Greek colours, white and blue. This was Piraeus then, the port of Athens; the usual installations, a few chimneys with industrial plumage, tawny hills beyond. He was glad to have arrived.

As the ship slowed, the breeze dropped and Kennedy felt a prickle of sweat on his upper lip. He had always been prone to sweating, and here, though still only the end of April, it was very hot. The sky, a pure blue earlier, had whitened and glazed in mid-morning and the water of the bay was the colour of oiled gun-metal. The ship's wake was healed almost before foam showed.

'Soon be on the old *terra firma* again,' Kennedy remarked to several of the nearer passengers, none of whom quite looked at him and none of whom replied. He took out a handkerchief, somewhat discoloured, and wiped his mouth and palms. Then he walked forward a few paces, keeping near the rail, and stopped again on the covered part of the deck. From here he looked round once more for Mrs Pouris. Where could she have got to? She had not yet given him her address in Athens.

They were coming into their moorings now, to the accompaniment of much shouting from officers and crew, who continued to lack, in this final phase, the air of quiet authority which might, for an Englishman at least, have induced confidence in their management; contriving to look expert without suggesting competence.

The sense of this, not however highly articulated, since most of Kennedy's feelings remained in the undergrowth, the sense of potential disaster on the boat, had given him a certain pleasure throughout the voyage.

A small unshaven man in a white yachting cap jumped up and down on the quay, shouting. He made a gesture as if to ward the ship off. Kennedy had not had time to learn any Greek, but he observed with delight that a mistake had been made. There was a grinding noise as the ship scraped against the wall of the dock. That would cost more than his fare to put right, anyway. All breakdowns and untoward events, hitches in procedure, pleased him in some degree, aligning his personal irresponsibility with that of the cosmos.

A small group of people stood waiting below the ship, unmoving, gazing upwards, waiting to unload on the arriving voyagers their accumulated emotions. Around them swarmed those who might make money, conceivably: touts, pimps, porters, taxi-drivers, the agents for hotels. The gang-plank was down and the first passengers had begun to leave the ship. One or other group, the still or the mobile, would claim most of these, for whom landing meant a renewal of love or obligation. But not for him, Kennedy knew, with a faint, involuntary contempt. No one was going to profit in either way from his arrival. . . . Suddenly he saw Mrs Pouris getting off the ship. 'Mrs Pouris!' he called, smiling at her back, then again more loudly, 'Mrs Pouris!' But she did not look round, seemed in fact to accelerate. Surely she must have heard?

He glanced down over the side. The engines had stopped, water slapped against the hulk. He counted five oranges bobbing about in the dirty water. 'Will passengers please leave the ship now,' said a voice on the loudspeaker. Turning his head, Kennedy saw the pale young Greek standing alone at the rail quite close. He had been alone throughout the voyage. Kennedy had seen him occasionally in the bar and on deck, always alone, but had not spoken to him, concentrated as he had been on Mrs Pouris, whose eyes were the colour of raisins, who smelled of hot silk and lotions not immediately nameable. Each evening he had slipped through the barrier into the first-class section of the ship, to pace with Mrs

2

Pouris up and down the deck. And now she had fled – there was no other word for it. She had received, perhaps, a warning, read a horoscope? Or, Kennedy wondered uneasily, perhaps he had not been sufficiently delicate in the insinuation of his poverty?

He had just decided to speak to the Greek when the latter glanced round at him and smiled, so there was a moment of what seemed recognition between them, something acknowledged in common. This was encouraging and Kennedy returned the smile promptly and on a larger scale. Perhaps something yet could be salvaged. His was a face constructed, it would seem, for smiling, broad, high cheek-boned, the wide mouth notched as it were for gradations of glee, curving up towards freckles and very round blue eyes. The eyes did not change much, whatever the degrees recorded below, and they had a lingering boldness of regard.

'Bit of a crush down there,' Kennedy said, hoping the other understood English. '*Ce n'est pas encore possible de sortir,*' he added haltingly. A lot of them knew a bit of French. He had learned his as an army clerk at S.H.A.P.E. headquarters in Paris, before certain dealings had led to his dishonourable discharge. 'No sense in going down there yet, *c'est pas la peine . . .*'

'I understand English,' the Greek said. He had a small oval face and very beautiful dark eyes. And he spoke English perfectly, without a trace of accent. 'One might just as well wait,' he said. This linguistic accomplishment was unexpected, disconcerting, hinting at a familiarity with Kennedy's countrymen, a faculty of assessment, that might be inconvenient. Kennedy paused, somewhat warily.

'Just coming back from your holidays then?' he said at last, in a congratulatory tone.

'No, I have come for a visit. I am Greek, but I have been living in England for several years.' He turned to look over the side again, at the passengers still descending. They were predominantly Greek. Speaking in loud tones, using their elbows freely, they jostled for precedence. It seemed to him that he remembered this fractiousness, this way of seeking in every occasion small personal triumphs. He was back among his people, many of whom were carrying huge Italian dolls wrapped in polythene.

'That explains why you speak English so well,' observed

Kennedy, taking out his handkerchief. 'It will be good to get on to *terra firma* again, won't it?' he added.

'*Les passagers sont priés . . .*' began the loudspeaker. Time was getting short.

'Where are you staying?' Kennedy asked. 'Have you got somewhere to stay?'

'Oh yes, I am going to live at my cousin's house in Kifissia. That is near Athens, a suburb really.'

'I'm not fixed up yet,' Kennedy said, 'I'm looking for a place to stay, just for a few days.'

'There are some good hotels and not expensive, particularly in the neighbourhood of Omonia Square.'

'To tell you the truth, old boy,' Kennedy said, in a confidential manner, 'I'm a bit short at the moment. Just for the next few days you know, till my money comes through. Even a cheap hotel . . .'

The other said nothing to this.

'I thought from the first moment I saw you,' Kennedy said, 'that you were an understanding fellow. My name is Kennedy, by the way, Bryan Kennedy.'

'Mitsos, Stavros Mitsos.'

'Put it there,' said Kennedy. He boosted his smile. 'I've heard that the Greeks are a hospitable people,' he said.

'They are considered to be so,' Mitsos replied. 'I think it is time to be getting off the boat now,' he added. He took a few steps towards the stairway leading to the lower deck.

'Just a minute,' Kennedy said, falling into step beside him. He hardly knew himself why he was thus persisting with such an obviously unpromising subject. It was not as though he were without immediate cash, even. But the flight of Mrs Pouris had inflamed his predatory instinct, he was possessed by a vindictive desire to make a touch before he got off the boat. 'I know you are a complete stranger,' he said, 'but I've got something here I'd like you to see.' He fumbled in the inside pocket of his jacket and produced after a moment a frayed leather wallet. 'I have several testimonials here,' he said. 'This one is from the Bishop of Jarrow, written in his own hand. Read it. I think you will be impressed.'

'There is hardly time now,' Mitsos said politely. He looked up at the pleasantly smiling face of the Englishman, striving as he did

4

so to keep his impression general, preserve the other's humanity, not succumb to the details of the features, the configuration of the nostrils, the large-pored skin, the shine of perspiration round the mouth. It had been increasingly difficult for him lately to spread his scrutiny over the whole area of anything without becoming helplessly impaled on the details. The man was very tall, well over six feet, and broad-shouldered. He had short untidy hair the colour of wet straw. His round blue eyes had a delinquent fixity of regard and his green tweed suit was too heavy, quite unsuitable for this weather. A man, on the whole, difficult to place. But no words or gestures he went in for now could redeem the gross haste with which he had revealed his needs to a stranger.

Mitsos left the rail and moved towards the head of the stairway. 'They will be swilling the decks down,' he said, 'and they will swill us too, if we do not hurry.' And in fact sailors had appeared with buckets of water. Reluctantly Kennedy restored the wallet to its place in his bosom and they descended the stairs together to collect their luggage from outside the purser's office; Kennedy a single battered suitcase held together by a strap, and the Greek two rather sumptuous cream-coloured grips. He was a frail, small-boned person and had some difficulty in getting down the gang-plank with these. Kennedy did not offer to help. Immediately they were off the boat Mitsos began to look around for a taxi.

'I was wondering,' Kennedy said, without much hope, 'whether you might lend me a small sum of money, to tide me over. Two or three pounds, say. Say three pounds. On the strength of that testimonial, which you are quite at liberty to read. I have several others from Justices of the Peace, Members of Parliament, and so on.' His hand strayed towards his wallet. He had every confidence in the impact of these documents on any person who could be persuaded to read them, since he had written them himself, had expended, in fact, much labour on their composition. 'Let me see,' he said, 'in drachmas that would be . . .'

Mitsos said, 'I can't lend you anything, I'm afraid. I am not carrying much ready money with me.'

'I see, yes,' Kennedy said. 'Never mind, old boy. Just a thought.'

'I'm sorry. You can come with me in the taxi to Athens, if that suits you.'

'Really? No, but look here . . .' Kennedy hoisted his suitcase, gave the dock a comprehensive survey in the hope of seeing even now some sign of Mrs Pouris. But they seemed to be the only passengers left.

A man detached himself from a group standing near the dock gates and approached them. '*Oriste, kyrie?*' he said. 'Taxi.' He took their luggage and they followed him through the gates and out into the crowded street. Trolley wires netted the sky overhead and yellow trolley-buses trundled past continually. The glare of the sun on white buildings hurt Kennedy's eyes and he was confused by the shouts of men selling peanuts and lottery tickets and by the loud conversations between passing pedestrians.

'I've heard that word before, that word "*kyrie*",' he said. 'In masses.' He did not attend masses, but knew this word meant God, in whom he believed with a certain resentful clamminess. passed through his mind without any sense of impiety how marvellous it would be if he could have claimed divine authorship for one of his testimonials. 'Noisy, isn't it?' he said.

'Greeks like noise, generally speaking,' Mitsos replied. 'Though I do not, myself.'

The taxi-driver opened the door for them and his golden molars flashed. '*Oriste,*' he said again.

'Now I think I must discuss the price with him,' Mitsos said.

Rapid Greek ensued. Kennedy stood by. His was a resilient and essentially optimistic nature. Now he declined to consider the wounding behaviour of Mrs Pouris and the lesser rebuff he had received from Mitsos, and he suddenly felt delighted to be here and grateful to the thin-necked person with the carrying voice, whose face he had not properly seen, who had put him on to Greece; grateful to the impulse that had lasted long enough to set him down here, listening to an argument about a taxi fare conducted in an unintelligible tongue.

In the Chelsea Potter it had all begun. He had been standing there with a Guinness on a crowded Friday, wondering who to ring up. He had felt rich but chastened, with over seventy pounds in his pockets, commission from selling encyclopaedias from door to door to American service families, a job for which he had shown aptitude but which he had lost two days before through smelling of drink and making fairly determined overtures to some of the wives – the one with whom he had been most successful had subsequently complained. And then this voice from further down the bar: 'You want to go to Greece, old man. I would, if I were single. Marvellous climate, bloody marvellous, four thousand years of history. Four thousand bloody years of history. They're all dying to learn English over there. They need it, you see, being a commercial nation. Anyone could go over there and get a good living. You only have to be English.' Which Kennedy indubitably was. There and then, watching the froth on his Guinness subside, he had thought, why not? Scraps of myth had come into his mind, culled from his haphazard but abundant reading; garlanded heifers and raped nymphs, marble columns, angular e's. He would go. He would be a tutor. Amazingly his resolve had held, long enough for him to write his testimonials, get his ticket, look at summer suits without buying one; long enough to steer him through the people who would have liked to help him spend what remained of the seventy pounds. What remained of it reposed at that moment in his hip pocket.

Negotiation ceased, and they got in. The taxi shot forward, narrowly missing a group of small crop-haired boys playing with pebbles in the gutter, and inserted itself into the stream of traffic. Down the long straight road to Athens small box-like houses were strung out, many of their walls bearing advertisements for macaroni or Fixe beer. For some time they skirted a glittering sea. Numerous sections of the road were under repair and thunderous with drills. Half-naked men toiled in the dust which swirled up under the wheels of cars and buses. The taxi-driver drove nonchalantly, at great speed, one hand only on the wheel, the other arm outstretched along the seat. From time to time he turned his head completely round to make some comment. Kennedy felt frightened, and to lessen this feeling did not look at the road ahead at all, but only out of his nearside window. For this reason he did not see the Parthenon till Mitsos told him to look, and whatever he had been expecting it was not this delicate railing of pillars suspended above the noon haze of the approaching city, too remote to be quite believed in as a structure. Not that Kennedy had given much thought to the Parthenon beforehand; he was not

7

much interested in monuments, but he decided now on a demonstration, possibly flattering to Mitsos, from whom he still had some small hopes of gain.

He said, 'I've read a lot about it, of course, but . . .' craning his head forward to look again. Mitsos watched him curiously. His pleasure and interest seemed genuine. Now he had slumped right down in his seat, twisting his large head to get a better view. No Greek would willingly have adopted so ungainly an attitude. Mitsos had never understood this physical carelessness of the English. His own body insisted on graceful reclinations. And what was this greed for an alien past?

The taxi proceeded more slowly now, among the thicker traffic of the city. They came out into Omonia Square. The fountains were playing there and the pavements were crowded. They went round the outer rim of the hub, selected finally the spoke of Stadion Street. Mitsos looked out of the window at rows of tall hoardings concealing, it seemed, areas of demolition. What had been there he could not now remember, though he struggled to do so, and this small failure caused him something like despair. Every lapse of memory or recognition seemed to threaten the purpose of his return, formed suddenly after so many years, his desire to readopt the city.

'Where can I put you down?' he asked.

Kennedy had been experiencing some disillusionment, travelling down this spacious but quite ordinary avenue with its shops and cinemas and restaurants. Though what he had been expecting he could not say. He glared sideways at Mitsos' watch, conveniently exposed just now. Twelve-fifteen nearly. An awkward time. He felt thirsty. From the top pocket of his jacket he took a folded piece of paper. 'This is where I want to go,' he said, passing the paper to Mitsos. The address of the Cultural Centre was the only one of any use he had in Athens and he had made up his mind to go there first of all.

'Ah, yes,' Mitsos said. 'That will be quite easy. The taxi will go up Vassilis Sofias. We can put you down quite close. A few minutes' walk.'

'Splendid,' Kennedy said. 'Perhaps I can give you a ring in a day or two? I don't know anybody here.'

'Athens is like a village, in some ways. We shall be sure to meet.'

'Yes, but if I had your phone number . . .'

'Here we are,' Mitsos said. 'This is where you must get out.' He spoke to the taxi-driver and the taxi drew into the kerb and stopped. Kennedy disentangled his long legs from below the front seat and seized his suitcase.

'Thanks again, old boy,' Kennedy said. 'We shall be seeing some more of each other, I daresay.'

'I hope so. That is your way up, through there.'

Kennedy scrambled out and then leaned back into the taxi, extending his hand. They shook hands solemnly. Looking back as the taxi gathered speed again, Mitsos saw the Englishman standing tall and irresolute, holding his suitcase, his unseasonable green tweed suit patterned with the shadows cast by one of the acacias that lined the avenue. So much for that. He wondered about Kennedy for a few moments, then he forgot him completely. He stared out of the taxi window, rigidly holding off the sense of unreality that threatened to descend on him in the absence of familiar landmarks. I am coming home, he told himself.

Kennedy found the Cultural Centre without any difficulty. It was on the far side of a hot little square with a railed garden in the middle, planted out with large purple pansies. Cars going round it took the corners almost always too fast and their tyres made tearing, ecstatic sounds. Entering, he was immediately grateful for the coolness, the subdued light. The floor of the entrance hall looked like marble, there was a large gleaming reception desk behind which sat a plump, rather pretty girl with glasses. Kennedy advanced on her with respectful eagerness, noticing, however, that her eyes were fixed on his suitcase, which he at once regretted having brought with him: it was not the suitcase of a man to whom interviews are spontaneously accorded.

'I have called,' he said, 'to see the Director.'

'Have you an appointment?' the girl asked.

Kennedy smiled and leaned towards her, putting both hands on the edge of the desk. 'No,' he said. 'I haven't. I've just arrived from England, as a matter of fact. But I'm very anxious to see him . . .'

He had the gift of enmeshing certain people – and not always the least discerning – instantaneously in his life, his purposes and projects. The girl looked at the curve of his mouth. Her manner lightened perceptibly. Besides, there was nothing here for her to withhold: Mr Jennings would see this man, after the statutory waiting time had elapsed; he always saw them – why, she did not know.

'Mr Jennings is engaged just at present,' she said, 'but he will be free in a few minutes if you would like to wait.' She indicated a row of chairs against the wall.

Kennedy said, 'Thank you very much, Miss. . . ?'

'Diamantopoulou.'

'Miss Diama . . .' He made a comical face. 'How was it again?'

'Dia-manto-poulou.'

Kennedy continued the comical face. 'Thanks anyway,' he said, and the girl laughed a little. He had found without knowing it a way of pleasing Greeks: by stressing the difficulties of their language. He went over and sat down on one of the seats, first placing the suitcase carefully against the wall. When he raised his hands to straighten his tie he saw that his fingernails were rimmed with black, and though this was their usual condition, the sight of them now caused confidence rapidly to leak away. He entered on one of his periodic moods of personal unworthiness, feeling not dishevelled, merely, but unclean. He should first have found a hotel and had a wash and brush-up, applied brisk friction to his dandruffed scalp, scaled the yellow off, untangled his armpits. Knees together on the hard little chair, perspiration cooling on his back, he glanced uneasily round the room and was soon able to blame what he saw for his condition. It was a room that undermined one, as ante-rooms do. The marble floor had a fishy gleam, the mahogany desk was too effulgent. The walls were glazed cream and bore pictures Kennedy had seen before, sailing ships at sunset and dawn, on seas resplendent or leaden. On a stand in one corner was a bowl of white and waxen lilies. The heavy swing doors shut out the noises of the square. The room in its sealed-off, menacing composure was familiar to him; he had waited in such rooms in his institutional childhood, waited for the attempt of authority to effect some inevitably painful dislocation of his personality – for this was always the purpose of such interviews, whether the voices were kindly or severe; held meanwhile in this glazed calm, knowing how far anterior to suffering it was, how impossibly far therefore from healing. . . . Through his heavy and uncomfortable body stirred some return of the stubborn hatreds of those days, the beginnings of hostility towards the much occupied Mr Jennings. . . .

The girl looked up with a vague expression and raised her hands to her hair. The gesture thrust upward her plump breasts. Under her thin black jumper the exact location of the nipples could be easily divined. Kennedy looked at them fixedly as an antidote, an evidence of organic life. She became aware of his gaze and lowered her arms again, leaning forward slightly in self-protection. She was not, however, annoyed.

'You are coming from England?' she said.

'Yes, that's right.'

'Perhaps you look for some teaching hours?'

'That's it exactly,' Kennedy said. 'I look for as many teaching hours as possible. How did you know?'

'It is generally the reason why you come and look us up,' the girl said, dwelling on the idiom somewhat proudly. She forbore out of kindness and the linguistic complexities involved to tell him of the long succession of derelict or eccentric Britons she had seen occupying these chairs in the two years she had been working there. She found this one rather attractive, in a dishevelled sort of way, but knew he would not get a job. None of them who came like this ever got jobs because those qualified for jobs never came like this. She did not know why Mr Jennings saw them at all.

'All the posts of the institute are filled now,' she said. 'It is late in the year. You should come at the beginning of October. Now we have the diploma examinations only a few weeks away.' She looked at him with a faint air of interrogation. It was an odd time to come.

Kennedy, who had never heard of the diploma examinations, maintained his smile with an effort. 'That's a facer,' he said.

'Sometimes I am hearing about works, private teaching.'

'Are you indeed? My name is Bryan, by the way. What's your first name?'

The girl's mouth became somewhat less full at this directness. She replied, however, after a moment, 'My name, it is Sophy.'

'That is much easier to remember,' Kennedy said, and the girl laughed again. Rapidly he began a process of calculation. He did not find her very attractive, but she seemed to like him and if what she said was true might prove a useful ally. On the whole she would be worth buying lunch for. He was about to ask her when she picked up the phone and spoke into it about him.

'Mr Jennings will see you now,' she said, looking up, a certain stateliness descending on her with the official phrasing. 'You go up the stairs to the next floor. His door is on the right. You will see the name.'

'Thank you,' Kennedy said. He decided that he had better wait to see what emerged from the interview with Jennings; Jennings might very possibly invite him somewhere; home perhaps or to some good restaurant; a fellow countryman, just off the boat. 'I'll see you later,' he said, giving her his maximum smile.

He mounted the stairs and proceeded down a red-carpeted passage, past a door which said 'Administrative Officer' and another which said 'Assistant Director', until he found the one he wanted: 'H. Jennings, Director'. He tapped discreetly and put his ear close to the door. Listening there he became aware of the beat of his heart. For some reason he felt sure that the 'H' was for Herbert.

'Come in! Come in!' said a voice of such carrying power that Kennedy recoiled a little. After a further pause to pull himself together, he entered, closing the door with some care behind him, and found himself regarding a fattish, white-faced man with prominent ears, tiny eyes behind rimless glasses, and an expression of great blandness, who was sitting at a desk similar to the one below.

'Good morning, sir,' Kennedy said, with the brisk deference he had found best when selling encyclopaedias. He was somewhat disconcerted by the unathletic appearance of Jennings, having expected someone a bit bluffer, after the resonance of the voice. On the desk were papers, a bronze vase containing more of the funereal lilies, and a round *papier-mâché* tray with tea things and a plate of biscuits on it.

'Come in, come in,' said Jennings again. 'Mr Kennedy, isn't it? I am pleased to make your acquaintance. Do sit down; take a seat here.' He articulated with a quite extraordinary, a loving, precision. The normal elisions of fluency were abandoned and each word came out separately with a little trimming of silence round it. Words thus treasured could never be lost, as other men's were; they seemed to fall into a place prepared for them, like smooth round pebbles falling into putty. While Kennedy still hesitated he brought one bloodless hand from below the desk and indicated the chair before him with a courtly gesture.

Kennedy walked to the proffered chair with a firm tread, the gait of a man who has confidence in his credentials. Looking at Jennings he became aware of a pale inquisitional gleam behind the glasses.

'Now, what can I do for you, Mr Kennedy?' Jennings said.

'Well, I have just arrived from England, sir,' Kennedy said, in his best manner. 'And I was wondering what the opportunities for employment in your institute were.'

'Ah, yes, I see.' The Director raised his upper lip slightly in a mild snarl. 'This is rather an unusual juncture in the academic ah, session, to be seeking a teaching post. We conduct our recruiting normally at the beginning of the year. Not the end.'

'Yes, I realise that, sir, and of course I know the diploma examinations are quite close upon us now, but circumstances, *family* circumstances, made it impossible for me . . .'

'You are qualified, of course?'

'Yes, I think I may say that I am qualified.' Kennedy smiled modestly.

'I mean, to put it in a more precisely delineated fashion, have you a degree?'

'Oh, yes,' Kennedy said, without hesitation. The lie agitated him a little, but Jennings paused at this point and lifting from the tray a brown earthenware teapot poured out tea into a blue willow-pattern cup, added milk and tweezered three lumps of sugar into it.

'You will excuse me, I hope,' he enunciated, stirring. 'This is all I take for lunch. The worst thing you can do in this country is to have a heavy lunch. It induces a feeling of somnolence, a certain

13

disinclination. . . .' He snarled again, rather hideously. His teeth looked very false.

'Quite so,' Kennedy said, his eyes on the steaming tea. 'The cup that cheers,' he said. Jennings made no reply to this, but continued stirring for some moments, his eyes lowered. Kennedy wrenched his gaze from the tea things and looked round the room. On the cream walls were pictures of people with complex abdominal structures inhabiting some sort of inferno, and other pictures of what looked like undergrowth, with tuberous objects tangled up in it. In one corner was a marble bust of some personage with a Balkan moustache. While Kennedy watched, a fly settled on the bald head and began to crawl diagonally across it. From the open window behind Jennings, voices came up from the square, a sudden jangle of music, and more or less continually the urgent clamour of tyres as cars went on swerving round too fast. In a bookcase against the wall were books by people he had never heard of, Eckersley, Hornby, Gaterby, Glover: *Essential English for Overseas Students*, Basic English for Students from Abroad, Fundamental English for Foreign Students.

Looking back towards the desk he saw that Jennings had been following his gaze with what might have been an access of interest.

'You are interested in Structures?' Jennings said.

'Very much so.'

'I am writing a book about it. For anyone who considers grammar carefully, Mr Kennedy, there is a way of life to be found in it. A whole philosophy.'

Kennedy maintained a respectful silence for some moments, then he said, 'I have some testimonials with me, if you would care to see them.'

'Tell me,' Jennings said, 'do you adhere to the direct method in your teaching, or are you of those who believe that a certain knowledge of the students' mother tongue is necessary?'

'I'm all for the direct method, myself,' Kennedy said promptly. 'I think that when you come right down to it, direct methods are always best.' In saying this he felt at least morally unassailable. They were shortbread biscuits, he noted. Jennings must have been nibbling one before he came in because there were crumbs on the

14

lapels of his dark suit. 'I've only been in the country a couple of hours,' he said. 'It's a tiring journey, rather.' He attempted a laughing tone. 'They don't give you much breakfast on these boats. Well, you know what these wogs are. All I had this morning was one of these cups of Turkish coffee. A couple of mouthfuls. And most of that was sediment.' Surely now a buzzer would be pressed, an extra cup summoned.

'Everything lies, of course, in the examples you choose,' Jennings said. 'If you had to explain the difference, let us say, between the Past Simple and Present Perfect tenses, how would you go about it?'

You old bastard, Kennedy thought. He had started sweating again. 'I would need notice of that question,' he said, aiming at a jocular, parliamentary tone.

'But what examples would you take?'

Kennedy was unable to reply to this and for some time the two looked fixedly at each other across the desk.

'I *lived* in Tibet. I *have lived* in Tibet,' Jennings intoned at last. 'The one describing an action completed in the past, the other describing an action in some way related to the present. I don't think we can offer you a post here, Mr Kennedy.'

Kennedy made a motion towards his wallet. 'I have a number of testimonials with me,' he said, 'as to my character and so forth, which you might like to see.' He had provided himself with a set of secondary testimonials, people who had actually known him, to whom written reference could be made, though he had calculated he would be well out of Athens before any of the replies could be received: a ship's doctor at sea for half the year; an ex-army major now an alcoholic of no fixed address; a retired headmaster who had died of a stroke while gardening; all of them, despite delirium and even death, asserting Kennedy's brilliant gifts. Much care and concern for the concordance of style with character had gone into these compositions, and to see Jennings greedily reading them would have given him joy.

'That will not be necessary, at this stage,' Jennings said. 'There are at the moment, in any case, no vacancies at the institute. None whatever.'

Kennedy met the pale eyes again. It seemed to him that their gleam had intensified. Jennings had never meant to employ him, then. Not at any time during the interview. Chatting thus with odd visitors was evidently one of his ways of passing the time. 'I see,' he said, and stood up.

'Before you leave, call at my assistant's office, will you?' said Jennings, without moving. 'His room is next to mine. He can give you a list of the commercial institutes in the city. In one or other of those you might conceivably find yourself a place.'

'That is very good of you,' Kennedy said, pausing at the door. His eyebrows felt charged with moisture. The insolence which was never far below the surface rose in him. 'I want to thank you for your invaluable assistance and advice, old boy,' he said loudly. 'To a fellow countryman, just off the boat. To say nothing of the offer of refreshment,' he added, lowering his head slightly. From this angle Jennings' glasses reflected the light strongly. Kennedy closed the door rather sharply behind him.

The name of the assistant director was Robinson. He was a tall, thin man with close-set brown eyes, a boyish hair-do and a watered-silk bow tie of pale blue. He had a rather spurious briskness of manner, and a way of making his face go shrewd from time to time.

'You want the list then?' he said forcefully, after Kennedy had spent some time explaining that he wanted the list. 'Well, to put you in the picture, we don't guarantee the quality of these places. We merely provide the information. You must bear in mind that they are all *commercial* institutes.'

Kennedy nodded. He had come to the conclusion that there was nothing much to hope for from the Cultural Centre, and so was not disposed to be deferential. 'You mean they aim to make a profit?' he said. 'Nothing wrong with that, is there? It's only common sense.'

'That is not how we look at it,' Robinson said. He tapped his teeth with a pencil. 'Do you play the English flute, by the way?' he said.

'The English flute?'

Robinson narrowed his eyes shrewdly. 'It is sometimes called the recorder,' he said.

'No, I don't.'

'We have musical evenings – Wednesday evenings. There is a good deal of musical ability in the British community here. The person who played the English flute has gone to Chile. We were sorry to lose him.'

'Yes,' Kennedy said, 'I can see he must have left a gap.'

'Here you are then,' Robinson said, handing him a typewritten list.

'Thank you.'

'Have you a degree, by the way?'

'Yes.'

'What class?'

Kennedy fought briefly with temptation and won. 'Second,' he said.

'I'm getting up a series of weekly lectures through the summer, starting next week actually. People talking on their own subjects. Greeks are invited too, anyone can come. That's the idea really, liaison with the Greeks, cultural liaison. I regard myself as a cultural liaison officer. There is a woman coming to talk about her childhood in British India, her father dispensed justice at the gates of Jawnpore, it should be very good. Then there's an extremely able man coming to talk about the "Harley Lyrics". Wetherby Croft, perhaps you've heard of him?'

'Of course.'

'We still have some vacant dates. Is there something you know a bit about, in that way?'

'It is paid, I suppose?'

'There is a fee, yes.'

'Never do anything for nothing,' Kennedy said. 'I took that in with my mother's milk.' He thought for a moment. He could not afford to turn up any prospect of money. 'My special subject,' he said, 'is modern poetry.'

Robinson's face went shrewd again. 'Who would you consider,' he said, 'to be the most *representative* of modern poets?'

'Well, let's see now,' Kennedy said, already regretting his rashness. 'When you say representative . . .' During his frequent and prolonged spells of unemployment he had read quite widely and he knew the big names. 'There's Auden and Eliot and Dylan Thomas,' he said.

'Ah, yes, but I was not thinking so much of that generation. Two of them are dead, and the other is an old man now with his main achievements perhaps behind him.'

There was a fairly lengthy pause.

'Philip Larkin,' Kennedy said.

'Yes,' Robinson said. 'Larkin, of course, yes.' He nodded encouragingly.

'Malcom Rutherford,' Kennedy said experimentally. Seeing that Robinson continued to nod, he added rapidly, 'Iris Swann, Oberon Peel, Maxmilian Winter.'

'Yes, yes, yes,' said Robinson, giving at each name a little nod. Something had crept into his expression, however, a sort of anxiety.

'Jennifer Poole.' Kennedy was beginning to enjoy himself. Suddenly he remembered another real poet. 'Ted Hughes,' he said. 'And there's Gilligan, of course. We mustn't leave *him* out.'

'No, of course not,' said Robinson, ceasing to nod. A silence fell. Robinson looked briefly out of the window. 'I wouldn't place him so centrally, myself,' he said.

'Who?'

'Gilligan.'

'Oh, wouldn't you? More outside the main stream, as you might say?'

'Yes, that's it exactly. Well, all this has been most interesting, Mr Kennedy. No doubt we shall be getting in touch with you later on. You've got the list, haven't you? Oh, and by the way, if you want any help on the more, er, *practical* aspects of living here, there's a very useful person down at the institute. His name is Willey, John Willey. He has been on our staff several years now, though only on a locally employed basis. He could probably help you with accommodation and so forth.'

'Thank you.'

'Go any time after five and you'll find him there. He is there every evening.'

Kennedy said goodbye politely. The sense of having scored

heavily off Robinson had restored his temper. His suitcase was still against the wall, and Sophy was still at her desk.

'I'd like you to have lunch with me,' Kennedy said.

That evening, towards the end of the first period, Willey gave his class a written exercise to do. While he waited he cast an eye over the list of names. Four years now he had been teaching classes of Greeks and the names still had not lost their booming quality: Electra, Aphrodite, Sophocles, Miltiades, Antigone. Though the boom was fainter now.

The present incumbents of these legendary titles sat before him in varying degrees of concentration. Almost nothing, as every teacher knows, so much distinguishes people as their attitude to instruction. . . . Abandoning the register he looked from face to face, pausing finally at Miss Triandafyllou, a pretty, clumsy girl of about sixteen whose eyes had a lustre always that seemed close to tears. He enjoyed watching Miss Triandafyllou. In his pity for her the essential unchastity of his thoughts could go longer unchecked. . . . Now under the stress of composition she shifted sharply in her seat and parted her knees, disclosing a tunnel beige-walled at first, closing at the white join of her thighs beyond the stockings. Palms together as in prayer could be inserted there, moved softly inwards, still without touching. As always, his imagination recoiled before the actual infliction of pleasure; he looked away. He knew all possible movements of a girl's legs, below the desk, within the confines of skirts lighter or heavier; the startled movements of virgins in response to some itch or cramp; slower, more monumental shifts of others, adjustments it seemed to a heat between the thighs. . . .' Some day, he thought, I will write a poem from the viewpoint of the teacher-voyeur, full of sharply realised visual imagery, with an existential flavour as of gates never opened. The whole redolent of a solemn though furtive anguish. It ought to be good, he told himself. The poetry of perpetual tumescence. Other men would assist at the ultimate surrenders of all these legs, that much was certain. And a very good thing too.

Outside, beyond the window, he could sense the quickening life of the city, the beginning of evening. The sun would have lost its fierceness now, the light would be softer, yellower, but not hazy. The long crest of Hymettos, no longer estranged from the city by the sun, would be settling nearer for the sunset embrace. The streets would be filling, it was the time for ouzo, the little glasses rattling on the tin tables, the clear liquid clouding as the chips of ice melted in it; the interminable Greek conversations over the glasses, malicious, acute, animated without extravagance, shallow until it was realised that the awareness of being alive in the promising evening was being continually reaffirmed. Just as the strollers who would now be filling the streets, moving slowly, talking loudly, watchful for eccentricities, seemed aimless only until it was recognised that they formed a procession of celebrants, the exactions of the day over.

Willey felt suddenly a rush of love for this city of his adoption. *H Aθενα ηας*. I wonder why it is, he thought, that I, forty-three years old, of no distinction, disgraced in England, precariously employed in Athens, with a fiancée I can't afford to marry, should experience almost invariably at this hour of the day, a feeling of optimism, a feeling of coming into my kingdom? Inexplicable really. Well, if you put it that way, he could imagine Olivia saying, in the tone of one making concessions.

It was a tone she often used. She would be at home now, her day at the Embassy School over. Home in the little flat in Kolonaki with the parquet floor and the green-tiled Turkish stove and the colourful lambs-wool rugs. She would have been out to the kiosk in Kolonaki Square to get a *Telegraph* and might be reading at this very moment of the doings of royal children, with her slippers on, pink-trimmed fur edges and a pom-pom. Her kind, heavy face intent. He liked always to know if possible where Olivia was, what she was doing. Her possessions and observances were essential to his knowledge of her. She was a woman, moreover, not easily detached from her chosen setting. Marrying her, which he wanted most of the time to do, would mean a placing of himself somewhere down in the midst. . . .

The bell rang for the end of the lesson. 'We will go through the exercise after the break,' Willey said. He affected not to see the upraised hand of Mr Rallos, whose questions were always veiled grievances, and made for the door. As he was crossing the hall to the little staff-room where his coffee, always prepared at this time by Nikos, the porter, would be waiting for him, a tall, broadly smiling, rather dishevelled person rose from a chair and came towards him.

'Is your name Willey?' this person enquired with great geniality, and Willey now saw that he had fragments of what seemed vegetation in his hair.

'Yes,' he said. 'It is.'

'Kennedy,' the other said, and thrust out a large hand towards him. 'Bryan Kennedy.'

'How do you do?'

'Mr Robinson suggested I should come and see you,' Kennedy said, and paused for some moments, smiling. He had not consciously formed any picture of Willey from the few remarks Robinson had let fall, but found his appearance in some way unexpected, the long, burdened-looking neck surmounted by a small neat head in which eyes blinked with a nervous frequency. This head seemed like something proffered, a target perhaps, because of Willey's very sloping shoulders. 'He said you might be able to help me find a place to stay,' he continued. 'I've just arrived from England, you see. Just today.'

'Oh, have you? How was the weather?'

'Eh? Oh, not bad. A bit drizzly.'

'Perhaps you'd like a cup of coffee?'

Kennedy was so pleased by this offer that he stopped smiling. 'I *would*, old boy,' he said. 'There's an old bastard over the way . . .' He stopped short abruptly. Tact with Kennedy was merely another word for caution; in moments of expansion he was always completely lacking in it. It only now occurred to him that Willey and Jennings might be friends. 'No offence meant,' he said.

Willey glanced quickly round. Nikos and several students were within hearing. 'Can we have another cup of coffee, Nikos?' he said. 'Come into the staff-room,' he said to Kennedy. 'We can talk in there.' At this moment he saw Mackintosh emerging from his classroom. Typical of Mackintosh to go on teaching five minutes past the hour, he thought. We know how keen he is, without that. He led Kennedy into the staff-room, which was empty. Nikos brought in the coffee. A moment or two later Mackintosh came in and Willey introduced them.

'Just arrived, eh?' Mackintosh said. He was a thin man of about thirty, with sandy hair, a cold-morning, shiny face and protuberant blue eyes. He had taken off his jacket, his short-sleeved pullover was skimpy and he wore armbands. 'I've only been here myself a few months,' he said. 'Since the beginning of the session.' He rubbed his hands together. 'Very interesting lesson, that,' he said. 'And very successful too, I may say. It's amazing really. They are only a first-year class, but believe it or not,' he said to Kennedy, 'they have already mastered the Anomalous Finites.' He looked with his prominent eyes from one to the other, continuing to rub his hands, taking in Kennedy's somewhat crumpled appearance, the scraps still adhering to his hair.

'That's good going,' said Kennedy. He had disliked the armbands from the start. He and a treasuring Scot like this, whose zeal was indistinguishable from self-interest, were archetypal foes, as Kennedy knew well. In a more permissive society he would have clubbed Mackintosh on sight.

'Congratulations,' said Willey with extreme coldness.

Mackintosh drank his coffee in a series of quick gulps. 'I think it would be a good idea,' he said, looking at Willey, 'if we sent in progress reports from time to time, once a month say. Outlining the work covered and the degree of facility reached by the students. It might be helpful. I intend to suggest it to the Director.'

Feeling himself included in the conversation, Kennedy nodded his large head several times. Willey made no reply at all.

'Well, I must get back,' Mackintosh said. 'I've got some writing to do on the board before the lesson begins. I don't think we should take up lesson time with blackboard work if it can possibly be avoided, do you?' He nodded at Kennedy. 'Nice to have met you,' he said, and went out.

'Well, well,' Kennedy said. He glanced at Willey's expressionless face, divining with a perceptiveness rare in him the other's dislike for Mackintosh. 'Forward into the sunlight,' he said. 'Marching towards mastery of the Anomalous Finites.'

Willey smiled suddenly. 'You've got things in your hair,' he said.

Kennedy put up a hand to his head. 'I went for a walk this afternoon,' he said, 'in the National Park, and feeling rather tired at one point . . . I suppose I must have picked them up.' He began extricating the pieces.

Willey heard tinkling laughter from just beyond the door. That would be Miss Watson. 'I've got another lesson in a few minutes,' he said. 'So I can't tell you much about things in general. But I suppose it's a place to stay you want first of all. Flats are easy to find, you know, in Athens, both furnished and unfurnished.'

'To tell you the truth, old boy, a flat would be a bit beyond my means just at present. Until my money comes through.'

'In that case perhaps the best thing would be Kitty's. That's a sort of lodging house. You get a single room that you pay for by the week. No meals. It's quite cheap, I believe. Quite a lot of foreigners are there already.'

'It sounds just the thing.'

'I'll give you the address then.' Willey wrote on a slip of paper. 'She's a Greek of some sort, from Constantinople. Everybody calls her Kitty. Here you are. If you want to get in touch with me you can always do it through the institute. I am by way of being a fixture here.'

'It really is very good of you,' Kennedy said.

'Not at all. I expect we shall be seeing more of each other.'

Kennedy tucked the paper into his breast pocket. It briefly occurred to him to ask this good-natured fellow for a loan on the spot, but he decided against it. No sense in rushing things. 'Bye-bye then,' he said. 'And thanks a million.' In the hall he passed Mackintosh, his blackboard work apparently postponed, talking to a little grey-haired woman with long ear-rings. He beamed at them but did not stop.

Left alone in the staff-room, Willey cast his eyes with habitual distaste over the books that lined the far wall: books containing passages for précis and comprehension; books listing idioms and

24

proverbs; books of extracts from other men's books; compilations of all sorts. Not an original idea among them. And always the same words on the covers, claiming to convey the essence: 'Comprehensive', 'Basic', 'Fundamental', 'Concise'. From Borneo to Bagdad ambitious youth was buying them, hoping to find an infallible guide to success in the examinations. Every week, it seemed, a new version of what was essential for foreigners to know was being published. Reviews in *The Times Educational Supplement*; elaborate circulars to schools and colleges everywhere; royalties, of course, since there was always a few more shillings to be scraped together in Borneo and Bagdad. . . . And now, he reflected, Jennings' book would be appearing soon, that chaotic mass of grammatical precept and mystical brooding. He was familiar with the contents as he had been all through the manuscript at Jennings' request, checking for errors, departures from usage. Hours of excruciating boredom for which there had been as yet no hint of payment. He had not, however, dared to refuse. And Jennings knew he dare not. . . .

The bell rang for the second period. Willey made his way back to the classroom, preparing a suitable face.

Kennedy went first to pick up his suitcase from Sophy, who had been minding it, and then, feeling rather tired of walking, he got into one of the little yellow trolley-buses that left from a point near the square. He thrust the address at the person nearest to him, and was told where to get off. Small boys moved quickly along the pavement balancing trays piled high with little hoops of bread. Kennedy bought two, suspected that he had been overcharged, and sat on a low wall to eat them.

He began to review his situation. Twenty-six pounds in drachmas, enough possibly for a month if he was careful. The prospect of a cheap place to stay, but no job yet. However, he had the list of institutions. Giving Sophy lunch had proved well worth while. She had promised to look after his suitcase, for one thing. And then in the course of conversation two distinct prospects for private lessons had emerged. One of them she had actually suggested herself, a girl of her own age whom she knew wanted private lessons, rich too, the daughter of a ship owner, Logothetis by name. Kennedy had the telephone number. The other had been an item of information merely, he was compelled to admit, and perhaps Sophy would not be pleased if she knew that he intended to get in touch with the person, but that couldn't be helped. Eleni Polimenou, she had told him, had telephoned twice that morning asking for Mr Jennings. Eleni Polimenou. Sophy had been quite indignant at his impassivity before this name. Had he not heard of Eleni Polimenou, the celebrated, the *internationally* celebrated Greek actress, she who had been to Hollywood, won acting awards? Now she wanted help with some play from a suitably qualified member of the institute staff. Unfortunately Mr Jennings had been out on both occasions of her phoning. He would want to handle this matter himself, since it concerned so important a personage. Mr Mackintosh she thought he would probably send. He had a high opinion of the abilities of Mr Mackintosh. Nothing, however, could be done for some days, as Miss Polimenou was out of town. She would be returning to Athens on May the 5th. . . . There and then Kennedy had resolved that on May the 5th he would be stirring early. Willey too, he thought, might prove a good source of private students. Things on the whole were not too bad. He ate steadily; the rolls were quite pleasant, stuck all over with little seeds. What were they, sesame seeds? When he had finished he crossed the street and set about finding Kitty's.

Her house proved to be a gaunt, four-storeyed building with narrow, railed balconies jutting out from the stuccoed façade, and a pervading smell of the urine of cats; and she herself obese and sleepy-eyed with a great curving nose and ceremonious manners. Yes, she informed him in a mixture of French and English, there was a room vacant, recently occupied by a young gentleman who had been *expedié*, for what misdemeanour Kennedy could not make out, except that it had been *quelque chose de dégoutant*. An American, of course, *ce pays barbare*. A civilisation sterile. Kitty's flesh below her pink flannel dressing-gown could be sensed constantly to eddy, even when her body was at rest. There were other Americans in the house, and Germans also, but she herself preferred always the English. Monsieur was English, was he not? *Ah ça se voit.* The rent, payable in advance, payable, in fact, immediately, was one hundred and fifty drachmas a week. Kennedy paid and was shown his room, one of those with a balcony.

Kennedy sat some time in silence on the narrow bed. There was a kind of rustling in the room, as of cockroaches, but he didn't mind that unduly. Unpacking would not take long, he had few possessions. Perhaps it would be a good idea to wash, there was a handbasin against the wall. As he was rising there was a light tap on the door and a second or two later the door was opened and a person in a maroon baseball cap poked his head into the room. 'Visitors,' this person said. 'You got visitors.' After a few seconds more of scrutiny he advanced fully into the room in a loping, rather rubbery, manner. His face beneath the cap wore a dazed smile. Immediately behind him followed a short young man with a bald spot, dressed in a somewhat shabby, but respectable grey pin-stripe suit. 'I am Simpson,' the man in the cap said. 'This is Roland, he is British.'

'Bryan Kennedy,' Kennedy said, and felt his hand taken in a surprisingly vigorous, almost convulsive, grip.

'I extend to you, sir, the freedom of this goddam city,' Simpson said. He had a rather agreeable light voice, with an odd tendency to trail the final syllables of his words. And he was, as Kennedy now saw, in a fairly advanced stage of drunkenness.

'That is very good of you, old boy,' Kennedy said, somewhat disliking the other's grandiloquence. 'You haven't any booze left over, have you?'

'Sharp,' said Simpson, who was swaying slightly, 'sharp. I can see you are a sharp one. By God.' He fumbled for a moment in the top pocket of his gabardine jacket which had the look of having formerly belonged to a bulkier man, and brought out a little white oblong. 'My card,' he said. Kennedy looked down at it. It was inscribed in gilt copper-plate with the words: 'Ken Simpson, American Artist, Exhibitions in all the Capitals of Europe.'

'Mr Simpson is an artist,' Roland said, speaking for the first time. 'Our rooms are just over the way. We heard you being shown the room. We thought we'd come over and see you had everything you wanted.' His face creased in an anxious conciliatory smile. 'Mr Simpson has been drinking a little,' he said. 'He has had a certain amount of disappointment.' He drew confidentially nearer, emanating a faint smell of hair oil. 'I've been here longer than anyone else,' he said. 'I'm the oldest resident.'

'The person who had this room before me . . .' Kennedy said. 'Why was he kicked out?'

'Nobody knows,' Roland said, looking uncomfortable.

Simpson sat down heavily on one of the two hard-backed chairs that together with a chest of drawers and the bed was all the furniture there was in the room. He crossed his legs and Kennedy saw that he was wearing the sort of shoes that basket-ball players wear, and no socks. The sole of the right one had a hole right through it and a neat circle of Simpson's skin was revealed.

'How did you get on today, Kenneth?' Roland said suddenly, in a sociable manner, as though encouraging a diffident guest. 'How did you get on down at Piraeus?'

Simpson adopted a look of sagacity. 'They all know me,' he said. 'All the officials down there. I go every day. You have to keep at them if you want results. I go down there . . . "My easel, where's my bloody easel, for Christ's sake?" "Ah, Ken, hello Ken, *ti canis*? Have something to drink? Vino, Birra? *Cognac.* Americano, eh?" ' Simpson paused, waving his arms about to indicate the friendliness of the officials at Piraeus. His face, which was extraordinarily mobile, had veered from his own initial sternness in demanding his easel, to wavering, pleased surprise at such a welcome, and then to the rather frantic Greek bonhomie of the officials themselves. 'I go down there . . .' he said. ' "Ah! Artist Americano. No money . . . do not speak of money, what you take, birra Fixe, ouzo, cognac? *Cognac* . . ." ' Simpson stopped talking altogether to mime with a dazed delighted smile the courtly behaviour of the dock officials, pouring out cognac, savouring the drink, setting the glass down. It was as though he had forgotten the verbal equivalents for all these actions. Abruptly his expression changed, became angrier. 'I have filled in the forms,' he said. 'That easel was made for me. I couldn't put a value on that easel. Ten thousand drachmas.'

'His easel,' Roland said, 'which has special fittings, made to his own specification, and is therefore much more valuable than an ordinary easel, has been mislaid, I trust temporarily, by the railway authorities somewhere in Germany. He has made a claim for compensation from the German authorities through the Greek authorities, but it seems to be taking a long time to come through. Every day he goes down there.'

'It's those bastards in Germany,' Simpson said. 'They are keeping it on purpose. Someone has seen how much that easel is worth. That's what they say down at Piraeus. "Americano good. Deutsch . . ." ' He made a face of disgusted antipathy. ' "You have drink with us; down with those fucking Germans! Those fucking Germans have stolen, yes stolen, your easel! *Cognac*." ' He went through the mime of pouring out again. 'By God!' he said. His eyes had an unusual opacity, a kind of grey film covering a large part of the iris, and the lashes remained quite stiffly apart for long periods.

'What I am afraid of,' Roland said to Kennedy in low tones, 'is that with all this delay Kenneth may lose his sense of purpose, the issues may become obscured.'

'They sound to me pretty fogged already,' Kennedy said. 'I had a nap in the National Park this afternoon and when I woke up I saw hundreds of girls marching down the avenue, all in these white blouses.'

'Bribes, they take bribes,' Simpson said. 'They all know me. "Ah, Americano, what you take? Birrz, ouzo? *Cognac*." ' He enacted polite reluctance, shrugging assent. 'I got a hollow leg for the stuff,' he said.

'Think of all the expense,' Roland said.

'A sort of parade it must have been,' Kennedy said. 'This afternoon about four o'clock. Greek schoolgirls, hundreds of them, marching down that avenue past the park, what do you call it, Amalias? What would it be for?'

'No idea,' Roland said. 'They have parades quite frequently. For birthdays, and Independence Day, and the day they said no to the Italians.'

'I'd like to think that this was the day all those girls were saying yes to someone. About fifteen they were. Marching along, swinging their arms, carrying all before them, as you might say. I swear to you, I have never seen so many lovely tits assembled together in one place. And they kept on coming. It was torture to watch them. English girls could never have put on a show like that, not at that age.'

Simpson emerged from his preoccupation with the easel. 'It's the olive oil,' he said. 'It goes to the breasts. They take olive oil with everything. Well, it stands to reason, doesn't it? I mean, think of all that oil. Bad for the skin of course, but bloody marvellous for the breasts, nourishing, fills 'em out. See the way their hair shines? Same thing, it's all the work of the olive.'

'I wonder if it lubricates their passages,' Kennedy said, leering at Roland.

'I don't know, I'm sure.' Roland wriggled a little. His face had gone quite red.

'Well,' said Kennedy, 'let's go out and have a drink. On me.'

When his lessons for the evening were over, Willey decided to take a walk before going to see Olivia at her flat. The meeting with Kennedy, something in the other's breezy disrespect, had unsettled him. Removing the scraps from his hair, Kennedy had somehow managed to suggest a larger life. Not a trustworthy person, however, he decided.

There was a scent of orange blossom in Kolonaki Square, though the flowers were mostly hidden in their clusters of sharp leaves; and below this immediate sweetness Willey sensed the harsher odour of the city compounded of dust and lime and cooling masonry. He crossed the square and began to walk along Scoufa Street. The buildings became shabbier as Kolonaki was left behind. At the intersection of the street with Hippocratous, in the arcade of some Ministry buildings, a young blind man was sitting on a low stool, singing and accompanying himself on an accordion. Willey stopped to listen. The voice was thin, whining, and somehow cruel too, beneath the complaint. The long quavering cadences were broken by snarling quarter-tones during which the singer raised his head with its fixed cataracted eyes and bared his teeth at the crowd. Willey was impressed by a quality of vulnerable savagery in the performance, like that of a maimed animal, reinforced by the violent but immediately checked movements of the arms expanding or contracting the accordion. It was apparently a love song he was singing. By listening intently Willey was able to make out some of the words.

'The bird of love is caged in my heart, I cannot free him. The night, which should bring my joy, takes my love away from me.'

The singer inclined his head, snarling softly. The song came to an end. Several coins clattered into the tin box on the pavement. Willey put in a drachma and began to make his way slowly back towards the square. He had only gone a few yards when the singer commenced again and the song followed him down the street as though there was something still that he had forgotten to do.

Wisteria was out on the walls of the Turkish Embassy, and a little below this, at the side of the steps, a mimosa tree was covered with yellow balls of flower. From the open doors of a *taverna* further down the street came the smell of lemons and retsina and burning charcoal. Willey went up the steps a little way, past the Embassy. He climbed until he could see over the white blocks of apartment houses to the Acropolis and the pale sea beyond. To the south was the long, intensely human line of Hymettos, violet along the crest; so great was the clarity of the light that the mountain seemed to take its rise from just beyond the square he had left. In his mind he could see its subsequent slow tilt to the sea, the ochreous knuckles of the foothills dipping at last into the glittering waveless water at Kavouri.

Willey stood looking. He loved this time of evening in Athens, the spent, faintly luminous pallor of buildings and pavements, the purity of the sky, the pause before night came. Below him the thin leaves of the mimosa stirred briefly. Suddenly he was filled by a feeling of loneliness and deprivation and by a sort of aching, objectless tenderness. Margaret's face came quite unexpectedly into his mind, her face framed by the school hat, sullen, not fully awake, as she said the rehearsed things: the facts arrayed exactly in narrative form, so that no real truth could strain through them, the terrible instilled resentment. Yes, on the evening of June the 8th it began, at his lodgings, I went there to get help with a lesson. . . . Those June evenings were cool, showering, sharp with the smell of privet and lawn from the little garden below his room, shrill with the voices of disputing children. And she had been different, in a way her flat young voice could not indicate, a different person, away from her companions; not school uniform

31

now but in a tightly fitting skirt and a blouse partially transparent so that the skin of her shoulders glowed beneath it. Why she should have decided to come to his lodging in this way he did not know – she had never shown much interest or attention during his lessons. She was wearing nylon stockings and he remembered the faint rasp of the nylon caused by the friction of the insides of her thighs as she shifted on the sofa beside him. She had shifted continually all the time he was attempting to explain the lesson. This in fact was what he chiefly remembered of that evening, the terrible restlessness of her body which no résumé of the facts could reveal; the carelessness of her legs which he had known at last was deliberate. Only when, hardly able to see, the blood beating in his temples, he had reached and laid his hand on her, only then had her body become still, stilled instantly as though by a blow. . . . Yes, always during the summer term, on several occasions, I can't remember exactly, ten or twelve times . . . A pupil of yours too, fifteen years of age, no isolated instance but what I can only call . . . No alternative but to . . . No possibility of a testimonial, of course, lucky to have escaped a prosecution. If you will take my advice . . . *No thank you.*

He walked slowly back down the steps. He had not thought of Margaret for quite a long time. One day he would forget her completely. . . . This prefigured forgetfulness appalled him suddenly as he went on, like an intimation of his death – only the dead do not bleed any more. . . . He emerged finally on Queen Sofia Avenue, quite close to Constitution Square. He crossed the avenue and walked past the row of little flower stalls that lie side by side against the outside wall of the Old Palace. Acting on impulse he stopped before one of these, still without definite intention, and the proprietor rose from his chair on the pavement and approached him, smiling, establishing already a shared admiration for the flowers. He was an old man and looked ill. '*Oriste,*' he said, and Willey's heart contracted at the brave attempt at blandishment, the word of welcome from the lined, pale face, pale with an indoors pallor, the pallor of hours spent behind the glass of greenhouses, coaxing blooms out of season, in foetid atmospheres. Great trays of gardenias were displayed on the stall, the blanched flowers closed for evening, and a bank of sharply budded roses, and sprays of mimosa. He stood before the flowers bewildered, helpless, caught in odours and colours as in a net. '*Oriste*,' the old man said again. He must buy some flowers, of course; that, surely, was why he had stopped here. Too expensive, the gardenias and roses. Easter lilies stood in vases, but these were too ceremonial, too austere. His mind flinched from the delicate mimosa. He chose finally tulips, a dozen yellow tulips. The old man nodded, approving his choice. '*Malista, malista,*' he said, the flowers vivid beneath his seamed face.

'How much?' said Willey, resigning himself to the haggling that must take place in Athens before any purchase could be made. For such beautiful flowers, personally grown, and as he could see quite fresh, sixteen drachmas. Twelve they agreed on finally, and the old man tied the stalks with twine and wrapped the bunch in silver paper.

Holding the flowers loosely, Willey went back along the avenue towards Kolonaki. Olivia lived just beyond the square on the ground floor of a three-storey family house. In the small garden of the house opposite there was a fig-tree in leaf now, the bright green buds unfurling into fans, the unripe fruit much darker, dusty-looking. He rang the bell and almost immediately Olivia opened the door, swinging it wide open with a gesture of exuberant welcome he knew so well.

'You wretch, you said you'd be here at half past seven and it's nearly . . .' Her eyes widened when she saw the flowers. Backing into the room she slithered a little on the mat. 'Oops!' she said.

'I have brought you some tulips,' Willey said. In the living-room he began to untie them, clumsily. He handled the twine too roughly, cutting some of the stems, and sap came out on his hands.

'I'll find a vase for them,' Olivia said, disappearing into the kitchen.

The flowers had an intense, an almost incandescent, yellowness in the dim, cluttered room. Fumbling with them, standing there on the figured carpet, among the carefully arranged objects, he thought how strange it was he should be doing this, standing here, making this particular series of gestures. The flowers would provide Olivia with an image of herself that had nothing, perhaps,

33

to do with his intention, and that was already beyond his power to amend. There was nothing, therefore, but to accept it as true. Ceaseless, he thought, the human need to shape experience, render motives acceptable. We are all artists in this respect, chipping away at life with our furtive little chisels. Why he had bought the flowers, for whom he had bought them, would never now be established. He had brought them, however, to Olivia. They were a correlative to his pain on the steps just now, with which she had really nothing to do; bridging, then, past and present, flowers for the dead and for the living.

'I don't think you've ever bought flowers for me before,' she said, returning with a glass jug. She turned on him a face bright with pleasure, and he was bewildered again by the enormous difference between the complexity of his purchase and the simplicity for her of the token. He smiled, nevertheless, affectionately at her.

'I think tulips are your sort of flower,' he said, and realised that this was true in a way; they were orderly flowers, not fussed with leaves, having deep colours without much gradation.

Olivia put the flowers into the jug and set it in the middle of the living-room table. 'They look nice there,' she said. She came to him awkwardly and kissed him on the mouth. He put his arms around her, feeling comforted by the familiar angularity of her body. She was a little taller than he was, and seemed always to bestow, in their embraces, more assurance than she received. After some moments she drew away and he saw that she had made a sort of recovery.

'Absolutely divine,' she said, in her rapid, rather gobbling voice. 'Where did you get them? I haven't seen any tulips about, have you your own sources of supply? Speak, unfold your secret.'

'Aha!' Willey said. He gave a twist to an imaginary moustache. 'Question me not, proud beauty,' he said.

They smiled at each other, both grateful that the situation had become thus facetious and manageable. Later she brought out the supper that had been waiting for him, and they ate it together: chicken and rice with cabbage salad, followed by American coffee, an extravagance this last.

Willey took off his jacket and lit a cigarette. 'Another homeless Briton dumped on me this evening,' he said.

34

'Oh *Gawd*,' Olivia said. 'Not another.' She was engaged in knitting him, very slowly, a canary-yellow pullover.

'I rather liked this one, though.' He told her about Kennedy. 'Not a usual type,' he said. 'Not a professional teacher at all, by the look of him. There's a sort of unauthentic heartiness about him, rather untrustworthy, really. I couldn't quite make him out.'

'It's all very well,' Olivia said. 'But you are always being used in one way or another by these people. It's a case of the willing donkey. I think you ought to protest.'

'I can't protest too much, you know that.' He had told Olivia early in their acquaintance about the circumstances in which he had left England. She had never directly referred to it since.

She said, 'I just hate to see you being used like this, you are so much better than any of them. Look at that appalling book of Jennings that you had to wade through.'

'Yes,' Willey said. 'Yes, I know.' He was silent for some moments. 'If only they would offer me a permanent post,' he said. 'A proper contract. I've been on the locally employed staff now for four years, longer than anyone else. My results in the examinations are always good.'

'They will, this year,' Olivia said. 'They're bound to. You are miles better than any of the other teachers there, and they must know it. They're not such fools as that.'

He looked at her in silence. Her loyalty touched him as always, but it was too constant a response to be in the present circumstances very reassuring. They were not such fools, it was true; but, of course, he was useful to them as he was. He had been for ten years at that one school in England, almost his whole teaching career. Ten years unaccounted for would have been far too suspicious a circumstance, so he had had to give the name of the school to Jennings, who offered him after some days the temporary post. But he must have referred to the school. A special knowledge informed every glance Jennings gave him, every bit of hack work he was asked so politely to do.

'If only they would,' he said. There was a vacancy, he knew, to be filled from the locally employed staff. What a difference it would make. It would mean that he could no longer be dismissed in any arbitrary, local fashion, for a start; no more scrambling for teaching hours, courting the secretaries to put in a good word for him; no more worries in the long summer holiday. It would be a salary they both could live on. There was not much time. Olivia was thirty-six and she wanted children.

'Mackintosh was there tonight,' he said. 'Teaching his first-year class. Exuding keenness as usual.'

She said quickly, 'But they couldn't possibly . . . He's only been there two terms.'

'No,' he said. 'I suppose not.' But the fear he had experienced from the first about Mackintosh, seeing the immediate identification the other had made, between his own advancement and the progress of his pupils, reasserted itself now with the effect of a chill, in the cosy little room.

3

For three days following his arrival at his cousin's house Mitsos did not go into Athens. He remained at Kifissia and went in the mornings for solitary walks through the straight, tree-lined streets of the suburb. The afternoons he spent on the terrace of a café in the main square, under the great-plane trees, reading the newspapers, drinking coffee.

He read in the papers the political slogans of the party in power, promises of construction, references to the achievements of the recent past. They had an effect on him of complete unreality, hollow-sounding; protestations not policies. He turned the pages, impatient of the words printed there, hoping however, irrepressibly, to find an item of marvellous relevance, something to chime with his own existence. When it was approaching five o'clock he folded his newspapers carefully, drank some water to clean his mouth of coffee grounds, and clapped for the waiter.

Alexei, his cousin, was worried about him, not so much worried as faintly outraged. It was not Greek, seemed moreover in some way belittling. He had known Mitsos well as a boy. They had been at school together, attended each other's name-days, competed in examinations and carnival costumes. It was Alexei's father, with the shipping office in London, who had found Mitsos the post. And it was he who had written to tell them of Mitsos' wish, after fifteen years, to revisit Athens.

Alexei had made resolves to help Mitsos if he could; but fifteen years is a long time; their differences in temperament mattered much more, now that their lives had taken such different directions; Mitsos was like a stranger in the house.

'There is something odd about him,' Alexei said to his wife Kikki. 'I would know this even without the letter. He looks too carefully at everything. Every time he looks at me I have the feeling he has never seen me before. Do you have this feeling too?'

Kikki assented. She was a beautiful girl with slow-moving, heavy-lidded eyes and a general air of being well satisfied sexually. She came from a land-owning family in Volos and had brought Alexei a good dowry, which he, as more in keeping with the times, insisted on calling 'contribution'.

'I know,' Alexei said, 'we must be considerate with him. He has suffered much. To see your father killed before your eyes and your mother violated, that is very terrible, Kikki. But the past cannot be changed. *Ti na canome?* We have to live. And there were many others, after all.' He bore a resemblance to Mitsos, especially about the eyes, but was more strongly built and heavier in feature; and of recent years he had acquired a barbered look, a managerial gloss.

'His father was a collaborator,' Kikki said. 'He was one of the first to go into the security battalions, when the Germans formed them. A volunteer officer.' Although she had taken on her husband's conservatism since her marriage, Kikki came from a district traditionally left-wing, a district, moreover, where memories were long.

Alexei frowned a little. 'I don't think we ought to speak of collaborators as though we meant by it always something bad,' he said. Many men in public life, highly respected men, had been collaborators to some extent. 'The guerillas did a lot of harm,' he said.

He tried to discuss these things with Mitsos sometimes, in the evening after supper. '*De mou les*, Stavros,' he would begin. 'Our job, the job of the young in Greece, is to build for the future. In our days in this country material considerations have the force of moral imperatives.' (He had read this in *Kathimerini*.) 'Greece does not need ideologies,' he said. 'She has made her contribution in this respect, as the world knows. She needs stability. We must have time to repair, rebuild, we must cement our differences. To revive the dissensions of the past, that is criminal, *den eine*?'

Alexei's face worked energetically as he spoke. Mitsos looked into that face, so like his own. Sensing his less than complete concurrence, it was charged already with a combativeness ironically at odds with his general theme. Alexei was a lawyer, working for Shell and doing very well.

'*Den eine?*' Alexei said again. If only, Mitsos thought, his cousin were not doing so well, if only his views were a little at odds with his interests. The English suits, the four-bedroomed house in the fashionable suburb, the Volvo in the garage, the maid: fruits of stability.

He said slowly, 'According to the Ministry of Justice, the bodies of over one thousand persons were exhumed during the winter of 1944 in Athens alone. They were victims of E.A.M. Nearly all of them were civilians and quite a lot were women. A high proportion of these people had been blinded, or in some other way mutilated, before being killed. The men who did these things survived, many of them. They are walking about Athens now. Respectable middle-aged men. Certainly they would want that cement applied. Don't you think it strange, Alexei, you might sit with one of these men in the café, a man who had deliberately blinded someone, *before killing him*, and you might find in him a complete agreement with your views?'

'There are criminal elements, I agree. That must always be so, not only here. There is violence in the people, yes, but Greeks are not cruel, on the whole. At least, they cannot sustain cruelty. It is the cruelty of impulse. Things were done that were later regretted. The people were envenomed by the Occupation. It happened all over Europe.'

'To blind a person that you intend subsequently to kill, that is . . . gratuitous. It is not something that can be "regretted".'

Alexei became impatient. 'It belongs, in any case, to the past. There is no point in unearthing these things now, *paidi mou.*'

Mitsos looked at him in silence. He thought he could see the line of Alexei's life: managerial rank; after the Volvo a Mercedes; the committee perhaps of the Athens Tennis Club; a *garsonnière* in town somewhere and a series of affairs, conducted with discretion and generosity. Kikki would get fat, of course, and spend much time playing *prefa* with her friends.

'I am not trying to unearth things,' he said. But the evil had first to be acknowledged, if there was to be any effective collision with it of repentance or resolution or even caution merely. Alexei dissociated himself from the past, which had not been of his contriving. Perhaps this was the healthy way. Perhaps he too would feel the same if he had gone on living in Greece, trammelled in the days that succeeded. 'It is not a question,' he said, 'of digging things up. The act of internment for everyone is personal and private. For me these things have never been buried, you see. . . .'

On Saturday they decided to make an excursion to the beach at Vouliagmeni. Kikki kept them waiting while she got ready, and Alexei spent the time dusting the cream Volvo; he kept a long feather brush in the boot for the purpose. Finally Kikki appeared and they were off down Kiffissia Avenue, skirting Syntagma, and then along Syngrou, slowing for the roundabout near the racecourse, coming out at a rather choppy sea at Faleron, where they turned left along the excellent coast road, pink oleanders whizzing past all the way down the middle of the carriageway, on the other side the glittering sea.

'*Vracho, vracho, to kaimo mou,*' Alexei sang, throwing back his head. He seemed very happy and Mitsos understood suddenly that this was the Greece his cousin was at home in, the complement of Alexei's soft-footed competitive, air-conditioned weekdays. These were the fruits, this Saturday hedonism, the machine that obeyed, the triumphal singing progress beside the brilliant sea.

Later, on the beach itself, he felt for a while self-conscious about his thinness, the whiteness of his skin, among these assured, sun-bronzed bodies that sprawled or sauntered all around him, beaded with sea-drops or smooth with oil. The whole beach smelled of salt and hot flesh and lotions.

The sea was pegged out with rafts at exact intervals. The rafts were covered with matting and anchored in place. Little paddle-boats bobbed across the captive sea, capsizing from time to time, plunging the paddlers into water that cleaved open for them like oil. No tremor of a tide in this sea; but it was alive with light, hot clear light; the surface glittered in uniform brilliance to the horizon where it paled, the blue turned misty to meet a paling sky – sea and sky attenuated themselves there, reduced their harshness, like lips that intend kissing.

After some minutes Alexei and Kikki ran down to the water leaving Mitsos alone at the table. He held himself still. The movement and light were like assaults on his senses. All around him limbs were flexing or reclining. Light rained from the sea, the teeth and eyes of bathers, the spine hairs, shin hairs, chest hairs, all burnished. Mitsos felt his gaze becoming irresponsibly selective: dwelling now on a thick forearm, now on the umbilical whorl of a girl, or the vast quaking buttocks of some Athenian matron. All at eye-level, all equidistant from his eye, none more beautiful or pleasing than the others, mere attributes of flesh. . . .

Kikki and Alexei returned from the bathe, laughing. 'Why don't you go in?' Alexei asked. His body was deeply tanned, compact and muscular. Water gleamed on the dark hairs on his forearms and chest. Kikki's skin was paler, almost golden. She lay down on the sand, laughing widely, her eyes closed against the sun. 'I'll bury you,' Alexei said. 'Let us bury her, Stavros.'

He began to heap the hot pale sand up round her thighs and shoulders. Where the skin was dry the sand slipped away, but it adhered to her in patches. Alexei persisted, grew intent. Soon the lower part of her body was completely covered. He took a handful of sand and creasing his palm like a funnel poured a trickle of hot grains deliberately down the front of her costume in the valley between the breasts. She squirmed in the sand, which partly fell away from her, and the frontal convexities of her thighs showed through. . . .

Abruptly Mitsos rose and made his way down to the water. He swam out to the farthest of the rafts and hauled himself on to it. From here he could see the whole sweep of the coast as far as the headlands hiding Cape Sunion, the whole south-western flank of Attica, abutting on its blue, enamelled sea. Thus, or almost thus, would the invading Persian fleet have seen it, lying off Salamis; at this distance the sort of changes that had occurred were not apparent; the same colours, sage and olive and terracotta; the same scents wafted from the land, pine and thyme and summer dust. Thus they had looked at it, secure in their power and the omens, surmising beyond, Athens, basined in the hills, guarded by its divinities.

He felt the sun hot on his back and the taste of salt on his lips. It seemed to him that he, no less than they, had come with an intention of conquest. To conquer a city is to make it habitable for oneself.

That Saturday morning Kennedy had shaved carefully, paid particular attention to the details of his toilet. He gave his tweed suit a good dusting. It was three days since he had arrived in Athens, high time to start looking for a job. The previous days he had spent in what he called 'getting the feel of the place', but he knew himself well enough to know that if he allowed the settling in process to go on too long his deep distaste for work of any sort would submerge him altogether and he would have to be helped home by the consul. He had drunk large quantities of Greek brandy the evening before, in company with Simpson, and was not looking so debonair as he could have wished. This morning, he told himself, nodding and winking at his shaving mirror, he would try the commercial institutes. The veins in his eyes, he noticed, were inflamed, his tongue the palest shade of sulphur. Coffee was what he needed.

But he met Kitty at the bottom of the stairs, grieving over one of her cats who had returned that morning with his right eye destroyed. She thought it the work, not of other cats, but of Athenian hooligans, though Kennedy could not discover the basis for this belief.

'*C'est dommage*,' he said politely.

'*Le pauvre*,' Kitty said. 'The unfortunate animal.' Sorrow had infused her great cheeks with a bluish tinge, the prow of her nose lifted nobly. The cat, pressed against the pink flannel of Kitty's dressing gown, regarded Kennedy steadily with one golden eye, the other was gummed with mucous. 'They are not compatriots of mine,' Kitty said. 'I throw back the connection. I am a Greek from Constantinople, *de l'ancienne race*. It is we, the *émigrés*, who have taught them to live. *La cuisine*, everything. Before we came they lived like beasts. Constantinople was a Roman city. But Athens — *c'est l'Orient, monsieur*.'

He escaped finally and found a little café where he got coffee and rolls. Then, refreshed, he began to plan his morning. Which one to begin with? he wondered. He bought a street plan of the city at one of the kiosks. He was, he saw from this, quite close to Constitution Square, where several of the institutes were situated. He chose one at random: Brittano-Hellenic Institute, Director Mr Melas. He would try that. Hermes Street. Ten minutes' walk brought him to the square itself.

Hermes Street proved easy to find, the institute itself even easier, since a large board jutted out over the pavement with the full name in white letters on a blue background, visible for hundreds of yards in all directions. It consisted of the two top floors of a rather expensive-looking six-storey block. Kennedy rode up in a smooth German lift and went into a small room marked 'Enquiries'. He asked the girl inside if he could see Mr Melas. He had not an appointment, he explained, but he had recently arrived from England. . . . The girl asked him to wait for some minutes, and then returned to say that Mr Melas could see him immediately. She led the way along the corridor and tapped at one of the doors. After a moment she opened the door and ushered Kennedy into the room, closing the door softly behind him. He found himself facing a heavily built, dark-jowled man, younger than he had expected, wearing a grey suit with a broad pink stripe.

'How are yaw?' this person said. 'Glad to see yaw, my dear felloo.' He had the weirdest accent Kennedy had ever heard, an almost unbelievable parody of English upper-class speech.

Kennedy shook the hand offered to him. It lay inert and podgy, slightly moist, inside his own. 'Kennedy,' he said. 'Pleased to meet you.'

While he was explaining the reason for his visit, Melas wriggled with the utmost understanding and said 'Haw' several times. He had a dark and coldly lustrous eye and a wide almost lipless mouth, like a frog's, that looked both exultant and suffering.

'Which universitair were you at, Mr Kennedair?' he said at last. 'Oxford, Cambridge?'

'Oxford,' Kennedy said.

'I was at Oxford *and* Cambridge, matter of fact, old chap,' Melas said. 'I was five and a half years in England.'

'Oh, were you?' Kennedy said, observing the complacent stretching of the other's mouth. He was having very considerable difficulty in comprehending Melas, who spoke in a series of extraordinary bursts or gushes, each of about five seconds' duration and each terminating in a long-drawled aspiration of ineffable aplomb.

Melas indicated the room where they were sitting, the large desk with its swivel chair, dove-grey carpeting, cream telephone. 'What do you think of it all, old chap,' he said. 'Haw?'

'Very nice.'

'My Director of Studies is also an Oxford man. He is in England at present for a spot of blightair.'

'What was that? I didn't quite catch . . .'

'Blightair, spot of blightair. Here he is, in his Oxford uniform.' He pointed to a small framed photograph on the desk. It was of a large-nosed, rather scrofulous-looking man in a mortar-board and gown.

'*Blighty*,' said Kennedy. 'I see, yes.'

'Tophool felloo,' Melas said. 'Invaluable. Let me show you round, Mr Kennedair.' They went out together into the corridor. Melas talked continuously, his vowels alternately gobbled and drawled. He was full of schemes. He spoke of his friends in high places, his belief in tours, visits, courses, culture, modern literature. But he did not seem eager to discuss in any concrete way the possibility of employing Kennedy in his institute. 'We have five classrooms,' he said. 'Three on this floor, two on the upper floor. I cannot show them to you now, because they are all in use. But I can show you the lavatorairs.' He opened doors, stood aside beaming to reveal lavatory pans with imitation mother-of-pearl seats, immaculate hand-basins, folded towels on racks. 'Try the chain, my dear felloo,' he said. 'Give it a jolly old pull.' Kennedy gave the chain a gentle tug. It flushed immediately. They stood smiling at each other, waiting for the roar of waters to subside.

'Excellent,' said Kennedy at last. 'Light, airy, spacious.'

'The emphasis is on education, of course,' Melas said. 'But these are aids, visual aids, old chap. Haw.'

They stepped outside into the corridor again. 'Well,' Kennedy said. 'I would enjoy working for you very much . . .'

'Oh, no, no,' Melas said, raising his hands. 'Not these Teutonic terms, to work for, work under. Here we prefer to speak of collaboration.'

'Well, I should very much like,' Kennedy said laboriously, 'the opportunity of collaborating with you in . . .'

'Do you know the works of Mr Thomas Eliot?'

'Yes.'

'I know them all, the poems, the plays, completelair. *Murder in the Cathedral*, *The Familiar Reunion*, *The Bottle Party* – a great play. I am going to organise Thomas Eliot tutorial groups all over Greece. You have not yet seen my new canteen.'

The canteen took up about half of the upper floor. It had polished parquet flooring, little tables covered with flowered oilcloth and a long counter decorated with Pepsi-Cola advertisements. It was quite deserted.

'What do you think of it, haw?' Melas said.

'Very nice indeed.'

'Canteens are the up-and-coming thing in education. It is entirely an idea of my own. I do not know of any other institute in Athens that has a canteen. They will come flocking, Mr Kennedair, in the breaks between lessons. They will arrange to meet their friends here, new students will be enrolled.'

'I think it's a great idea,' Kennedy said.

'It has not been opened yet, officially. I am still searching for a reliable person. Difficult to find in Greece, Mr Kennedair. People are often not honest.' Melas shook his head sadly. 'I was five and a half years in England,' he said.

'Yes.'

'What will you take? Pepsi-Cola?'

'I don't want anything, really.'

'Please, you will take something. From the new canteen.'

'All right, thank you. I'll have an orange juice.'

'Certainly,' said Mr Melas. 'Certainly.' He went behind the counter and poured out a Fixe Orange into a glass. 'Orange juice,' he said, beaming, handing the glass to Kennedy. 'Cheerioo!' He watched carefully while Kennedy was drinking. 'Good, haw?' he said. 'What do you think of it?'

'Very good.'

'What do you think of my accent, Mr Kennedair? Very British, haw?'

'Very British, yes. Coming back to the question of my position, I believe you said earlier that you were needing instructors?'

'I did, yes.'

'How much would you be offering?'

'Well, of course, old chap, you will appreciate my position, I am only at the beginning. I have had a lot of expenses. You have seen the lavatorairs, the canteen. . . .'

'How much,' Kennedy said, 'in round figures?'

'I could offer suitably qualified instructors twenty drachmas an hour,' Melas said.

'But that's only five shillings. I mean, at that rate, I'd have to work forty hours a week to make ten pounds.'

'I could not promise you forty hours,' Melas said. 'Oh dear no, haw, haw.'

'That's absurd,' Kennedy said. He felt cheated. He had paid his dues of admiration to the Melas establishment and was, it seemed, to get nothing back except the sweet taste of orange juice still lingering in his mouth.

'Think it over,' Melas said. He glanced at his watch. 'I have to go out now,' he said. 'You have not seen my car, have you? Did you see it when you came in? Perhaps I can give you a lift?'

'All right,' Kennedy said, somewhat moodily. 'If you are going anywhere near Kolonaki Square.'

They descended in the lift together. At such close quarters Melas smelled of after-shave lotion and garlic. He asked Kennedy what he thought of the lift, and Kennedy, who had been expecting the question, said that he always distrusted German machinery, which, while often presenting a superficial appearance of efficiency, nearly always turned out to have radical faults. This kept Melas quiet, except for a 'haw' or two, until they reached the car, a primrose-coloured machine, parked round the corner from the institute. Without this time waiting to be asked, Kennedy related one or two unfortunate experiences friends of his had had with this car.

'British car,' Melas said, reproachfully.

'Yes,' said Kennedy, 'but they don't make them like they used to.'

Inside, before engaging gear, Melas put a hand on Kennedy's knee. 'I could show you Athens by night,' he said. 'All floodlit.' He gave the knee a slight squeeze.

'I've seen it,' Kennedy said.

Melas deepened the exultation, or possibly anguish of his smile. 'I can help you a lot in this city,' he said. 'Any time you want any help . . .'

They skirted Constitution Square and turned left along Academy Street. Whatever confidence Melas had lost when Kennedy criticised the lift and the car he soon regained while driving. He was a very showy driver, one of those drivers whose hands register awareness of their own dexterity. When he changed gears his hands followed through, rather as though he were making strokes at ping-pong, and returned to the wheel with a flowing, omnipotent gesture. And he kept up a running commentary on the ineptitudes of other drivers: 'Did you see that felloo cutting in there, Mr Kennedair? No signals at all. And look at that beastlair rotter over there, he thinks by sounding his horn to make a way for himself. Haw, I remember your splendid Highway Code.' His right hand detached itself from the wheel and made circular gestures. 'The Greek people, Mr Kennedair, are not yet accustomed to the automobile. Look at that felloo there, I ask you.' He leaned over to point out the offender.

'Look out!' Kennedy said urgently. The traffic lights at the corner of Kanaris Street had changed while Melas was looking away, causing the car in front, a Citroën, to pull up quite suddenly. Melas was able to reduce speed but was still travelling at ten or fifteen miles an hour when he collided with the rear of the Citroën. Kennedy had seen the accident coming, so was able to brace himself and avoid being thrown forward against the windscreen. He saw at the moment of impact something, some fitting from the car in front, go flying across the road and at the same time the head and shoulders of the driver were suddenly jerked rather grotesquely forward and upward.

Melas for some moments preserved a complete silence. The driver of the other car, white-faced and evidently furious, had emerged and was shouting and gesticulating fiercely towards them. Cars behind had stopped. People were already beginning to gather.

'*Vlacha*,' said Melas, rather snarlingly. Then, remembering his passenger, he said, 'Did you see how the rotter cut across me, Mr Kennedair, haw?'

'No,' Kennedy said. 'As a matter of fact, old boy, I didn't.'

Melas descended from the car slowly, and Kennedy followed. Melas addressed himself magisterially to the crowd. The dignity of his manner was marred, however, at the end, when he spat dangerously close to the other driver's shoes. Cars behind were hooting. A policeman appeared and began pushing his way through. Melas, whose behaviour seemed to be deteriorating, spat again, more copiously, and began shouting and waving his arms. The policeman looked unfavourably at Melas. It seemed to Kennedy time to be going. He edged his way out of the crowd, and walked rapidly away up Kanaris Street in the direction of Kolonaki.

Not far away, in Jennings' office, the fortnightly staff meeting was proceeding.

'It was good of you to come,' Jennings had said, making urbane shapes with his mouth. Then he had lowered his gaze to the papers on his desk and sat in silence, waiting for the shiftings of his audience to subside into the receptive hush which after long experience of articulating he had come to recognise as his element. He enjoyed these meetings, which were held every second Saturday; always, in fact, marking the day with a white carnation in his button-hole. 'I have your remarks here in front of me,' he said, still without looking up. 'I found them most interesting.' His plump white hands lifted papers, allowed them to fall again. 'It helps us all, I think,' he said, 'to pool as it were our resources. And it seems to be particularly valuable at this stage, with the examinations approaching, to know your general plans for revision. I must assure you, of course, that you have by this time covered all the material required for the examinations. . . .' He glanced from face to face as though seeking confirmation of this. Mackintosh was nodding gravely, but none of the others made any sign. Jennings paused for some moments to twitch his features, establish their sensitive mobility.

'What I wanted,' he continued, 'was a more or less general statement of your intentions, but one or two of you have seen fit to go into some detail.' He picked up one of the papers. 'There is someone in our midst,' he said, 'who shall remain nameless, who intends to revise what he calls the Past Progressive Tense. He will point out, he says, that this tense is used for an action initiated in the past, not necessarily completed, extending over a period of time. He will illustrate this with examples.' Jennings paused, smiling, teeth improbably white. 'Well now,' he said, 'is this really true? Can we really talk about language in that way? I think that person would be embarrassed by some of the questions I could ask him.' He was silent for a moment, then said suddenly with a deepening of intensity: '*All the time I was staying with my aunt, I heard the sound of the sea!* There you have a strange, indeed a baffling, conjunction of tenses, simple past and continuous past. Yet the actions are *co-extensive*. When we are faced with such illogicality there is nothing for it but to accept.' Jennings raised his hands, palms upwards, in an oriental gesture of acceptance.

Willey cleared his throat. His face was rather flushed. 'It appears,' he said, 'that you are referring to me. I realise that there are exceptions, of course. But the rule covers nine cases out of ten in my opinion.'

Jennings continued to finger the paper. 'I do not think,' he said, 'that rules as such will get us very far. Language is behaviour, it is meaningful activity. Anything we say *about* language will be largely irrelevant. What confronts us, on every hand, is *usage*. The essence and the existence are one.'

Willey knew it was rash of him to prolong this discussion; he should never in the first place have emerged from the anonymity which Jennings had intended for him, but the unfairness of the thing had disturbed his judgment. Also, he hated, intensely, the manner Jennings assumed for such pronouncements, the blandness, the spurious philosophical poise. He forgot for a moment Olivia, his desire for a permanency, the plot of land in Ekali he hoped some day to buy. 'That won't get us very far in the classroom,' he said. 'We have to teach particular groups of people to use English, communicate in English. We see them for six hours a week, sometimes only four. We have to use rules valid in the great majority of cases. The students must acquaint themselves with usage in their own time.'

'If I may be allowed to intervene at this point, sir,' Mackintosh said. He leaned forward alertly, his face shining, protuberant eyes under pale lashes looking deferentially at Jennings.

'By all means, Mr Mackintosh.' Jennings made one of his courteous unfolding gestures.

'Well, I must say I disagree with Mr Willey. We must relate everything to a natural context, it seems to me. As you yourself have pointed out quite frequently, sir, it is the language as it is actually used that we must teach. Too much language teaching these days' – here Mackintosh glanced briefly round and smiled at Willey – 'is completely divorced from context. In a void, so to speak.'

'Quite so,' Jennings said. He nodded approvingly at Mackintosh. 'I liked your suggestions for the drills inculcating particular usages,' he said. 'There is this one for the use of the distinguishing relative.' He referred to one of the papers. 'Yes, here it is. *That is the moon. Which moon? The moon we see every night. That is the sun. Which sun? The sun we see every day.* Yes, very apt, I think, Mr Mackintosh.'

Mackintosh smiled modestly. 'Not too rapid an extension of vocabulary,' he said. 'Each usage embodied in a key phrase . . .'

'But on what conceivable occasion,' Willey said, 'and among whom, could such conversations about the moon and the sun be conducted? Such words could not be uttered by dwellers on earth. They are more unreal even than the examples we used to get in the old textbooks, things like "my cousin is deaf and lame but my uncle is a hunchback". At least those contained some vocabulary . . .' He was aware, while he was speaking, of people turning to look at him: Miss Watson, earrings swaying; the dark remotely frowning face of Drakakis, the translation teacher. 'I must confess,' he said, 'that I cannot understand what you mean by context, if those are your examples.'

'A certain divergence of opinion,' Jennings said, smiling steadily at Willey. 'I see that we are not altogether agreed. A sign of health, perhaps.' His head pivoted smoothly away from Willey. 'I found your remarks concerning prepositional usage extremely interesting, Miss Watson,' he said. 'Would you like to, ah, elaborate a little?'

Damn them all to hell, Willey said to himself some time later, as he was walking from the meeting. He felt depressed. His foolish argumentativeness had served only to advance Mackintosh. To object to the latter's examples when Jennings himself had specifically approved them, that had been utter folly. What in the world had possessed him to do it? Suddenly he felt that he needed a drink rather badly. He paused on the pavement wondering where to go. The 'Lykis', outside which he was standing, was on the sunny side and all the tables under the awnings seemed to be already taken. It was too hot in the direct sunlight, and he was already turning away when he heard his name called. Looking over, he saw Kennedy alone at one of the tables under the awning, smiling and waving.

'Come and have a drink,' Kennedy called.

Willey crossed over to him, feeling for some reason delighted at the meeting.

'Did you get fixed up at Kitty's?' he asked, lowering himself into the seat beside Kennedy.

'Oh yes, thank you very much,' Kennedy said, smiling broadly. 'There was a room vacant because of this American fellow who had to leave because of disgusting behaviour. I haven't found out yet what he did.' The sunshine had brought out the freckles on his nose and cheek-bones and his fair hair was in the same dishevelled state that Willey remembered from their first meeting. The cuffs of his tweed jacket were frayed. He was sitting at his ease, legs splayed out across the pavement in front of him. 'What will you have?' he said. 'I'm having this ouzo stuff, I rather like it.'

'Yes,' Willey said. 'I'll have ouzo too.'

'I've had a bit of a fruitless morning, this morning,' Kennedy said. 'I'm just recovering from it, as a matter of fact; learned a bit, though.'

He told Willey about his adventures of the morning. The story of the accident amused the other considerably. 'So he reverted to Greekness under the stress?' he said. 'There ought really to be a verb in English "to Greekle", to behave in a Greek way. As "they stood there Greekling". It would be a great enrichment. I know

51

this Melas slightly. He is widely regarded as consummately British. His institute should do well.'

'He didn't seem too keen to employ me. He showed me round the place, but he hedged when it came to a job. And when I asked him point-blank he offered me twenty drachmas an hour. Twenty drachmas, that's only five shillings!'

'I shouldn't think he wanted you to work for him at all. He would have to pay you too much, a native English speaker. There are plenty of Greeks who would jump at twenty drachmas an hour. What you ought to try is private teaching. You can get up to a hundred an hour for that and no tax to pay. No qualifications needed, you only have to be English. And now is just the time that people are getting panicky about the exams. I have a couple of prospects, if you're interested. No time to do it myself.'

'Thank you very much,' Kennedy said. 'I would be very grateful. Let's have another drink. This same Melas could seem to be something of a twister,' he added. 'In fact there's trickery in the air of this city. That's my impression anyway. Trickery and antiquities and the old drachma going clickety-click.'

'Well, yes,' Willey said. He was beginning to feel a pleasant muzziness. 'It is a commercial nation. Sharp practice is condoned here – more than that, admired. I sometimes think that in Athens chicanery rather than virility has become the measure of a man. No, I am exaggerating, of course. Anyway, I don't mean illegal practices necessarily, though many laws here seem curiously lacking in definition. I mean taking short cuts, getting one up on people.'

Willey paused for a moment smiling. 'Of course,' he said, 'they are so *personal*, when they conduct official business of any sort, they always try to breach the hierarchy at some point of personal acquaintance. What in the Army used to be called the old-boy net. They are intriguers by instinct. There's a permissiveness towards all forms of deceit, and that's what often outrages the Anglo-Saxon.'

'It doesn't outrage me, old boy,' Kennedy said. 'And you seem to get along with it all right?'

'Well, my principles have been eroded over the years,' Willey said.

'You've been here for some years now, haven't you?'

'Yes, Athens is my home, really. I haven't any other.'

'You don't go back to England much then?'

'I don't go back at all.'

'I see,' Kennedy said. There was silence between them for some moments. Then Kennedy said casually, 'Spot of bother perhaps?'

For a moment Willey was disposed to be annoyed. He looked sharply at Kennedy. But in the smiling face of the other he could detect neither sympathy nor complacent insight – only a sort of careless geniality. 'Yes,' he said. 'You might call it that,' and he smiled slightly. Kennedy's own obvious rascality removed it from anything like a confession.

'I've been in spots of bother myself,' Kennedy said. 'At one time or another. Let's have another one.'

'My turn.' Willey clapped his hands for the waiter.

'You must like it here then,' Kennedy said.

'Yes, I do.' Willey paused, oppressed by the difficulty of expressing his feeling for the city, the whole country. He wanted, with the ouzo working within him and the spot of bother conceded, to convey something of this to Kennedy. But his emotion was distilled from many particular moments, a complex blend, not now easily expressible: the sum of evenings when Hymettos bloomed before dying and the moon stared at the sun across the flushed city; the sanctity of dusk in the streets, unsullied by contacts or deliberations; the constant interaction between the animate and ephemeral and the ageless, pulseless; red anemones on the hill of Pnyx, cropped children squabbling on the marble steps of the theatre of Dionysus,' songs of fishermen and their bright nets on Homer's sea, at Delphi the slow song of a bird near the temple of Apollo, cicadas round the Portico of the Athenians, white dust and olive groves, an eagle flying high; everywhere the throb of continuity, in the grass between stones, the eyeholes of statues dredged up from the sea, the green of the sea-bloom still on the bronze. . . . None of this was communicable to Kennedy, not because of difficulties in language really, but because this was his own Athens, his own Greece: like a loved person she depended on a recognition of her qualities which none but he could accord; and he had accorded it early, when his own pain and loneliness compelled the sort of attention that shapes things for ever. . . .

'It grows on you,' he said.

'I suppose it does,' replied Kennedy, who had been watching his face with some intentness. 'I've never been anywhere long enough for that to happen to me. Except London, but you can't count that; I was born there.'

Willey returned no answer to this. He looked across the square, where traffic flowed and eddied ceaselessly. The ouzo, to which he was not really accustomed, had confused him and the light hurt his eyes a little – outside, beyond the striped awning, the world vibrated with light, as though sheathed in glass. Mica in the pavements glittered. The urge to confide in this clearly undependable person was strong in him.

'I've had rather a trying morning myself,' he said, and suddenly, almost before he knew it, he was telling Kennedy about the staff meeting, the terrible agility Mackintosh displayed in scaling the heights of official approval, his own diminishing prospects. Under Kennedy's by this time serious regard it had all come out, his precarious and difficult position at the institution, Olivia and his desire to marry, buy a bit of land – she had the money for this, carefully saved over years – but he needed a guaranteed income, because Olivia would want to start a family fairly soon.

'Everything, you see, depends on Jennings,' he insisted, feeling the onset of drunkenness.

'Yes,' Kennedy said. 'Yes, I see, old boy – I can think of people I'd rather depend on.'

'We'll have another, I think,' Willey said. 'One for the road, as they say. Please note,' he added, while they waited for the drinks. 'Please note, my dear fellow, that my ambitions are not inordinate. I am not asking a great deal.' He paused, aware of the absurdity of the pontifical manner that was descending on him, helpless, at the same time, to evade it. 'I do not,' he said, 'demand anything in respect of *permanence*. I leave that quest to nobler minds. No, simply a *permanency*, my dear fellow – what is your first name again?'

'Bryan.'

'I require, my dear Bryan, only a permanency.'

'I wish you the very best of British luck,' Kennedy said. 'You won't forget to give me those addresses, will you? You know, the people who might want private lessons.'

4

Mitsos stopped for a few moments outside the Old Palace. On the paved area, before the Tomb of the Unknown Soldier, pigeons gobbled and strutted: people were throwing corn for them from little packets. From time to time children rushed shouting into their midst, scattering them in all directions.

He looked across the wide avenue towards Constitution Square. The paved walks were the same, with their borders of cannas and wallflowers, the garden of olives and orange-trees in the centre, all this was the same, but he could not have recognised the buildings around the perimeter. Everything seemed much higher than he remembered. The enormous American Express building dominated the square now, and the big stores round Hermes Street, linked by new travel agencies and airline offices. The Hotel Grande Bretagne on the right was as he remembered it, with its sharp marble steps, the braided and constantly saluting person on the pavement outside, and the perpetual swarm of taxis at the kerb. A group of elderly, pastel-coloured American ladies came down the steps as he watched. It was as though the garden and hotel had been transplanted from some place totally familiar if he could only find it, and set down here in this strange square. He had come here quite often as a child, with his mother, after the ritual walk in the National Gardens, the ritual feeding of the ducks, for an ice-cream – a *Special*, with pistachio nuts and caramel. How long ago that seemed now, his greed for ice-cream conflicting with his desire for a distinguished seemliness of behaviour. . . . His mother's face of that time too he could recall in every detail, the great delicacy of temple and cheek, the beautiful, shortsighted eyes, the mouth mild, too small for beauty. . . . He was swept by the feeling of desolation that had accompanied all his wanderings through the city. Whatever he recognised seemed arbitrarily transposed, as though some vast and pointless reorganisation had taken place in his absence. And as though to confirm the changes that had happened, he heard once more as he stood there the sound of this new Athens, the steady remorseless chipping of steel on stone, repeated at exact intervals. It came from across the square in the direction of Philhellinon Street, but for Mitsos this sound had ceased to be local: everywhere he went in the city it pursued him, sometimes light and quick, almost gay, sometimes heavier, more solemn, frequently overlaid by the screeching of traffic or the voices of people, threading the more abrupt and dramatic evidences of change, the roar of demolitions, the stuttering of drills; re-emerging in every pause, every lull, every interval of silence. It was the sound of Athens continuing her renewal, continuing to elude him.

He crossed the avenue and went past the kiosk at the head of the steps leading into the garden. The man in the kiosk was picking his teeth with customary Greek discretion, holding his hands as though playing a flute, although he was alone there, behind *Corriere della Sera* and *Athens News*. Mitsos did not go directly through the garden but turned and proceeded round the outer edge in the shade of the orange-trees. He came out on the wide area of pavement covered with green tin tables and little stiff cane chairs. It was deserted now, in the hot mid-morning – clients went over the way to Zabaritis, where there was shade.

After hesitating for some moments Mitsos himself crossed over and sat at one of the tables just off the square. He asked for coffee and, while he waited, thought again of earlier that morning, walking along Partriarchou Joachim, striving to persuade himself of a destination, past the new apartment houses, the new boutiques, the new florist with great sheaves of lilies and irises in his window, precisely on the site surely of the little shop where he had once gone for the breakfast yogurt. Round the corner and up a little, over the steep cobbles to Charitos Street, where he had been born, spent his whole life, until the night of his father's death. He had known the house was no longer there – Alexei had told him – but he had expected at least to be able to see where it had been. The whole block was a maternity clinic now, with swing doors and a glimpse within of hushed green carpeting. Indeed in all the street only one original house was left standing, with its graceful wrought-iron balconies, wide-eaved roofs, tall narrow windows. It had clearly been empty, probably condemned. Jasmine grew over the closed green shutters. He walked up and down, past the clinic with its green neon cross, the sharp-edged apartment houses. The change was too radical, it denied his experience; the street denied him a past. He had not known that by new styles of architecture the past could be denied. As he walked up and down, the fig man with a basket on his head had passed by, uttering his trailing sibilant cry of *Sica! Sica!*, a sound well remembered from childhood in this street which was then another street. And into Mitsos' ears as the calls receded came the slow, almost stealthy sound of hammering metal against stone, from somewhere further up on Lycavettos.

Opposite him now was an obese pale woman in a black silk dress with short sleeves from which her soft white arms came billowing. She was eating with solitary greed a tiered cream cake, using for the purpose a tiny fork, almost lost in her plump white hand. Mitsos watched the fork dig deftly into the yielding cream, saw it freighted and conveyed to the moist lips above, saw the mouth shape itself at the last moment, the lips widen in a sort of grimace before closing over the fork completely in a perfectly round pout, to suck the cake softly off the prongs.

Mitsos experienced a slight feeling of nausea. He closed his eyes for a moment. There were times when the obsessive observation of detail descended on him, like a sort of visual cruelty, that he was helpless to prevent. Without finishing his coffee, he put the money for it down on the table and walked slowly away.

Not far away, in the Cathedral Square, Kennedy and Roland were having a beer together. It was one of Roland's days off. He worked four days a week, Kennedy had discovered, for a big firm of architects and civil engineers with many foreign employees, correcting the inter-departmental minutes, which were always written in English, of a sort. He had got this job because of his training as a draughtsman in England.

'I'm worried about Simpson,' Roland said.

'Oh yes?' Kennedy was wary. He had not yet been able to discover who was parasitic on whom in Roland's relationship with Simpson. Until he could unearth the self-interest he felt curiously hampered and powerless. There was no doubt that Simpson occupied a central place in Roland's life. Roland had adopted, it seemed voluntarily, the rôle of translating Simpson's predicaments into coherent form for the benefit of third parties. What did he get out of it? Kennedy dismissed as monstrous the suspicion that Roland might be really disinterested, might be experiencing, merely, a human concern. He was himself quite capable of the sudden anarchic impulse of generosity, even self-sacrifice, but he never gave considered kindness to another without some motive of gain, however blurred or impractical. And a faculty he did not possess himself he could not believe in in other people. 'Simpson's all right,' he said. 'He'll still be all right when you and I are on the scrap-heap.' He smiled suddenly and looked down at the tubby beer bottles on the table before him. On the whole he felt pleased with life this morning. Things were beginning to move. He had already secured three private students and had an appointment later with the girl that Sophy had told him about. Also, Eleni Polimenou, the actress, was back in Athens now. Kennedy intended to visit her later in the morning and offer his services.

'Yes, but the drinking, Bryan,' Roland said. 'I do hope he recovers his easel soon.'

'You believe in this easel, then?'

'Believe in it?'

'Believe it exists, I mean.'

'Of course I do,' Roland said indignantly. 'Don't you?'

'Well, it strikes me as a bit fishy, if you want to know the truth.'

'I know a dedicated man when I see one.' Roland was quite flushed.

'Listen,' Kennedy said, 'he's dedicated all right, he's dedicated to surviving.' Artistic bums like Simpson he had met before and always disliked, mainly for their spurious sense of caste, the way their cadging always got muddled up with feelings of privilege.

Roland's flush had faded. His face was pale, deeply lined for one so young. He declined his head a little and Kennedy could see the pale gleam of scalp beneath the thin hairs on his crown. He would in a few years be quite bald. It seemed to Kennedy that this was a particular result of a general lack in Roland of nutritive oils. He was essentially a *sparse* person. What impulse, what sudden image of himself, had taken him from his parents' home in Wimbledon, his safe job in a drawing office – for he had told Kennedy something of his life – to be Kitty's oldest resident, Simpson's defender, lay almost beyond speculation.

'You may be right,' he said now. 'But that wouldn't stop you from being hopelessly wrong too. I mean wrong from beginning to end. You don't care about anything, that's your trouble. Everyone should care for something; Kenneth does.'

'Here endeth,' Kennedy said. He was somewhat disconcerted by this unusual directness of Roland's and to cover this he looked away across the square, smiling broadly.

Roland took a nervous swallow of his beer. 'They are an extraordinary people in some ways,' he said, with an abrupt change of subject. 'Just look at this city, marvellous natural site, between the sea and the hills. Numerous eminences commanding extensive views. Wonderful climate, brilliant light, almost no industrial pollution. An architect's dream, you might say. And yet there is hardly a building of any distinction in the whole place. Excepting the antiquities, of course.' He looked across the square at the pigeons, the slowly moving people, the vast straight shadows of the cathedral. 'Just look at this ghastly cathedral,' he said. 'It has no merit of any sort, unless size is a merit. Certainly it's *big*. You'd think they'd know, wouldn't you, with all these beautiful little Byzantine churches in Athens. . . . Well, just compare it with the little Metropolis over there. About seventeen centuries between them . . .'

They looked for some moments in silence at the tiny church, the exquisite proportions of cupola and façade, the warm flush of the walls, in which fragments of antique marble were inset, the Byzantine reliefs of symbolic birds and beasts, the coats of arms of the Frankish lords of Athens. Then, because any claim on his piety irked him, Kennedy shifted suddenly in his seat and said, 'By the way, the fellow who had my room, what are the theories?'

Roland immediately began to look uncomfortable. 'There are conflicting stories,' he said reluctantly. 'Some say he exposed himself to Kitty one morning on the stairs. Others that he misbehaved in some public way on the balcony overlooking the street.'

'I shall wait for a favourable moment,' Kennedy said, 'and ask Kitty.'

At this moment they saw Simpson approaching from the direction of the Plaka. He was wearing his maroon cap. He walked with outlandish loping steps, his head lowered so that his features were quite concealed beneath the long peak. For some reason he was walking close to the walls of the houses, and so he was frequently held up by the steps from the street doors on to the pavement. Instead of swerving to avoid them he stopped dead at every one and side-stepped sharply. It was as though he were demonstrating his powers of co-ordination.

When he reached their table he raised his hand in a sort of salute before sitting down. 'Jesus,' he said, sticking his jaw out, 'I've had a hell of a morning.' He always conveyed the pressure of events, though what he did when he was not at Piraeus enquiring about his easel nobody knew. This morning, not being drunk, he had his features more under control. There was still, however, that curious staring quality, the grey film round the irises.

'I got a commission,' he said, 'for some paintings of Hydra. Rich bloody Americans. How the hell can I give of my best without an easel?'

'What will you have?' Kennedy asked.

'Cognac,' said Simpson. 'Without ice,' he said to the waiter. 'Don't you put any ice in it. It's perfect,' he said, 'if only I had my easel. They say they want views of Hydra because they've just been there. I've never been there of course but all these bloody islands look the same, anyway. I could do it easy, if only I had my easel.'

'Maddening,' Roland said.

'Can't you just work on a table or something, for this once?' Kennedy said.

There had been something derogatory in his tone and Simpson stiffened. 'I've got my reputation to think of,' he said. 'These

61

paintings will be shown to friends, back in the States. "That's a Simpson", they will say.'

'Quite so, Kenneth,' Roland said. He gave Kennedy a reproving glance.

'It's like what I said to Halpin the other day – I met him in the Plaka, he is often there hanging about, he's been telling people I don't pay my debts, the bastard – I was talking to him about these blisters I get in my heels from wearing baseball shoes all the time and he said to me . . . he wears these coloured scarves and he has these long sideburns. God, I hate his guts! He knows it too.' Simpson looked at them triumphantly as though this was the end of the story, Halpin's knowledge of his hate.

'What did he say then, Kenneth?' Roland prompted.

'I happened to meet him in the Plaka, he lives down there, and I was showing him these blisters and he said to me, "Ken, you're a bum, admit it, Ken." I looked at him a minute, then I said to him, "I've got my talent, Halpin, what the bloody hell have *you* got? I hate those bloody scarves you wear," I said to him.' He fixed Kennedy with the look of considerable animosity, then he delivered a right hook at the air before his nose. There was a remarkable savagery in the gesture. 'What the bloody hell have *you* got?' he said.

'Look, old boy,' Kennedy said. 'I don't give a monkey's for any bloody Halpins, but are you telling me you can't paint anything at all without your easel?'

'I'm telling you,' said Simpson in a loud voice. 'I'm telling you . . .' He paused for a moment as though baffled.

'You're up the creek, that's what it is,' Kennedy said.

'Please, Bryan,' Roland said.

'You may be all right at kipping in parks,' Simpson said, 'but you don't know your arse from your elbow when it comes to painting. I hate that bloody suit you're wearing.' Saliva had collected in the corners of his mouth.

'Don't get excited, Kenneth,' Roland said.

'I asked a civil question,' said Kennedy.

At this moment the waiter returned with the drinks. 'Look,' Simpson said, 'the bastard has put ice in my cognac.' He stood up suddenly. 'Take this fucking ice out of my cognac,' he said.

'For Christ's sake,' Kennedy said, in some disgust. 'If you can't behave like a gentleman, piss off.' He was about to say something else when he saw a person he knew passing across the square. It was the Greek he had tried to touch for a pound or two on the boat. 'Hey!' he called. 'Come over and have a drink. Hey you,' he called again, as the other did not appear to have heard him.

Mitsos turned his head and looking across the square saw a tall gesticulating person in a red cap with a strangely long peak. Then he saw the Englishman who had shared his taxi from Piraeus sitting at the table together with a worried-looking young man. While he looked, Kennedy beckoned to him, smiling broadly. 'Come and have a drink,' he shouted again. Slowly Mitsos walked towards them. He saw the man he knew reach up and draw the capped person down into his seat again. He stood smiling and inclining his head while Kennedy performed the introductions.

'What was your name again?' Kennedy said.

'Mitsos,' he said. 'Stavros Mitsos.'

'Stavros, that's right,' Kennedy said. 'I remember your sur-name, of course. Come and sit down. What will you have?'

Mitsos said he would have a coffee.

'How's it going?' Kennedy said. 'You said we'd be sure to meet, didn't you?'

'I did, yes,' Mitsos said. 'Athens is small. Or, rather, the area where people congregate is small.' He looked from face to face for some minutes. He could not understand how it was he came to be talking to these people. Suddenly he became aware that the person in the cap was speaking to him in muttered conspiratorial tones.

'Ken Simpson,' he heard this person say. 'American artist, exhibitions in every European capital. If you are interested in buying paintings I hope to be doing a series of impressions of Hydra shortly, or Mykonos, or Poros – Greek islands, you know. When I recover my easel, they lost my easel, not the Greeks, the bloody Germans.' There was something odd about this person's eyes.

'I do not know a great deal about paintings,' he said.

'All the better,' said Simpson. 'The response will be fresh.'

The other man, who had been shifting and fidgeting in his seat, now broke in with the air of a person performing a familiar duty of interpretation. 'Mr Simpson,' he said, 'is at present without his easel which has been mislaid by the railways authorities somewhere in Germany. It is a very valuable easel with various unique attachments.'

'I see,' Mitsos said. 'That was very unfortunate.'

'*Unfortunate*?' said Simpson unbelievingly. 'I'll buy that.' He had begun groping in his top pocket and after a moment produced one of his cards, which he handed to Mitsos with old-world courtesy. 'My card,' he said.

'Thank you,' Mitsos said. He was holding the card and seemed about to look down at it when the others saw his expression change suddenly. He stood up, looking across the square. 'Excuse me,' he said.

'What's the matter, old boy?' Kennedy asked, looking up at him curiously, then following his gaze across the square. There seemed, however, nothing remarkable happening there. People passing, that was all. The pigeons. A *pappas* on the cathedral steps talking to a woman dressed in black.

'Excuse me,' Mitsos said again. His face had gone whiter. Still holding Simpson's card in his hand, he took a few steps from the table.

'Wait a minute, here's your coffee,' Roland called, afraid, it seemed, of further offending the waiter. But Mitsos began walking rapidly away from them towards Odos Mítropoleos. They watched in silence while he disappeared from sight.

'Extraordinary way to behave,' Roland said.

'He saw something that shook him,' Kennedy said thoughtfully. 'I wonder what it was.'

Simpson said morosely, 'Look, that's my card on the ground there. The bastard dropped my card.'

All three of them looked for some moments at Mitsos' cooling coffee, as though the explanation might be there.

Simpson's card fluttered down unnoticed from Mitsos' fingers. His whole being was concentrated on keeping in view the man before him, the man whose face he had glimpsed on the square a few moments before. The man was bulky and walked slowly and was carrying, moreover, a very large black umbrella loosely furled, which he from time to time rested on his shoulder like a rifle, so he was not difficult to keep in sight.

But as they proceeded slowly up Hermes Street his surrender of will, his present complete dependence on the other for direction and purpose, began to seem like faith – needing at least, if not exactly guarantees, yet certainly a revision of the steps that had led to it. He recalled the man's features as though this constituted evidence: the face full, very pale, clean-shaven, a shallow cleft in the heavy jaw; memorable really only for the strange light eyes, almost yellow in colour, set at a slight downward slant in the head, like the eyes of a sad dog. . . . That look of mournful belligerence he had seen on the square just now, but he could not, at such a distance, have noted the colour of the eyes, that was a memory, not a present impression, a memory of fifteen years ago, when the men had come from Epirus to his father's house, the man with yellow eyes among them, he who had turned at the door and looked back, at his father's body, the whimpering woman beyond it, looked for some moments and then come back into the room. . . .

At Syntagma the man in front paused briefly on the edge of the pavement, as though undecided. He had a slow, lordly way of moving his head on the short thick neck. His linen jacket was crumpled and ill-fitting, strained too tight across the heavy shoulders. The black umbrella was like a symbol of office. After hesitating for a moment he crossed over to the inner square, and Mitsos followed, to the left down the central path, where the man installed himself on one of the green wooden benches under the orange-trees. The sun was hot now, high in the sky, it was desirable to be in the shade. Mitsos chose another of the benches, at a considerable distance. He was not so much afraid of recognition – he had been, after all, only a child then, only twelve years old – as reluctant to be registered at all in the other's awareness, at least for the present. The distance, however, was a disadvantage, in that he still could not see the man's face clearly. The man himself was quite motionless, a fawn sprawl on the bench, the rusty black umbrella hooked on the seat beside him. Suddenly, while he watched, it moved to unbutton its jacket, loosen its tie. Paunchy, sluggish, without apparent occupation, encumbered with an eccentric black umbrella, what could such a person have to do with him? Everything that had occurred on that distant evening had seemed sealed off from all possible aftermath, since his father had died violently then, and his mother within a year, and he himself, the only victim to survive, could refer to no one for mitigation nor even for confirmation of what had happened – the others, the men who had done these things, having no objective existence for him at all, as though summoned only for that time, to perform that one rôle, afterwards too monstrous for any other imaginable context. And now by some chance the only face among those others that his memory had culled and retained was possibly across the square before him, possibly. In the continuing uncertainty of this, only faith on his part could persist in asserting the identity, since he had seen the face again so briefly, for those few seconds on the square, and age and daylight had altered it. The face he knew had been younger, leaner, ruddy in the lamplight, with glinting stubble along the jaws. It had looked back with those queer yellow eyes from the door at the three of them, his father's body on the floor, himself crouched still partly stunned in a corner, and his mother standing in the middle of the room, body slightly stooped in an attitude of readiness as though awaiting the signal for a race, a repeated moaning note coming from her open mouth. That face had turned smiling at the door and glanced at them all in turn, his mother finally. For some moments the face had smiled, regarding his mother. Then some fixity, like earnestness had come over it, and the man had come back into the room. It was as though, it was exactly as though, those irrepressible noises of grief and shock had aroused the man, acted as the equivalent of female heat. Crouched there in his corner, he had seen it all happen, seen his mother straighten her body at the last moment, before the man reached her, straighten and raise her hands palm outwards and her moaning changed, not into words, but a higher more continuous note and then she was thrown down on to the carpet already soaking with his father's blood, a bundle that jerked and threshed. He saw everything that was done to his mother and he did nothing, made no sound. The man rose from the body of his mother whose exposed legs were strangely inert now and shameless. While he fumbled with the front of his trousers he had looked at the boy in the corner and the boy had known that it was in the man's mind to kill him. It was then that the man's face had laid its final impress on his memory, the yellow eyes grave now, almost impersonal. The man had stared a moment longer, shrugged slightly, and gone. His father's outstretched hand had quivered.

The person opposite Mitsos stirred suddenly. After a pause to adjust his tie and unhook his umbrella he made his way diagonally across the square in the direction of Philhellinon Street. Mitsos watched him for some moments, saw him pause again at the pavement, waiting apparently to cross the street. Then he got up himself and, keeping the other continuously in view, emerged from the square at a point somewhat higher up. There he waited. He knew that on no account must he allow the man to be lost to him ever again. To do so would be to offend irrevocably, put himself beyond help.

Kennedy left the others sitting at the table, involved now in an animated discussion of Simpson's easel, the favourite topic, it seemed, of both, and made his way to Carneadou Street, where his prospective pupil lived. The apartment was on the third floor of a new and imposing block of flats. An elderly woman in black with several whiskery moles, whom he assumed to be a retainer of some sort, came in answer to the bell and led him into a large sitting-room crowded with very new-looking furniture and with a great many pictures on the walls. Pride of place was held by a huge and shiny cocktail cabinet with a front of chrome and glass, and massive, incongruous webbed feet. It was not a room in which people would readily unbutton. Sitting on the sofa, wondering whether to smoke, Kennedy felt a growing discomfort. People, of whatever sort, could rarely abash him. He had considerable resources of effrontery and, moreover, a sort of naïve cynicism, an almost helplessly denigratory habit of mind, which did not permit the recognition of aspirations beyond the level of his own. But things, inanimate objects, especially when they were glossy and redolent of the wealth of their owners, had this power of discomfiting him when he was left alone among them. He felt belittled by these evidences of a fixed abode. He had had on occasion the impulse to defecate on deep pile carpets. There was an armchair opposite him now which especially aroused his resentment, fashioned in pink leather, encapsuled still in polythene. He was thinking of the joy of ripping out the stuffing when a stout, handsome woman, with the faintest of moustaches, wearing a green silk dress, entered the room and approached him, holding out her hand.

'Ah, Mrs Logothetis,' Kennedy said with considerable relief, uncoiling his legs and rising.

'How do you do, Mr Kennedy? I am afraid,' she added hesitantly, 'that my English is not good.'

'It doesn't matter,' Kennedy said, allowing his eyes to linger on the lady's abundant, scarcely differentiated green bosom. She belonged to an age group in which he had scored some notable successes in the past.

'I have not called my daughter yet, as I wanted to have a little word with you before you begin.'

'Naturally.'

'She has the diploma examination very soon now. She has a good basis in grammar and vocabulary. But she lacks the confidence to speak. She is not like her mother in this respect.' Here Mrs Logothetis laughed a little and looked somewhat gaily at Kennedy, as though inviting him to approve her maternal freedom.

'Ha, ha, no, that's only to be expected,' said Kennedy. 'Perhaps she's a bit on the timid side?'

'Yes.' Gravity once more descended on Mrs Logothetis. 'And this causes me to be worried about the oral part of the examination.'

'It is a problem,' Kennedy said, with a sense of brilliant improvisation, 'with which we often have to deal. Practice, constant practice, is what she needs.'

'You think?'

'Certainly. I suggest she has at least three hours a week.'

'You think?' said Mrs Logothetis again. Her seriousness deepened. It seemed to Kennedy that her bosom heaved somewhat. 'She is not accustomed to being alone with a young man. We could send her to an institute, but these institutes are not always . . . The parents think the girl is in class applying herself, but often it is otherwise. She is walking out with boys. We do not want this for Lydia.'

'Quite so.' Kennedy nodded slowly, striving to assemble his features into a compound expression which would indicate his full realisation of the dangers of such contacts, his own professional integrity, setting him far above suspicion, and at the same time, in order to establish a vital link with Mrs Logothetis, the sense they shared of the potential delights of such contacts once the period of sheltered youth was over. It was a difficult expression to achieve.

'We believe in protecting our girls, Mr Kennedy. We accompany Ketty everywhere, the beach, the cinema. We take her for excursions in the . . . Studebaker. Do you not think we are right?'

'Well,' said Kennedy, 'I think you are.' His concentration had lapsed a little and he was no longer sure whose virginity they were talking about: Ketty's imperilled one in the present, or Mrs Logothetis' judiciously abandoned one in the past. What emerged as the only real positive was the general randiness of the male population of Athens. 'In England' he said, making a slight recovery, 'as you probably know, our young people have more freedom. It is what you might call a more permissive society.'

Mrs Logothetis pursed her full, rather pale lips and shook her head sorrowfully. 'All that is for after marriage,' she said. 'How much do you charge for the lessons?'

'One hundred drachmas an hour.'

'Ah yes.' Mrs Logothetis looked simultaneously pleased and worried. 'The last teacher only charged sixty. We were not pleased with the progress Lydia was making with her. A hundred, however, is too much, I think. You will take eighty?'

'A hundred is the official charge,' Kennedy said, 'among us qualified teachers.'

'But since it is for three hours a week . . .'

'Let us say ninety, then,' said Kennedy, conveying by his smile that for Mrs Logothetis' sake he was lowering standard hitherto strictly maintained. Ninety drachmas was twenty-two and six, after all, he reflected. Not bad for an hour's gentle dalliance with the delicately nurtured Lydia.

'I will bring her now,' Mrs Logothetis said.

Lydia must have been waiting in an adjoining room, because after only a very few moments her mother returned with her. She was short and plump with shining shoulder-length hair, a completely round face, puffy lips, pale like her mother's, and an extraordinary passivity of demeanour. Her face registered no expression during the introduction. Her hand was soft and cold.

'*Hairo poli*,' she said tonelessly.

'Ah,' said her mother, with a sort of raillery, 'you must speak English now. "How do you do?" That's it.'

'Yes,' Kennedy said, smiling broadly. 'That's it.'

'How do you do?' Ketty said. She regarded him steadily. Her eyes, though large and well shaped, were not clear, but yellowish round the almost black irises. And in the depths of them, unrelated to any change of feature, he discerned the light of a pure and relentless hostility. He also divined in that moment that these English lessons were entirely an idea of her parents.

'I will leave you together now,' Mrs Logothetis said. 'For today I suggest not a complete lesson, but to discuss your programme and become acquainted. Lydia knows the times she has free. She has private lessons also in French, German and piano. And this year she has the final examinations of the Greek Gymnasium. So, you see, she is quite busy.' Mrs Logothetis smiled richly.

That might be it then, Kennedy thought, but without much hope, as he smiled goodbye to the retreating mother; possibly he had been mistaken, and the girl was not antagonistic at all, simply dazed with study and controlled trips in the Studebaker.

'Well,' he said, 'shall we sit down? I won't keep you long today, since it is the first time. Your mother wants you to have three hours a week of English.'

There was no reply to this and after waiting some moments Kennedy said, 'How do you think we should arrange the lessons?'

Lydia said something in Greek in a low and rapid voice.

'I'm afraid,' Kennedy said, keeping up his smile, 'that we shall have to talk only in English. This will be practice for you and, besides, I don't know any Greek.'

Looking once more into the girl's unwavering eyes, he knew that he had not, after all, been mistaken: the inimical light was

70

blended now with what seemed the beginnings of a more personal antipathy. There was a fairly prolonged pause which Kennedy spent calculating how much this girl's father must be spending on private lessons alone. Ten pounds a week at least. Straight down the drain. He had no idea at all of how to proceed, having never given an English lesson, nor any other kind for that matter, in his life before.

'Well,' he said with something of an effort, 'this is what I suggest. You read something in English in your own time, something on the shortish side, of course, a story or such-like, and then I can ask you questions about it, and then . . .'

Suddenly, without warning, without any preliminary tension of features, without even turning her eyes away, Lydia opened her mouth wide and uttered straight towards him a loud and piercing cry.

Kennedy was horribly surprised. He sat bolt upright in his seat. For a moment he wondered if Lydia was subject to fits. But no further sound came from her, her face was quite impassive. 'What on earth. . . ?' he said.

At this moment a full-bodied girl in the uniform of a maid came into the room and stood quietly at the table at which they were sitting. That screech had been a summons, then. Still in the grip of the surprise and alarm it had aroused in him, Kennedy looked up at her and immediately Lydia and all disagreeable thoughts faded far away. The maid was beautiful. In Kennedy's mind, as in the minds of many men, there was an ideal feminine type. It could perhaps best be summed up in the word bovine. And in the first hasty upward glance it was that sort of serenity in the face that impressed him, a quality of mindlessness. The eyes were widely spaced, very gentle and cow-like, not brown, however, but luminous grey, the colour of a shallow pond; very level under rather deep brows. The whole face was broad, inclining to heaviness, but the cheek-bones were high and the large mouth well shaped, with a tendency to hang open a little. A face almost breathtakingly reposeful.

'*Fere mou ena potiri nero*,' said Lydia, with graceless abruptness.

'*Amesos!*' the girl said. Her voice was rather deep, Kennedy noted. In the moment before turning away she gave him an unhasty neutral gaze. He watched her leave the room, observing the square, steady shoulders, the regular, unselfconscious sway of the hips, the high firm buttocks. The back of her thighs and legs were heavy, but her ankles neat, even in the thick stockings and clumsy black shoes she was wearing.

Kennedy breathed out audibly. He looked once more at Lydia, with renewed astonishment that such a creature should have a goodess like that at her behest. Nothing could so well have illustrated the power of the drachma. He had still not fully recovered when the maid returned with the glass of water that Lydia had apparently demanded and which she took from the tray without a glance or a word of thanks. Again the maid met his glance, this time it seemed a fraction more lingeringly. He forgot to smile at her, and this too denoted the impression she had made.

The rest of the conversation with Lydia was conducted on his part with a sense of unreality. Somehow they arrived at an agreement about the hours to be set aside for the lessons, and Kennedy stalled on the choice of a textbook, since he did not as yet know of one. He made a mental note to get some advice from Willey on the matter at the earliest opportunity. Lydia herself conducted him to the door, which was a disappointment, because he had hoped to see something more of the maid at his departure. Still, there would be time for that. Lydia had a curious and rather touching way of walking very close to the wall. As she led him along the passage her left shoulder was actually rubbing against the wall as though she would have liked to vanish through it.

Once more on the pavement Kennedy found the harsher aspects of life obtruding. He had now to find Neofiton Vamva, where lived Eleni Polimenou, the celebrated Greek actress. He stayed the first passing Greek with a smile and a broad gesture. 'Neofiton Vamva?' he said, stretching his mouth round the vowels to assist comprehension. 'Neofiton Vamva?'

Meanwhile, about half a mile away Mitsos was following the man carefully down Philhellinon Street. The man moved slowly, as though conscious of leisure, moving his head from side to side in a way that seemed lordly, swinging his umbrella. Just before the

72

English church he turned into a doorway and disappeared. Coming up to it in his turn, Mitsos saw it was a café bar with half a dozen steps leading down. The bar was below street-level, but outside on the pavement there were two small tables, and Mitsos, after a moment's hesitation, sat down at the first of these, with his back to the bar. From here, if he turned his head, he could see below him through the glass front of the bar, the top of the other man's head and the lower part of his face. Although there could not have been more than two or three yards between them, he was himself practically invisible to the man below because of a sort of ornamental trellis across the lower half of the bar front, through which had been trained the shoots of some creeper with glossy sharp leaves. The sun shone hotly on Mitsos, for there was no awning, and falling on the slatted trellis and faintly stirring leaves, dappled the interior of the bar with flecks of light, so that the man's lowered head and his face and his fawn suit were chequered with shifting patterns, and Mitsos had the impression of looking down from the upper air into some leafy cage. There was no one else in the bar. On the table before the man were *kephtedes*, bread and white cheese, and a glass of beer. One of his hands was out of sight below the table; the other, large and very pale, quite hairless, plied a fork busily. He seemed from this angle of vision to have no neck at all, his blunt head balancing by a sort of miracle on the thick shoulders, while he fed steadily, chewing with an open mouth.

Mitsos asked for bread and a little salad when the waiter came, and ate it quickly, without appetite, constantly turning his head to watch the man below. There was in that face and form as he was compelled to view it now no trace of the resemblance which had so shocked him in the Cathedral Square. Then the man's pause and smile had seemed almost like a deliberate reminder; a vague smile, perhaps no more than a clench of the features against the sun; but then there were the eyes too, so distinctive, and, above all, perhaps that moment of irresolution, almost of bafflement. Fortuitous, of course, but recalling so strongly, so irresistibly, the other, distant, pause at the door, that other smile, that had turned from relish to purpose at the stimulus of his mother's grief. . . .

They were from Epirus, this had been stated at the outset: men come from far, intent on something. He remembered the curious contained peace in the house in the days immediately before that evening, with his officer father home from the north, the first time for almost a year they had seen him. A professional soldier, commissioned before the war, who had fought both Italians and Germans and, of course, in the latter years of the occupation exclusively Greeks. He had returned from the north changed, grimmer, always preoccupied. Mitsos had been too young then fully to understand the disgust inspired in his father, fastidious, authoritarian, deeply conservative like almost all his class, by the activities of the guerillas, who had turned to rend one another even before the Germans withdrew, turning what might at first have been seen as a movement of liberation into a murderous gibberish of initials, E.A.M., E.L.A.S., K.K.E. '*Eamobulgarians*,' he had said, the bitter word of abuse twisting his lips under the neat moustache. 'The only minds that have a sense of why they fight are in Russia, not in Greece.'

He had known, of course, must have known, that he was in danger. This would be the reason for that grimness, that absorbed quality in his father. His mother, too, would have known. That calm then, remembered now as happiness because of the horror that succeeded it, but of a peculiar tension nevertheless, had perhaps been a sort of despair. For the departure of the German occupation force had delivered the country to the *andartes*, which meant increasingly, as Zervas was confined to his perch in the hills, to the groups of the extreme left. It was a time when public and private motives had become confused – a time for the settling of old scores. All the collaborators who could, including the rank and file of the Security Police, had sought immediate obscurity and there were some no doubt who had escaped detection and the certain death that followed upon it, survived until the following year when justice was again in official hands and the courts, moreover, disposed to be lenient. . . . His father, however, had been an officer, commanded a battalion. He had made no effort to hide himself. Where, after all, was he to go? He had come home to Athens to the house that had been his father's. No doubt, with customary cold incredulity he had misjudged the lawless temper of the people on liberation, trusted too much to the immediate re-

74

establishing of order now that the common enemy at last was gone. A bullet in the street was the worst he could have expected, otherwise he would not so have endangered his family. And Epirus must have seemed quite far away. . . .

'We are from Epirus,' had been the first words Mitsos remembered from the group of shabby men who had come in from the street that October evening. They had been frighteningly without gesture, without extravagance of speech or behaviour, confronting his father and mother in their softly lit living-room. 'Where is your uniform now?' one of the men had said quietly. 'Your fine uniform.' There had been in this colloquy a note, a feeling as though this were the beginning of a quarrel, rather than the end of it. What words, if any, his father had said he had not retained in memory. He did not know which of the men had moved, it was not the man with yellow eyes, he felt sure of that, an amazingly casual gesture of the arm but swift too, as though he was trying to dislodge something possibly noxious, possibly about to sting, from his father's collar, but there was a short knife in his hand, and his father stepped back sharply, he looked startled, exactly as if he had in fact been stung, and began to raise his hand to the side of his neck, but the blood came spurting over his hand, staying it, and he was suddenly red to the waist. He fell face forward on to the carpet, not as though collapsing but as though struck down, and he died then or a little later, died without another look at anyone, face pressed against the carpet. Mitsos himself, with that great jet of blood before him and his mother's cries in his ears, had sprung wildly forward, to minister to his father, not to attack the men, only to receive a heavy blow on the side of the head which flung him partially stunned against the wall, from where he had endured the rest, the smile, the hideous moments of irresolution, his mother's reduction to anonymity, his own mute plea for life.

He glanced down again through the trellis into the interior of the café. The man was fed now and still, stippled by the light that rayed through the leaves and bars. Mitsos clapped his hands for the waiter, wanting to be ready – time spent in paying his bill might result in the man's being lost to him, since no destination had yet been established. He had barely finished paying in fact

75

when the man came up the steps into the sunlight and stood for a moment with raised head and narrowed eyes as though himself seeking a scent or a direction. Mitsos had turned away, but there had been no need for this, the man did not look towards him at all, but, after that brief pause, proceeded steadily up Philhellinon Street.

And Mitsos followed. The pavements were crowded, but he had no real awareness of other people. He saw no faces, heard no individual voices. Noise and movement of people formed a sort of element through which he tracked the man, comforting as cover might be, more comforting, since they took away his particularity, gave him a reason for walking down this street where other persons walked.

Neofiton Vamva proved not difficult to find. Eleni Polimenou had an apartment on the sixth floor, with polished parquet and chintz and sketches of nude rotund females on the walls. There was a fine view from the window of the eastern side of the city, extending from the wooded hill of Pangrati across to the Byzantine Museum with the suburb of Kaisariani beyond it, and the tawny foothills of Hymettos in the distance. Kennedy had full leisure to dwell on all this because Eleni Polimenou kept him waiting for a considerable time. He had in fact abandoned the view and was looking fixedly at the photograph of a smiling man in a big black hat with the words 'Kindest regards, Eugene' inscribed in one corner, when a door must have been opened somewhere, for suddenly he heard a harsh voice talking, he realised after a moment, into the telephone.

'But, darling, shit! shit! shit!' he heard this voice say. 'What? Yes, I know, I *understand*, angel, but there are things in this play to make you vomit green, my love. . . . No, not bad, *impossible*. Yes. My meaning is, no human tongue could frame them. Some changes, yes. . . . Also, this, what do you call it, this biographical note. . . . Yes, I know they ask for it, darling, but I think it is better not to go on and on about the years as though I will soon be getting the gold watch. Nor do I like references to my middle period. You can say *mature*, if you like. . . . Better, yes. . . .' The voice spoke English with a plangent American accent, and this, in conjunction with the habit of heavy aspiration retained from Greek, made it a vehicle of considerable harshness and carrying power. The phone was replaced and a few moments later a slim middle-aged woman of striking and energetic appearance entered the room, smoking a cigarette in a short holder. She had auburn hair, narrow eyes and a mouth of slightly peevish sweetness. Guessing from the outset that Kennedy was a foreigner, she said to him in English, 'You want to see me?'

'I've heard,' began Kennedy, 'through the Cultural Centre . . .'

'Ah, so you have come from the man Jennings?' Miss Polimenou's eyes were chestnut-coloured and brilliant, but not very efficient, it seemed: she screwed them up and advanced her head a little to get a good look at Kennedy. Myopia, which lends to many an aspect of peering benevolence, did not achieve this for her.

'An odd little man, somewhat shitty,' she said, still referring apparently to Jennings. 'He said he would send someone. Well, this is what I want, darling, I will just tell you now because I have not much time, some men are coming to take pictures. I am appearing in a play on the British television in October and I have the script to look at now. It is a kind of family tragedy about Greek peasants in the Peloponnese. There is a good part for me, the mother, a strong part, but we have to make some changes in the script.'

'Yes, I see,' Kennedy said.

'Also you must correct my accent. It is too American. I must speak English as the English expect foreigners to speak it.'

Miss Polimenou produced from the pocket of her robe a leather spectacle case and donned tinted glasses of a greenish shade. She gave Kennedy a long look through them. 'My God!' she said. 'You are a tall man. How much do you weigh?'

'About thirteen and a half stone,' Kennedy said.

'Good beef, ah!' said Miss Polimenou. 'Do you think you can help me?'

'I'm sure of it.'

'You will not regret it, darling. How much is that in kilos?'

'I beg your pardon?'

'In kilos, how much you weigh?'

'I'm not sure; a kilo is about two pounds, isn't it? That would be . . .'

'I like a big man,' Miss Polimenou said. 'Let's have a look at the play now. We can do the first act maybe. It's in my bedroom.'

'But the men,' said Kennedy, suddenly disquieted. 'The men who are coming to take the pictures.'

'They can wait.' She laid a beringed hand on his arm. 'Let's go,' she said.

The bedroom was predominantly blue, Kennedy noticed. Miss Polimenou made no move to get the script. 'Got good biceps muscles too, I bet,' she said.

'They're not bad,' Kennedy said, 'I suppose. I don't really get enough exercise.' He was unable to prevent his voice from quavering a little during this utterance, for Miss Polimenou, while still apparently looking through her tinted lenses at his arms, had laid her hand elsewhere.

Jennings sat at his desk, wheezing very slightly, tapping softly with his fountain-pen on the blotter before him. Beyond the blotter was his *papier-mâché* tray, with tea things and shortbread biscuits. He was musing on the inconsistencies of the English language and on the imminent arrival in Athens of an English mandolinist for whom a recital and afterwards a cocktail party had to be arranged. The difficulty was that although the hall had to be booked in advance and the invitations for the cocktail party issued, the mandolinist had not yet said definitely when he would be arriving. I hope, Jennings said to himself experimentally, that the fellow arrives in time. But, of course, that was ambiguous. It might mean arrive in time to perform at the appointed hour or it might merely mean arrive in the course of time. There existed, it was true, the radiantly precise *on time*, but that argued an attitude to a mandolinist (admittedly a minor one), more appropriate to a person one directly employed – a plumber, perhaps, come to mend a pipe. The amazing range and complexity of the English prepositions, no other language could approach them. The puny French *à*, for example, the heavy German *mitt*, made to do service in a dozen different contexts, they came nowhere near the ease and grace of the English. Once the prepositions were abandoned,

78

of course, one met with difficulties. Consider clauses, some extraordinary things happened in clauses. If he, Jennings, for example, were to say to his assistant Robinson, during the cocktail party, 'It will soon be time the mandolinist was going,' then they would both, clutching their glasses, be confronted by this stark, this inexplicable, this mystical past tense. *Was going*. Robinson, of course, would notice nothing, make some glib reply. Not a spiritual man, Robinson. There was an alternative, to be sure, *time for him to go* – the boundless infinitive, spanning like the participles all times, without number, without tense. Still, he was reluctant to abandon that dark irrational past. It gave power to the user. 'It will soon be time the mandolinist was going or went.' He heard himself answering with impeccable modulations the flurried questions of foreign students rendered distraught by this inconsistency. 'If you will permit me to observe, ladies and gentlemen,' or 'If I may be allowed at this point to observe, to your many questions my only answer can be, that this is the language we use,' accompanied, as he glanced from face to face, by the impenetrable blandness of the Zen master.

Some of this blandness had appeared on his face, but it faded as he thought once again how undesirable it would be that the mandolinist should return to London in any way dissatisfied with his reception. It must not be thought that he, Jennings, was indifferent to the arts. Perhaps Robinson had some news. He did nothing for the moment, however, to summon his assistant. He sipped tea for some while and nibbled a biscuit. The biscuits, he noted, were not quite fresh, unduly friable; little crumbs fell over the dark serge of his lapels. He must register a complaint, a sharp one, to the administrative office about the quality of the biscuits that were reaching his table. Hard, when one could eat almost nothing else, to have crumbly biscuits sent up to one. He made a note on the blotter, and this purposeful activity recalled to him the question of prepositions. It would be a good idea, he thought, to get Willey to prepare a paper for him, taking a single substantive and proliferating examples to give, as it were, in miniature a demonstration of the richness of English in this respect. It might make a useful appendix to his book. *Hand* for example 'to hand', 'by hand', 'in hand', 'on hand', 'at hand'. That would serve admirably. Willey's was a temperament perfectly suited to this sort of research. The donkey work, as Jennings humorously put it to himself, without which no scholarship was possible. Not an original mind, of course, no feeling for the marvellous paradox at the heart of grammar, a structure monumental yet always in flux. All right in his place. Latterly, though, he had not seemed to know that place. Jennings had not forgotten his insolence at the staff meeting. 'Permit me to observe, Mr Willey, that I know something of your previous history, and to your many requests for a permanent post I can only say . . .' Mackintosh was the man for a permanency. He had recognised Mackintosh's promise from the outset, his devotion to grammatical forms, the absence of any sentimental reluctance to inform on less-conscientious colleagues. Jennings even felt some slight affection for Mackintosh, who recalled his own first faltering steps as an untried Teacher of English as a Foreign Language, in Istanbul, all those years ago. Mackintosh would be waiting outside for him now. Presumably he had been in touch with Eleni Polimenou, in accordance with his instructions. It was of the utmost importance that nothing be allowed to ruffle Eleni Polimenou. There must be no reservations in the glowingly favourable report Jennings hoped she would make of him in London as courtier, scholar and wit. Besides this any number of mandolinists paled into insignificance. Eleni Polimenou's word carried real weight.

He pressed a button in his desk and after a few moments Robinson appeared, wearing a navy-blue blazer and a green cravat. Jennings looked at him sourly. His assistant's sartorial pretensions always affected him disagreeably. They marked Robinson as a man without real interest in English as a Foreign Language.

'Has anything further been received,' Jennings said, 'regarding the arrival of Mr Slingsby-Merd?'

'Nothing, I'm afraid. There is a cinema on Stadium Street which would be available in the mornings, but they require to be told exactly when.'

'Naturally.'

There was a short silence during which Robinson assembled his shrewd expression. 'By the way,' he said at last, 'are you acquainted with the work of a poet, a contemporary poet, named Gilligan?'

'Just a moment,' Jennings said. 'Gilligan, did you say?' He never read poetry of any sort, being unable to tolerate the violence done to syntax. His reading consisted almost entirely of books about linguistics with, for light relief, property advertisements in newspapers of the sort that are accompanied by photographs. 'The name has a certain resonance,' he said. 'It, ah, rings a bell.'

'None of the people I've asked so far have been acquainted with his work,' Robinson said.

'Gilligan, Gilligan, Gilligan,' Jennings said with a remote expression, as though summoning something from the depths. 'Why do you ask?'

'Well, you remember a person named Kennedy who called here some time ago?'

'Yes,' Jennings said. His alertness increased visibly. 'I remember him quite clearly. Not a good type.' He had made a note on his blotter about Kennedy while still in the grip of the rage those insolent sarcasms had roused in him.

'Well,' Robinson said, 'he offered to give a lecture on contemporary poetry at the institute. Of course, I pressed him for details' – Robinson shrewdness intensified – 'I mean to say, anyone could just walk in here, couldn't they? He mentioned this Gilligan as a key figure. I haven't, as I say, been able to find anyone who has read him, or even heard of him.'

'In my opinion,' Jennings said, 'that is not a young man to be trusted. An ill-bred and coarse-grained young man. He spoke of the Greeks as wogs, for example. In my hearing.'

'That's a bit thick,' Robinson said. 'I am coming to the conclusion,' he added, 'that Gilligan does not exist. Gilligan is simply a name he invented on the spur of the moment. It seems incredible.'

'There was something inherently untrustworthy and semi-educated about him.' Jennings lifted his upper lip in a slight snarl. 'Also, if I remember, he had a cockney accent. Quite unmistakably.'

He looked fixedly at Robinson, who narrowed his eyes even further and looked back. 'So he did,' Robinson said. 'So he did.'

The two men looked at each other in silence for some moments, then Jennings placed his fingertips together with renewed urbanity. 'Is Mr Mackintosh out there?' he asked.

'Yes.'

'Ask him to come in, will you? And let me know as soon as anything further is received concerning Mr Slingsby-Merd.'

'Will do,' said Robinson, who was inclined at times to brisk abbreviations.

While he waited, Jennings found Kennedy's name on his blotter and put a ring round it, enclosing as an afterthought the date. 'Ah,' he said, when Mackintosh came in. 'You wanted to see me?'

Mackintosh inclined his head sideways to an angle of about forty-five degrees. His delivery, while lacking Jennings' plopping virtuosity, had an exaggerated distinctness that promised well for the future. 'Well, sir,' he said, 'it's only a suggestion, sir, of course, but what I thought was, why don't we have a sort of extra-mural weekly lecture?'

'H'm,' Jennings said. 'Extra-mural. I see; yes.'

'Yes; perhaps on Saturday mornings, but that would be for you to decide sir, of course. Each member of staff could deliver a lecture on successive Saturdays, on some aspect of English Language teaching, to a selected audience of students and practitioners.'

'It sounds promising, promising,' Jennings said. 'I will give the matter my full consideration, Mr Mackintosh. Did you come to an arrangement with Eleni Polimenou?'

Mackintosh righted his head, which he had been keeping tilted while he watched the effect on Jennings of his suggestion. 'No,' he said. 'As a matter of fact I didn't.'

Jennings looked at him in surprise. 'Why was that? You went to see her, didn't you?'

'Oh yes, I went to see her, only about half an hour ago, as a matter of fact, but when I got there she said she was fixed up already. She said she was quite satisfied. She's got rather a *raucous* laugh, hasn't she? Not what you'd expect at all. Someone from you had already been, she said. A big boy, she described him as. I thought this was hardly likely, so I asked who it was. She said a man called Kennedy. I was introduced to a person of that name some days ago, by Mr Willey. It might be the same man.'

'Did you point out to her that he was not in any way an official person?' Jennings spoke even more deliberately than usual, in order to disguise the rage which the mention of this name had awakened.

'Yes, I did. I said I was pretty sure the fellow had no official backing, but she didn't seem to care. She said Mr Kennedy knew his onions. Those were her exact words. She has a picturesque way of expressing herself.' Mackintosh commenced what was almost a chuckle, but seeing no response on Jennings' face, he tilted his head quickly and said, 'It's a bad show, sir, isn't it?'

'So he is one of Mr Willey's friends, is he?' Jennings said slowly.

'I gather so, sir,' Mackintosh said, restoring his head to the vertical. 'I gather so.'

After Mackintosh had gone, Jennings mused on Kennedy for a while malignantly. The man ought to be denounced, of course. But for a moment his hands were tied. If Eleni Polimenou pronounced herself satisfied there was nothing really to be done. She was not, Jennings sensed, the sort of person to be much disturbed by the illegality of Kennedy's proceedings. Better to leave things as they were for the moment. At all costs Eleni Polimenou must not be antagonised. Jennings sighed. It was all so difficult. How much better, really, if humanity could be approached like grammar, such persons as Kennedy classified once and for all as irregular, like certain verb forms, for example. Then everyone could read and be apprised of them, they would never be able to deceive again by false analogy with regular people. . . .

As a means of forgetting Kennedy and his own powerlessness, Jennings fell to imagining a perfectly arranged, rapturously applauded mandolin recital at the end of which people thundered, not for the performer, that mere adjunct Slingsby-Merd, but for the organising brain, Jennings. Jennings. *Jennings*. He stood blinking charmingly raising his hand for silence, waiting for a hush to fall over the vast audience. *Ladies and Gentlemen, if I may be permitted to observe, in reply to your many requests for further recitals, I can only say . . .*

83

The man Mitsos was following pursued a steady course, coming out on Amalias opposite the National Gardens. They passed the sponge seller on his customary corner, straw hat low over his eyes, his sponges strung round his body. Large-pored, ochreous, of all sizes, their soft organic shapes were in startling contrast to the hard edges of the kerb and the granite facings of the buildings behind.

They went past the massive columns of the Temple of Zeus, then to the right along the avenue of Dionysus the Areopagite, past the theatre of that older pagan Dionysus of wild celebrations. Above them on the right the slopes of the Acropolis with the pale gold of the Parthenon at its crest. All the way along the mosaic pavement of the avenue, like the echo of his steps, Mitsos heard the chipping of metal on stone, coming clear from the Acropolis on the still air, through the intermittent trilling of the cicadas; masons were squatting amid the vegetation with which these slopes had been planted, fabricating items needed for more extensive, more evocative ruins; cornice, pediment, the fluted drums of columns.

At the Odeon of Herodus Athens they left the pavement and mounted the steps towards the Acropolis. They climbed past flagged terraces, clumps of laurel and umbrella pine, emerging on the wide, level terrace which partially girdles the hill from north to south, the southern side leading to the little kiosk where those who intend to ascend to the Parthenon itself buy their tickets, the northern broadening into a coach park fringed with stalls selling postcards, coloured slides, reproductions in plaster of antique vases and statuary. This was an area devoted entirely to chicanery and the importuning of tourists; below precincts sacred to Athena and Poseidon, light gauges twinkled and the gold molars of lurking photographers, and persons vociferated in broken English.

The man exchanged some pleasantries with the vendors, was evidently well known there. Then, passing further along the hill northward, he took up finally a position directly beside the rough steps leading to the summit of the Areopagus. He was directly in the sun there, and proceeded to open his umbrella, the purpose of which was at last fully revealed. It was a vast umbrella of an old-fashioned sort with a long handle and strongly arched struts. The black cloth was very thin, especially where the spokes distended it, so that to Mitsos, standing somewhat below the man at a point further down the path, the umbrella resembled a symmetrically arched membrane, partially admitting the light, like the fully extended wings of a huge bat. The man stood quite still beside the steps, his head and shoulders in shadow. From time to time he spoke to groups of passers-by, appearing to make to them some proposition.

Mitsos looked over the westward side of the Acropolis where numbers of people, having obtained their tickets of admission below, ascended by degrees in a sort of slow swarm towards the massive portals of the Propylae. So pure and brilliant was the light that perspectives were obliterated, the slim pillars set into the sides of the hill among the Venetial bulwarks having the same apparent distance from him as the columns of the Sacred Way and the narrow summit of Lycavettos beyond, monuments and hills forming a great frieze against the depthless blue of the sky. The streams of new devotees, guide-books in hand, clambered up through the portals and disappeared into the blue distances beyond.

He glanced down over the florid Roman façade of the Odeon. From this eminence he could trace the steps by which, following the man, he had arrived here, the ascending terraces, the careful mosaic of the avenue, the jumble of streets beyond. Always in Athens there were these prospects, this visual recreation or reminder of the way one had come, which gave a sort of dignity to journeyings about the city, a sense almost of wonder at human mobility and the tremendous intricacy of choices this involves.

He stopped alongside the umbrella and stood there waiting. He had approached at a time when the other was looking away, and he thought in this moment how strange and probably un-precedented it would be for this man, who was accustomed to making the first move, to find a person standing waiting beside him in this deferential way, waiting to be noticed. Then the man turned his head and Mitsos was looking into the wide face, framed by the umbrella. The strange eyes, with their mournful downward slant, regarded him steadily. They were not the colour of the eyes he remembered, not yellow, but a sort of pale hazel. This confrontation must have been of the briefest, but seemed endless to Mitsos. He smiled painfully at the man, but as yet said nothing. He could get no distinct impression of the other's face yet, only its width, and the eyes, like a dog's. Surely the eyes were the same?

'You wanna guide?' the man said. 'A guide for the Areopagus?' His voice, which Mitsos had for some reason expected to be authoritative, was little more than a harshly intensified whisper. Somewhere inside that bulk, it seemed, vital passages were clogged.

'I am Greek,' Mitsos said. 'You can speak Greek.'

The man smiled. He had full, slightly everted lips and his front teeth were very widely spaced. 'Usually they are foreigners,' he said. 'You are not from Athens, then?'

'I am from Epirus,' Mitsos said.

The man lowered his umbrella and closed it. 'Shall we go up?' he said. 'This hill,' he whispered behind Mitsos as they were climbing, 'the Areopagus, or Areos Pagus, as it was known in ancient times. . . .' They stood together on the summit. 'Down there, it was down there, the temple of Ares.' He pointed down the north-west slope of the hill.

'Ah yes,' Mitsos said.

'The ancient assembly, the Senate of the Areopagus, met here. While primarily a political body, it had the right to try certain criminal cases. . . .' The voice whispered on laboriously, a few inches only from Mitsos' ear, continuing its regurgitation of fact and legend. Mitsos listened only intermittently. He was possessed by the strangeness of his position, the strangeness of knowing exactly what this man had eaten for lunch. . . . 'Also Orestes after the murder of his mother Clytemnestra is said to have appeared before this court. You have perhaps read *The Eumenides* of Aeschylus?'

'Yes.' Mitsos was impelled suddenly to get on to a more personal level with the man, the plane of opinion. 'I have always thought he was justified,' he said. 'Don't you think so?'

'It was the crime of matricide,' the man whispered. 'An offence against the gods. . . . You do not speak with the accent of Epirus?'

'I spent my childhood in Athens,' Mitsos said.

'The council was still functioning in the fifth century B.C., the Great Age. Pericles took away its political powers. Thereafter its chief purpose . . . The deserters of Chaeronia were tried here and condemned, in 338. Demosthenes also. . . . If you will come this way a little . . .' He led Mitsos along a rocky terrace on the eastward side of the hill. 'Here,' he said, pointing upward to a higher rectangular terrace. 'That is the highest point. It was there they conducted the trials of the criminals. And there, to the left, do you see that square stone, the big one, standing alone? That was used as a seat for the disputants. There were two originally it is said, the Stone of Outrage for the accused, the Stone of Resentment for the accuser.'

'Which is the one remaining?'

'No one can say.'

'I think it is the Stone of Outrage,' Mitsos said, with the same painful smile.

He was beginning now, with an almost unnerving distinctness, to take in the minutest details of the man's face, the fair stubble along the jaws, the dark pitting of the long lower lip caused perhaps by some infection of the mouth, the ramification of lines and wrinkles round the eyes, the ruptured veins over the cheekbones showing darkly below the tan.

'If we go round to this point . . . There you will see it, down towards the foot of the slope, that open space there, this was the sanctuary of the *Erynes*, infernal goddesses, avengers of murder, called also sometimes The Kindly Ones. Come once more this way . . .' He led Mitsos to the central part of the terrace. 'From here you have a good view. There is the Saronic Gulf, you see, and over there Mount Kithairon. Below us now the Agora, with the library of Hadrian beyond . . .

'In the year A.D. 50,' the man said, with suddenly increased power and volume, 'St Paul delivered on this hill his Homily on the Unknown God which converted the senator Dionysus, known thereafter as St Denis the Areopagite. St Paul gave utterance to many solemn truths here, which, though received at the time with mockery and jeering . . .' The voice went on rapidly, without faltering in the order of the words, though sinking at times into its former harsh and laborious whisper. 'St Paul extolled the exalted ideal of humanity, without distinction between Greek, Jew or barbarian . . . foretold the collapse of the Hellenic world at that time so glorious. . . . The new religion that he brought was destined . . . The single force to which we Greeks owe everything, our nation, our language, our literature. This way, please. Take care down the steps, *paidi mou*.'

They descended to the broad terrace at the foot of the hill.

'Thank you very much,' Mitsos said. 'That was most interesting.' He took out a twenty-drachma piece and handed it over.

'My pleasure,' the man said.

'What is your name?' Mitsos asked. 'In case I should need a guide again.'

'Ask for George. That is what the foreigners began by calling me and now everyone does. I am well known here.' He turned away, preliminary to raising the umbrella.

Mitsos was visited by a sharp feeling of discouragement. There was no legitimate pretext for detaining the man further. He was alone again. He went slowly back down the hill until he found a wooden bench under one of the pine-trees. From here he could still see George at his station.

While he waited many hundreds of people ascended to the Parthenon. George said his piece several times. Finally, just after six o'clock, he lowered his umbrella for the last time, furled it loosely, and began to make his way northward in the direction of the Agora. Mitsos followed circumspectly. The steps descended steeply, between red-roofed Turkish-style houses, with the mounds and rubble of the Agora on the left, towards Morastiraki Square. Before reaching the square, however, George turned off into a maze of very narrow streets, little more than alleys. Mitsos walked with an exaggerated lightness. If the man had turned to look behind he must have recognised him, but he went on his way, looking ahead, as one very familiar with his surroundings. They emerged on a street that Mitsos thought he recognised, without remembering the name. Here it was close and airless, with tall, dun-coloured buildings rising on either side. From a side-turning Mitsos heard the desperate tearing sounds of an accordion. George turned again down an alley-way that led between blank whitewashed walls into a tiny square, with a kiosk and two orange-trees, and at the further side a small dilapidated *taverna* built in one floor, with silent birds in cages on its front wall, around the entrance. Immediately alongside the taverna ran a narrow cobbled lane with the outer wall of the *taverna* on one side and the windowless backs of several small houses on the other. Standing at the corner of the square Mitsos was able to see George turn into the last of these houses, which was the only one to face on to the lane. A few yards further on the lane ended in a brick wall. Thus, although this was a densely populated district, no one could actually overlook the last house in the lane except from the exact position at the corner of the square where Mitsos was standing.

Mitsos waited. He was at peace now, sure that he had tracked George down. And this was confirmed a few minutes later when the other appeared at the street door in shirt-sleeves, holding a large teapot of blue enamel. Standing on the second of his three front steps and stretching out his arm to its fullest extent he began watering the little pots of purple and yellow pansies in a row on his window sill, giving to each pot a particular and loving care.

5

It was quite some time before Kennedy had an opportunity of speaking alone to the maid at Lydia's house. Each time he went there for a lesson he hoped for this, but each time he was disappointed. He saw her only briefly when, at a given pitch of boredom, Lydia broke into her harsh cry for water. The lessons, he was compelled to admit, were not proving very successful. The emphasis was still on oral work, as Mrs Logothetis had wished, but it was he, Kennedy, who was orally working. Although he continued to speak confidently to Mrs Logothetis about Lydia's progress, he had in fact soon ceased to expect any response from her, and now simply talked the hour away, aiming his remarks at various corners of the room. He relied to some extent on her obvious loathing for the subject: since he exacted nothing in the way of work from her, he hoped she would not complain of him to her mother. Thus his dismissal would be postponed until he had had time to get a bit of money together. He felt that at twenty-two-and-six an hour, tax free, the longer it could go on the better. He had five students now, two of them secured for him by Willey, the others by Sophy; and of course there was Eleni Polimenou. Things were building up, but slowly. What he needed, he told himself, was a breakthrough. Somewhere quite near, he could not help feeling, if he could once get through the hedge, there was grass of the most vivid green.

Today he purposely arrived for the lesson a good twenty minutes early. He was shown in and asked to wait by the same elderly retainer, and the horror of the polythene-encased chairs was beginning to close in on him again when Veta appeared at the door and came towards him. Even in this cluttered room the grace and dignity of her walk was apparent. Against the cheap dark cloth of her dress the contours of her figure stood out firmly. Her face was completely expressionless. Kennedy stood up, and this action caused her eyes to widen slightly.

'*O kyrios thelei ena kafe?*' she asked.

'Yes please.'

'*Nescafé y turkiko?*'

'Nescafé, please. Without milk.'

'*Oriste?*'

'You don't speak any English, then?' Now that they were both standing he could see how tall she was, only a few inches shorter than himself. She did not, however, shrink against her height, as many tall girls do, but faced him with shoulders held back and head up. He thought he discerned a speculative look in her large mild eyes, a sort of wonder, as if something had come through the gate into her field and she was trying to relate it to the rest of creation; something expectant also, in a primitive way, as though his foreignness was something potentially startling or comical. He put forth his smile and said rather helplessly, '*Elleniki, ochi.* . . . I'm afraid I don't know any Greek.'

After a short pause Veta said slowly, '*Moi parle un peu français. Pas beaucoup.*'

'But that's great,' Kennedy said. 'How did you learn it?' he asked in French.

'I am from Tinos,' Veta replied, speaking very slowly and hesitantly in her rather deep voice. 'My mother worked at the convent. *Les Sœurs*, they helped me. *Mais moi suis pas Catholique, suis Chrétienne.* . . .'

Perceiving that she meant Orthodox, Kennedy did not comment on this distinction. 'Well, it is lucky for me,' he said.

'I go now to get the coffee.'

'Black coffee, please,' Kennedy said, and watched legs, superb even in the thick black, stockings, move out of the room. She returned within a very few minutes and placed the coffee on a small table beside his chair.

'What do you do when you're not working?' Kennedy asked.

'*Plaît-il?*'

'How do you employ your hours of leisure?'

Veta continued to regard him silently, mouth somewhat open.

'What is the day you do not work?' he said.

'In the afternoon and evenings of all the Wednesdays I do not work.'

'But today is only Thursday,' Kennedy said.

'Sometimes I go out for one or two hours. But I do not know this before.'

'I see,' Kennedy said. 'It depends on the family. Not exactly generous amounts of time off. Do you think you could escape for a while on Saturday?'

'Plaît-il?'

'Do you think,' Kennedy said, spacing his words carefully, 'that you can come out for one or two hours on Saturday?'

'It is possible, yes, I think.'

'If you can, will you meet me?'

Before replying she looked at him steadily for some moments. Perhaps some process of calculation was involved, but Kennedy could discern nothing of this on her face. 'What will we do?' she said.

'Well, we could have a drink,' Kennedy said, 'and become better acquainted.'

'Yes,' she said, 'I like.'

'Good. What time then?'

'Saturday, that must be the afternoon. Four o'clock is best.'

'That's a date then. I'll wait for you outside that big building they call Zappeion. You've got it, haven't you? Saturday, four o'clock, Zappeion. For God's sake don't forget.'

Veta said nothing more, but she nodded quite emphatically to show that she understood all the aspects of their assignation. She smiled at him as she left the room. She smiled again when she came in a little later in answer to Lydia's raucous and peremptory cry. To excite himself Kennedy sought to detect in it a conspiratorial quality, but it was really not a very expressive smile.

The oral work was even more desultory than usual that day. At the end of the lesson Lydia asked him in muttered tones if he wouldn't mind waiting a little, her father would like to see him. She herself went out, leaving Kennedy a prey to some apprehension. Had it come then, already, his dismissal? After a very short interval Mr Logothetis came in with a smile that must have started outside, because it was at its meridian when he came through the door; and extended a narrow, yellowish hand, fairly liberally beringed. Kennedy, who had not met Mr Logothetis before, smiled as he had decided English tutors should smile, and for a moment or two they regarded each other with expressions of mutual esteem and gratification. Mr Logothetis was a short, plump and dapper man. He was bald on top and that part of his cranium which was hairless was tanned a pleasant brown. He had melting eyes and a curving, somewhat crafty, nose, and he was wearing a light tweed suit that looked English to Kennedy.

'I am happy to meet you, Mr Kennedy,' he said, in quite passable English. 'For a long time we are seeking a good teacher for Ketty, and now it is clear that we found one.'

'You are kind,' Kennedy said tutorishly. 'She is an apt pupil.' He looked down with considerable interest at Mr Logothetis, who was said to be one of the richest men in Athens – a city not lacking in rich men.

'Do you think so, do you think so really? I am glad you say that. Parents, you know, they worry, or perhaps you not know, eh? Not yet?'

'No, not yet,' Kennedy said, with his broadest smile. 'But we all come to it sooner or later I suppose.'

'You are from London, Mr Kennedy?'

'Yes.'

'I have agency there, for shipping. You want a reduction any time, I can get you one.'

'Thank you very much.'

'Tell me, Mr Kennedy, in confidence, what do you think are my daughter's chances for the examination?'

'Well,' Kennedy said cautiously, 'it's very difficult to say, really. Miss Logothetis has a very good general knowledge of English, but it's rather difficult to get her to, er, *flow*, if you follow my meaning.'

'Yes, yes, this is always her great trouble. In the mathematics, for example, she does well, but for the languages her approach is too . . . mechanical. Also, of course, for a subject like mathematics, there is a syllabus, you can know what you will be asked. With a language it is more difficult.' Mr Logothetis nodded his head sadly.

'Quite so,' said Kennedy, 'and of course everyone knows that an examination is a chancy business, if I might put it like that. What I mean is, you may happen to have prepared the right questions or you may not. . . .' He had been speaking without design, concerned only to keep up an appearance of academic expertise, but was halted now by what seemed a sudden fixity of Logothetis' regard.

'Subject to chance, you think?' said Mr Logothetis.

'Up to a point, yes.'

Mr Logothetis drew a gold cigarette case from his inside pocket and offered a cigarette to Kennedy. 'American cigarettes,' he said, 'you like?'

'Very much.'

'I can send you some.'

'That is very good of you.' Kennedy was beginning to feel quite well disposed towards Mr Logothetis, who was clearly a man of kindly disposition, a good parent too.

'Subject to chance is not justice,' Mr Logothetis said.

'No, I suppose not.'

'You see, Mr Kennedy, I want Lydia to proceed without loss of time to the higher diplomas. This one is a lower diploma, is it not?'

'That's right, yes.'

'It would be a pity for her to lose time over such elementary matters. Because, let us be frank, she might fail to pass.'

'She might, yes,' Kennedy conceded. He felt quite sure that Lydia would fail to pass.

Mr Logothetis regarded the end of his cigarette. 'I want Lydia,' he said, 'to go to the Girton College of Cambridge. For admittance there, certificates are of utmost importance, as I don't need to tell *you*, Mr Kennedy. The authorities there, they *insist*. Quite right too, square and above ground, standards are standards. For a university, only to pay fees is not enough.' He looked up quickly at Kennedy. 'I should be most grateful,' he said, 'to anyone who could help Lydia to obtain her diploma.'

'I can assure you,' said Kennedy, who was beginning now to feel rather bored by all this parental ambition, 'that I shall do my best to get her through the examination.'

'My gratitude would be *concrete*,' Mr Logothetis said.

'I beg your pardon?'

'I know you will do your best, Mr Kennedy. All reports of you that I have heard assure me of this. From my wife, from my daughter – she looks forward so much to her lessons with you.'

Kennedy realised suddenly that Lydia had at last allowed expression of her boredom, and her loathing for himself, to escape her. He was, as he all at once perceived, on rather dangerous ground. 'I am pleased with her progress,' he said.

'We have every confidence in you,' Logothetis said, almost tenderly. 'But since you yourself admit that chance is a strong agent in the matter and since it is agreed that Lydia is not, shall we say, greatly *gifted* in the subject, although of course she is very *keen* – she would be most distressed to hear me saying this. . . .' Mr Logothetis sighed. 'Her mother and I sometimes wonder whether it is not too much strain on her, whether it might not be better to put an end to these lessons for the time being.'

This threat, following so closely on the praise and promises, had an almost numbing effect on Kennedy. If they stopped the lessons now it would mean his losing nearly four pounds a week. 'I did not say,' he said, striving to keep up an appearance of scholarly dispassion, 'I did not say I thought she would fail. On the contrary, she has every chance of success. With continued coaching, of course. It would be a great mistake to stop the lessons at this stage, very bad for your daughter's morale.' He was aware of a certain dampness inside his shirt. 'What did you mean just now,' he said, 'when you said that about your gratitude being concrete?'

Mr Logothetis sighed again. 'You will take a drink?' he said. 'Scotch?'

'Thank you.'

Mr Logothetis moved to the cocktail cabinet and busied himself there for some moments. 'Soda or water?' he said.

'Just as it comes, if you don't mind.'

Stepping lightly in neat crocodile-skin shoes Mr Logothetis advanced on him holding a very large tumbler of whisky. 'Your good health!' he said.

'*Sigeia!*' returned Kennedy.

'Ah, you are learning Greek. That is very good. My people

thank you. If only, you know, it was possible for Lydia to know beforehand what she needed to prepare . . .' Mr Logothetis laughed a little. 'Eh, Mr Kennedy?' he said, still laughing.

Suddenly, belatedly, blindingly, Kennedy saw where all this might be leading. Holding his glass in one hand, he took out as stealthily as possible his by now deplorable handkerchief and wiped his upper lip. 'That would give her,' he said, 'what we British call a sporting chance, wouldn't it?'

'Exactly, my dear Mr Kennedy. Anyone who would do that for me, I would be very grateful. And since gratitude alone is not useful to anyone I would be prepared to make mine *concrete*, to the extent of seven, eight thousand drachmas.' Mr Logothetis took a drink and looked wistfully round the room. 'Not of course conditionally on the result,' he said. 'That would be too much to expect. No, simply some guidance. . . .'

There was a pause while Kennedy groped in his mind for a concept of eight thousand drachmas. That was nearly a hundred pounds, surely. If he'd give that much, he'd give a little more. He said slowly, 'I have, as a matter of fact, a friend who might possibly be of help. I can't be certain at this stage. And he might ask for a little more than eight thousand, since he would be taking something of a risk, you understand, contravening . . .'

'How much more?'

'He might ask for ten thousand. It would be exact information, if I could persuade him, not simply guidance.'

'I see, yes. Very well. What a lucky chance I mentioned this to you, Mr Kennedy.'

'Yes, isn't it? I'd better speak to my friend, I think, before I can be definite about it.'

'Of course. In the meantime we continue the lessons. I am glad not to deprive Lydia of such an excellent teacher.'

'It is good of you to say so,' said Kennedy. 'Old boy.'

'Not at all. I leave everything in your hands then. Always we can trust the English for the fair play. You are renowned for it.'

'Yes. Well, here's to you.'

'And here's to *you*, Mr Kennedy.' Mr Logothetis took a drink, and surveyed Kennedy. His face was only slightly smiling, but some interior jubilation must have disarranged his English, because after a moment he added, with some emphasis, 'Mud down your jolly hatch.'

6

Mitsos waited near the statue of Kolokotronis on a square whose name he could not now recall, while the man he was following had coffee with the proprietor of a radio accessories shop. In the time since he had been dogging George about the city Mitsos had encountered many such threads, little filaments of the other's life. George's existence in its external aspects was being slowly revealed to him, the routes he took through the city, his hours of rest and work, the cafés he frequented, the people he knew. Mitsos had developed an intense, a consuming, interest in the smallest details of this life. He was insatiably curious about George. He wanted to know everything. Somewhere in this accumulation of habit and taste a vital link would shine suddenly, associating their two lives; ignorance on his part, even in the smallest things, might enable the other not to escape but to disown him, repudiate the connection between them.

So he was content to wait patiently, full in the sun, beside the statue, keeping the entrance to the shop in view. He had been standing there quite still for a long time now. The shadows of pigeons wavered over his feet. In the middle of the square the proprietor of a flower stall slept under his awning, among carnations, roses, gladioli. There was no one else on the square.

Mitsos declined his head. His temples throbbed with pain. He could look nowhere without hurting his eyes. The white paving dazzled him, the tall white buildings round the square reflected the sunlight achingly. He was exhausted with walking and standing and with the oppression of the sun. But he could not leave this place, to sit somewhere, or even seek the shade, because lately he had grown superstitious about small observances, as though everything hung on particular patterns of behaviour, not

98

necessarily logical, compelling him to impose on himself quite arbitrary rules. He had stationed himself here. He would not move now until George came out of the shop.

He had eaten little that day, but he felt no hunger. He wanted only to have the man in his sight again. Prolonged periods without visual experience of him filled Mitsos with anxiety as though his own existence had somehow come into doubt. Beneath the pain in his head however, and combating this uncertainty, he was aware of his heart beating, the quietly enduring pulse of his blood. With these days of early June Athens had sprung into full summer, a summer for Mitsos of glaring days, aching reflections, spent evenings; and a curious readiness of the senses. Sounds carried to him flatly, without resonance, in clear detonations. The city was basined in its hills, brought closer by the hardening horizons of summer. The sea when it was glimpsed was bright and flat, not taking the mind to further distances; continuing merely the enclosing line of the hills. Mitsos felt contained in the city as though in a white bowl; and within the bowl this extraordinary clarity in which the senses reluctantly and painfully lingered on things. So great had been this helpless alertness of his senses that the sharp angles of kerbs, the concrete facing of buildings, the edge of marble steps outside hotels he had felt almost as wounding him, like a fingernail scored across his eyes.

Now, while he waited, demotic music came from somewhere across the square, wailing in quarter tones and swirling repetitions, thinning and sounding frantic like a wasp in a box. Above him Kolokotromis pointed heroically on his charger. The shadow of his extended arm had been a mutilated stump merely when Mitsos had first positioned himself there, had lengthened gradually to a lance as the sun dipped westward; and his helmet had run from a boss, a deformity, to a spiralling, immense crown.

The flower seller sat up and looked about him, then went behind his stall and came out with a slopping bucket of water which he scattered on the pavement around his flowers. And as though this had been a signal prearranged, during the next few minutes boys from restaurants and stores all round the square emerged with buckets and sluiced the pavements. The water glinted, and the sounds of its impact came to Mitsos like a long irregular respiration. There was a smell of wet dust, and the odour of flowers became more marked.

Mitsos straightened himself, sensing in this ritual of the water the beginning of a new phase of the day; and almost immediately George emerged from the shop, hesitated in the doorway in the nonchalant portly way that Mitsos had come to know so well, and then went along the side of the square and turned left towards Athinas Street. With a sense of gathering up again the reins of life, Mitsos followed.

'I'm afraid,' Kennedy said, speaking very slowly and deliberately, looking Mr Andronakis straight in the eye, 'that your essay is far below the standard required for the examination.' He paused for some moments before going on. He had given considerable thought beforehand to the way this interview was to be conducted. It was in a sense crucial, a test case. Andronakis, a private student of his, already unconfident about his English, needed to be shaken still further. 'Below the standard,' Kennedy said again, allowing a faint, regretful smile to appear on his face. He put up a hand delicately and undid the top button of his shirt. He was wearing one of Thorne's and it was too tight for him. Andronakis, a burly man with a manner that was ingratiating without servility, shifted in his seat and passed a hand over his short and wiry hair. The canary in its cage on the balcony behind him commenced an abortive trill. 'Give song, little bird, for Mr Kennedy,' Andronakis said absently over his shoulder. The canary became abruptly silent. 'It is not good, then, the essay?' said Andronakis. Kennedy grimaced, as if he did not quite know where to begin. The essay, which was lying at this moment on the table before him, was entitled 'Don Quixote'. Kennedy glanced once more over the opening paragraph:

'This is one of the innumerable plays, one hundred less, or two hundred that anybody with good education must know. On his days and until now, it had passed about three centuries. In spite of so long time his plays are so fresh as if it had issued yesterday. It is very often happens only with great authors and well known and masterpiece plays that such plays are monument immortal in eternal keeping ever knews, or as in classical language says, classic. *Don Quixote* was also classical of Thervantes . . .'

'No,' Kennedy said. 'Not very good, really. In fact you need more time, Mr Andronakis, before you can be ready for the examination. At least another year, possibly longer.'

'The future is forward,' Mr Andronakis said; one of his phrases, but he pronounced it now with less than customary conviction. He was a commercial agent, with some important principals in England, and he had now in middle age taken to English lessons because he had somehow persuaded himself that the Government was about to issue a decree making it illegal for anyone without the diploma to engage in such transactions with foreign firms. How he had formed this idea Kennedy did not know, but he had not attempted to rebut it.

'I have to be honest with you,' he said.

'Yes, yes. Much appreciate,' said Mr Andronakis, who was now looking distinctly discouraged. 'What can do?'

Kennedy looked austerely to one side and began speaking in measured tones:

'There is a solution to your problem, Mr Andronakis. Of course, I wouldn't do this for just anyone . . . but I flatter myself we have become friends during these lessons . . .'

'Friends, yes,' said Mr Andronakis, who had clenched his large fists in the effort of following Kennedy's words.

'And so I feel justified, as a friend, in putting this to you. As a matter of fact I have a friend who might help you with this examination.'

'Friends, yes. Help me. Much appreciate.'

'No, I mean *another* friend. As a favour to me, you understand, I might be able to persuade him to give you some information before the examination which would help you to pass it successfully. I couldn't guarantee success, of course. But it would give you a very great advantage.'

The canary on the balcony broke suddenly into a melodious cadence.

Kennedy glanced at Mr Andronakis's face. It expressed bewilderment.

'If you knew what questions were going to be asked,' Kennedy said very slowly, 'you could prepare yourself better for the examination, couldn't you?'

'You mean to let me know the questions?' A look of delighted comprehension dawned on Mr Andronakis' face.

'I cannot promise,' Kennedy said. 'I can do nothing myself. But this friend of mine in London . . .'

'Understand perfect,' said Mr Andronakis. 'Among friends is much possible. How can I say you my thanks, Mr Kennedy?'

'Of course he would do it to oblige me,' Kennedy said. 'But a gift from you would help things along quite a lot. Oil the wheels, you know.'

'Excuse, please. Oil wheels?' Mr Andronakis reached by force of habit for his notebook and pencil. 'Is this idiom?' he said.

'Never mind that now. If I could offer my friend ten thousand drachmas as a little gift from you, to show that you appreciate . . .'

'Much appreciate, ho, goodness, yes! Ten thousand drachmas is much.'

'Think of it, Mr Andronakis. You would have your licence safe. No further worries. Your rivals and competitors closed down because of their bad English. You safe, laughing, with your certificate hanging on the wall. The future is forward, Mr Andronakis, remember that. What is ten thousand drachmas?'

'Eight thousand.'

'Nine thousand.'

They regarded each other closely for some moments. Mr Andronakis looked serious and impressive. 'For nine thousand drachmas,' he said, 'there must be no mistakings, my good friend.'

'No mistakings,' Kennedy said. His little burst of oratory and his sense of being near a successful conclusion had brought him out in a sweat. Now he had two prospects: well over two hundred pounds. Another three, and it would be worth doing. Of course, he didn't know as yet whether he could get access to the papers, but there must be a way, he told himself. If people were willing to pay money for it, a way must be found. 'I will speak to my friend,' he said.

'Sing, sing for Mr Kennedy,' said Mr Andronakis, holding out his hand, sealing the bargain. 'The future is forward,' he added, which made Kennedy laugh heartily.

After this highly successful piece of business he proceeded to

Eleni Polimenou's flat. He would be glad, he reflected, in a way, when the lessons with her came to an end. They had been interesting certainly. He felt it a privilege to see an artist such as she undoubtedly was, actually at work on the script of a play. All this had been a novel experience for Kennedy. Nevertheless it had been tiring. Several times she had received him in her bedroom with no script in evidence; and she was demanding, quite without tenderness, needing much patient preliminary before her angry cries signalled his release. He bore the marks of her nails on his back. He had not minded it unduly. He knew that she regarded him as an instrument, just as the playwright was an instrument. But he was well able to perform without being attracted; and in this case his sense that Eleni Polimenou could be very useful to him was a sufficient stimulus. All the same, he hoped, as he ascended to her flat, that today's session would be theatrical, rather than fornicatory. He wanted to preserve his tissues for Veta, whom he was meeting later that afternoon.

He was relieved therefore to find her fully clothed in the drawing-room with the script of the play open on a table. They sat down and began reading the last act together, he making his responses in normal conversational tones, she in a more vibrant and highly charged manner. Occasionally he stopped her to correct a pronunciation. As always, towards the end of the play, when they brought home her shepherd son fatally shot by the police, her voice throbbed with feeling, quavered on the brink of sobs. Looking across at her, Kennedy saw the usual tears in her eyes. He wondered briefly if she had ever had children. He thought it on the whole probable that she had not. Suddenly the telephone rang. 'Shit!' said Eleni Polimenou. 'Excuse me, darling.' A moment later he heard her, shrill and blasphemous, in the passage. Amazing, he thought. He was repelled by these swift changes, much more so than if they could have been called hypocritical. Some lingering Puritan distaste was aroused in him.

At the end of the reading she sat back in her chair and smiled at him. 'Only one more time, darling,' she said. 'Next Saturday can you come?'

Kennedy said that he could. 'Are you leaving Athens?' he asked.

'I shall be busy now with rehearsals for the Epidavros Festival, the Greek Tragedy.'

'Oh, yes, of course,' Kennedy said. 'I would like very much to see you in that.'

'I can get you tickets. You tell me when.'

'That is very kind of you.'

'We must speak now about payment for the lessons.'

Kennedy said gallantly, 'I have had payment already, many times over.' He had surmised, however, from the tone of her words earlier and the quality of her smile, that there would be a further instalment next Saturday: they would end this coaching as they had begun it, in bed.

'Never do anything for nothing,' Eleni Polimenou said.

'Well, as a matter of fact, instead of giving me money,' he said, 'I would rather you did a favour for a friend of mine. An Englishman named Willey.'

'Yes? He must be a good friend.'

'He is a deserving case. I wonder if you'd mind if I brought him to meet you, just for a few minutes, one evening this next week.'

'Let me see. Yes, if you like. Wednesday evening I am here from seven to eight o'clock. Is it a healthy friendship, darling?'

'Oh yes,' Kennedy said. 'Nothing like that about it. I just want you to do something for him that I think you could do quite easily. He works for Jennings, whom you've met, I believe.'

'Yes, he came here. What is the favour you want me to do?'

'It's just to put in a good word for him, more or less.' In a few words he told her about Willey's position at the institute. 'Is it something you would be able to do, do you think?' he said.

'I'm not sure,' she said. 'I think probably yes. Jennings, when he came here, seemed to me mainly concerned with prestige. Perhaps if that aspect could be emphasised . . . These people, you know, I have had dealings with before in my life, cultural organisations, councils, bodies to sponsor the arts. They are sometimes difficult to manage, sometimes easy. This is because they are vague about their function. To a business man you can say, "Do this, it will make money for you," but these people do not aim at profits, their salaries are sure. They have no special skills, usually, like an artist or a doctor, for example. They are all the time simply *sponsoring* things, you see. They depend on the people they handle for glory. So they are sycophantic, usually. When they are not arrogant.'

Kennedy was impressed. 'I think that's a very sound analysis,' he said.

She looked at him rather narrowly. 'There is more to all this than you are saying, I'm sure of that. Still, if that is what you want I will try to do it, yes. You let me know when.'

'It is very kind of you,' Kennedy said. 'I'll see you on Wednesday evening, then, with Mr Willey.'

George and Mitsos walked for some time in the streets adjoining Omonia Square. Mitsos had lost all sense of direction now. This man might have killed my parents, he told himself cautiously and with wonder; almost indeed with reverence. True, his mother had not died of the rape. But within a year she had died. She had begun to forget the simple order of things, the normal sequences of speech, the way to lay a table. And shortly afterwards she had died, in hospital. Right up to the moment of death her face had worn an expression of perplexity, so that it was only after she had stopped breathing that she seemed once more certain of things. A cerebral tumour, the doctors had said, which might have been clambering for years inside that small skull, but which Mitsos in the obstinacy of his grief had attributed to the events of that one evening. Merely the suspicion of being the perpetrator conferred on the man before him a value unique in the world and a curious fragility despite his bulk. Only when it occurred to him how easily the other could still get away did Mitsos feel at all savage towards him. George might even now be contemplating a change of job, a journey. Perhaps the little house in the blind alley was not his at all, and he was only a lodger there, free if the whim took him to leave at a moment's notice, leave at a time when Mitsos was sleeping or unavoidably elsewhere, take a bus or a train to where he could never be found again. There was no way he could be certain of George's intentions, except by depriving him of intentions altogether, immobilising him — skewering him, as it were. But he was still too grateful, too indebted, to be able to want this, except in slack unguarded moments. It may not, of course, be the same one, he told himself. Latterly he had needed to remind himself of this quite frequently; it seemed to be mattering less, or rather mattering only to one who sought a pure metaphysical truth: his impure tangible truth was the man before him, who had been vouchsafed, surely, for something.

Today George was not carrying his umbrella; perhaps this meant he was not going to work. They were quite close to Omonia Square now, the long parabolas of water from the fountains in the square glittered at Mitsos as he glanced from street intersections. At the corner of Peraius Street, George turned into a very large, old-fashioned café with high chairs backed in dark hide, and heavy, marble-topped tables. After hesitating on the pavement for some moments Mitsos followed him in. It was cool and hushed inside. A few men sat alone with newspapers. As he walked between the tables, George was in the act of sitting down and pulling a newspaper from his pocket. He glanced up as Mitsos approached and their eyes met. George showed no sign of recognition, but Mitsos immediately smiled and held out his hand. 'Not at the Areopagus today, then?' he said.

No particular expression had appeared on the other's face. Mitsos said quietly. 'You showed me round the Areopagus some time ago. You remember me, don't you? It turned out that we are both from Epirus.'

'Yes, now I remember you,' the man said, and once again, even though Mitsos had been prepared for it, that harsh laborious whisper, issuing from such a heavy man, was astounding. 'But you are mistaken, I am not from Epirus. There are so many, you understand,' he added, excusing himself, it seemed, for his failure to recognise Mitsos.

'I beg your pardon,' Mitsos said. 'I thought you were from Epirus.' He looked down at the chair nearest him. 'How strange,' he said, 'that we should meet again so soon.' The other said nothing. Mitsos nerved himself to look into the pale eyes. For some seconds they stared thus at each other, then abruptly Mitsos sat down at the table. 'Excuse me,' he said. A weakness had attacked him under the scrutiny of the man, not out of fear of the other's recognition, but at the terrible familiarity of those features, that face which he had been constructing in the nights when he could not sleep – an exercise in his insomnia curiously calming. Every line and mark he had recalled, until it was like an image springing directly from his own creative energy, rather than a face existing in life. So intimately did he know it now that blindfolded he felt he could have identified it, just by the merest tracing of the fingertips: the complications of the soft, dark skin under the eyes, the pitting of the lower lip, the prickle of bristle round the mouth; minute indentations of his fingertips could even register the life below the skin, the local suffusions of blood and the patterns of little bloodbursts along the cheek-bones. The whole of that face was known to him, more fully than he had known any other, more fully by far than he knew his own; no object of love could have been better known.

'I happened to be walking,' Mitsos said. 'I came in for tea. They serve tea here, I suppose?'

George looked at him rather intently for some moments. He seemed to be trying to decide something. 'You are on holiday in Athens?' he said, after a while.

'Yes.'

'From Epirus?'

'No. I have been living abroad, in England, for several years. Since I was thirteen, in fact.'

The waiter appeared and Mitsos made an order for both of them: lemon tea for himself, ouzo for his companion.

'In that case . . .' the other said, shrugging his heavy shoulders.

'What?'

'I had a feeling that somewhere before we had met. Not very recently. But if you have been out of Greece so long . . . I myself have never been out of Greece.'

Mitsos looked down at his hands. 'It is not very likely,' he said. George's shirt, he noticed, was stained and crumpled, and his pale blue tie had darker stains where it broadened below the knot. The collar of his jacket was greasy and there was a scurf of dandruff on it. Seen thus, at close quarters and indoors, everything about him indicated poverty and neglect. Mitsos could smell him too, an acrid smell, as of clothes that have been put away damp. There was nevertheless a kind of authority in the set of the large head, the reclinations of the thick body as it shifted in the high-backed chair. 'Perhaps it was in Epirus,' he said.

'I have told you,' George whispered, 'that I am not from Epirus.'

'Oh yes, of course. Athens, then, perhaps. Here in Athens.'

'You were only a child then.'

'True, but children can be ... encountered, surely? And subsequently recognised?' Mitsos looked down at his glass. His headache had left him now and he felt alert, rather excessively alert, as though he needed to keep his responses in check. 'You must have to know a good deal about our monuments and antiquities,' he said, 'to do your work.'

The other's lips tightened briefly as though in scorn of this. 'You learn as you go along,' he said.

'But in the winter,' Mitsos said loudly, irrepressibly, 'what do you do in the winter? Do you leave Athens in the winter?'

George looked at him curiously. 'I never leave Athens,' he whispered.

'You are not an official guide then?' Mitsos said, recovering his former conversational tone.

'No. I have no friends, and those licences are coveted.'

'That is a pity.'

George met his regard squarely, smiling a little. 'Nevertheless,' he said, 'as you see, I live.'

'Yes, yes.' Mitsos smiled back. He felt a genuine happiness at being able to endorse this.

It was quite gay in the gardens as Kennedy walked towards the neoclassical facade of the Zappeion building to meet Veta. People strolled along the pavements between borders of cannas and dahlias. The orchestra was playing a familiar medley. Waiters passed frequently among the crowded tables, their white jackets gleaming in the sunlight. Altogether, Kennedy thought, a scene of some jollity. He chose a table in the shade quite close to the orchestra, which was running at that moment with spirit through the overture to *William Tell*, and settled down to wait.

To while away the time he took out the wallet from his inside breast pocket and began reading some of his testimonials. He had not yet been able to persuade anyone else to read them, but age and custom had not staled the pleasure they afforded him. In certain moods he could believe entirely in the Kennedy they depicted, a Kennedy of sterling qualities who could be recommended for any post to which his talents inclined him to aspire. Perhaps his favourite was that purporting to be written by the headmaster of the secondary school that Kennedy had briefly attended while he was living with a sort of uncle. This headmaster, a gaunt man whose lungs had been damaged by gas in the First World War, had caned Kennedy before the assembled school and afterwards expelled him for assaulting the music master. Now, albeit posthumously, he atoned for such barbarous behaviour, rating Kennedy second to none as athlete, scholar and natural leader. 'He is', Kennedy read, 'one of the most remarkable pupils who have ever passed through my hands, equally at home in the study and on the playing-field, a thorough all-rounder.' That caught the schoolmasterly tone exactly, he thought. God, he had been inspired when he wrote these testominials! Old Robson was dead now, of course, caught short one day while pruning his roses; his death gave an oracular force to the neat typescript; the absence of any possibility of contradiction made it into truth. Similarly with the praises of the ship's doctor to whom Kennedy had sold a radio set belonging to his landlady, and the forthright military appraisal of the major, now drunken and of no fixed abode, who had assisted at Kennedy's dishonourable discharge for breaking into a civilian store while absent without leave, and trafficking in stolen cigarettes. All these persons, with whom in fact relations had been less than satisfactory, now spoke for him in their several voices. He was beginning to leaf through the secondary set, testimonials written by persons who had never existed, when he saw Veta approaching. He recognised her immediately while she was still some distance away, even though this was the first time he had seen her in clothes other than her maid's uniform. It was her walk that made her so easy to recognise, the walk of a girl who had been barefoot and carried loads: head up and shoulders back, hips moving more freely than is usual among town girls, and a kind of thrusting motion of the thighs, very beautiful to Kennedy, as though she were wading against some element slightly resistant. He folded up his testimonials methodically, put them back in the wallet, and was in the act of replacing the wallet in its usual pocket when Veta arrived at the table. Thus she was in time to see him put the wallet away, and her eyes lingered very appreciably at the spot below his tweed where it reposed, so much so in fact that Kennedy had to wait some moments before he could direct his smile at her. She was chewing, with mouth somewhat open and a regular revolving motion of the jaws, some sort of gum. Her large mild eyes moved from the area of Kennedy's pocket to his face, the chewing stopped briefly while she returned his smile, then commenced again.

'So there you are,' Kennedy said, getting to his feet.

She was wearing a dress with a flowered pattern, square-cut at the neck and tight across her magnificent bosom: a dress that did not look as if it had cost much, but he knew it would be her best. He was not at all idealistic about women, or anything else; but as he stood there he was taken unawares by a confused but potent sense of her evolution, the ages and coincidences that had gone to fashion her, bestow on her that way of walking and standing, rounded breast and buttock, imparted that texture to her hair, that particular configuration of bone beneath the flesh of her face. The sense of this showed momentarily in his expression – a quality of wonder transcending admiration – for the girl herself lowered her eyes, not in coquetry but in what seemed a temporary bafflement, still, however, chewing steadily.

'Please sit down,' he said, recovering somewhat.

Veta did so, remarking a moment later, '*Qu'il fait chaud*,' and agitating the front of her dress to ventilate herself, in peasant fashion.

Kennedy smiled at the gesture. He was by now in a frame of mind in which he would have accorded approval to anything she did. 'But you must be used to the heat,' he said.

'In Tinos,' she said, speaking the French very hesitantly in her deep voice, 'We lived close to the sea. It was fresh. Here is like a *furnos*.'

'We will go to the sea one of these days, shall we not?' he said, and again he experienced that look of hers, the large eyes direct and somehow appraising, as though she was trying to gauge some meaning not immediately apparent in his words.

'What would we do there?' she said.

'Well,' he said, 'we could bathe, have a picnic.'

'Yes,' she said, 'I would like . . . Can I have an ice-cream?'

'Of course.'

'A *Special*?'

'Anything you want,' Kennedy said. 'You can have anything you want.'

She laughed a little. It was as though the inclusiveness of the promise reassured her in some way; of his eccentricity perhaps. 'You are rich, then,' she said. 'A rich English.'

'I am the sort of man,' Kennedy said boastfully, 'who, if he likes somebody, spares no expense.'

'*Plaît-il?*'

'I can be generous,' Kennedy said. He raised his hand and patted the right side of his chest, where his wallet was. Generosity was specified there, of course, among his other virtues. It was a pity, he thought, that she didn't know any English; he could have showed her his testimonials. Her eyes were regarding intently the area he had patted, only leaving it in fact when the *Special* arrived, a great mound of vanilla, veined with strawberry juice, bordered with marzipan, studded with pistachio and walnuts, winged with wafers.

'My! my!' Kennedy said, eyeing it. He looked at Veta. Her eyes were shining, as she considered the ice-cream, with a frank and childish pleasure. He had never seen her so animated. 'Are you sure you can eat it all?' he asked gravely.

'Oh yes,' she said, with complete seriousness. 'I had one before, when I first came to Athens, and I was able to eat it all.'

'Well, that's a comfort,' Kennedy said. 'How much do they pay you at that house?'

'They pay me three hundred drachmas,' she said, nibbling one of her wafers before taking the plunge with the spoon.

'A week?'

Again she laughed a little, at this further evidence of Kennedy's princely scale of living. 'A month,' she said, rather indistinctly – she had begun now on the ice-cream.

'Three hundred drachmas a *month*? But that is absolutely fantastic,' Kennedy said. 'It's slavery.'

'I have my food and bed there. I can save nearly all my money.'

'But you must never have any fun at all,' he said.

'I save, every month, two hundred drachmas. With the money I buy gold pounds. Soon,' she told him proudly, 'I will have fifty gold pounds.'

Little by little, as the ice-cream diminished, a certain amount of information about herself was somehow conveyed, with Kennedy first prompting, then guessing in the long pauses between monosyllables. He had to work hard at it, but discovered that she was twenty years old, and had been in Athens three years now, always at the same house. She had left Tinos because her mother had died and there was nothing for her to do there, no work at least that was not rough and ultimately brutalising. Tinos was beautiful, but in Athens, as she had heard of it, there were opportunities for improvement, domestic service offered softer influences. So she had come with the grief of her mother fresh, and a very small number of possessions, and delivered herself over to the Logothetis family, who had thus secured, for something less than a pound a week, someone to fetch and carry, wait at table, do laundry and shopping. She knew no one in Athens except a few of her fellow domestics, and had no relative nearer than Tinos. She was completely alone, saving steadily at the rate of twelve shillings a week. . . .

'Well,' said Kennedy, 'from now on you're going to have a bit of fun.'

The orchestra was battling now with Strauss. Veta's gum must have been stowed away in some recess while she was busy with the ice-cream, because now she recommenced chewing, with the ruminative motion, which, in conjunction with the mild steadiness of her gaze, Kennedy found quite captivating.

'Now that you've met me,' he said, 'things are going to get a bit brighter.' There was a little pause. 'I am a man,' Kennedy said, 'who likes to spread sweetness and light.'

'*Plaît-il?*' She had not been really listening, however, he could tell. Expressions did not flit across Veta's face, they settled and basked a while. Now there was one there he later came to know quite well, a sort of faintly luminous calculation. He gave her his broadest smile and waited.

'Can I have another *Special*?' she said.

7

On the following Tuesday, Willey and Olivia were able to meet
and go out to Pendelis in the morning, to look at building sites.
This was made possible because it was half-term at the Embassy
School, where Olivia worked, and because Willey discovered
when he went to the university to give his weekly lecture on the
Victorian novelists that the students were on strike again. They
went on strike every summer term, sometimes for a few days only,
sometimes for the best part of the term. It was the heat, coupled
with various political and economic discontents. Willey went to
his usual classroom to find only two students there, playing chess.
So he phoned Olivia and they met at a point near Canning Square,
where the Pendelis buses left from.

Olivia was waiting for him at the bus-stop. She was dressed in a
pink gingham blouse and a peasant-style skirt, black, very full,
with a broad folksy pattern stitched in gold round the hem. She
also carried a craft-shop bag with further Greek motifs. This was
better by far than the knapsack she would sometimes bring, with
the thermos-flask of tea — she was a great girl for thermos-flasks.
Olivia frequently affected home-woven things, she even sometimes wore wooden beads that clicked together, and what she
called chunky ear-rings. Willey suffered with her in this matter of
dress, suffered with her lapses of taste and her basic, ineradicable
assumption of defeat in advance. He had always thought that for
Olivia dressing up to go out was less an act of vanity to ensnare the
travelling eye than an act of courage to endure it. Lately, it was
true, perhaps emboldened by his love, she had gone in for more
sophisticated adornment, bought variously coloured headbands,
grown her hair longer. Once, staggeringly, she had met him with a
huge mauve artificial rose pinned to her blouse. He had compli-

mented her quickly on this, but something must have been wrong with his tone or his glance, for she had never worn it again. In fact he was helplessly opposed to these experiments. Olivia represented for him not abundance, but a due recognition of inherent limitation. He did not want the sort of love that breeds anguish and the expectation of marvels. Olivia and he, he told himself frequently, with mingled tenderness and pain, had settled for each other; any longings on the part of either that could not be met within their relationship – and some of his own were totally inadmissible – had had to be put beyond hope. Thus he was distressed by any tendency towards expansiveness that Olivia showed, any vagaries, anything unexpected, even if this promised to prove an enrichment. He wanted her as she was, unable or unwilling to realise that she, after so many years of deprivation, of being the unattached girl, did not need commending for the qualities – camaraderie, kindness, social availability – that she had developed in self-defence, but for those more specifically feminine traits for which in the past she had had small encouragement.

Today she greeted him easily and naturally, without that strained sense of occasion that sometimes afflicted her. 'Just in time,' she said. 'This bus leaves in about three minutes. Let's get in.'

On the bus he told her about the strike. 'Of course,' he said, 'they will be used by the Opposition as evidence of popular unrest. There is no popular unrest. There are simply numerous local discontents which never combine.'

'Why is it,' she said, 'that one only hears of *students* striking and demonstrating, never these poor labourers and people?'

He could tell by her tone that she had slipped into the rôle of female seeking guidance from male in public affairs. He said, 'They are the only ones with the necessary irresponsibility, I suppose. Everyone else has too much to lose. The unions have no power except in collaboration with the Government.'

The bus had passed now through the nearer suburbs of Athens, and the green foothills of Pendelis were quite close, gashed white higher up with the marble quarries. In the flat land before the hills were groves of olives, small orchards of apricot and peach. The bus turned down a long straight avenue planted on either side with eucalyptus, from which other, narrower roads branched off at regular intervals. They got off at the terminus, a little square with a trellised taverna, and walked slowly up the ascending street beyond it, which at a certain distance developed into a loose-surfaced track. After some minutes they came to a narrower track, branching away from this, and they followed it, since they had not been this way before, continuing to walk towards the hills as the track narrowed into little more than a footpath, rose, then dipped abruptly, so that suddenly they were out of sight of all habitation, among pine and scrub with huge poppies flaring everywhere. Now the characteristic colours of Athens were all around them: sage and speckled grey and terracotta. Wherever the land was cut it bled sandstone red. Here and there high above them they saw through the pines more quarries, neat white scallops in the hillsides. All the land in their immediate vicinity was scheduled for building development.

'That would be an interesting site,' Willey said, pointing a little up the hillside at a sharply sloping area of ground flanked by large rocks. 'You could have a splendid rock garden at the front there.'

'Yes, John, but it doesn't face south, I don't think, does it?' Olivia had two fixed ideas about the house they would have: that it should face south, and have an internal courtyard with a tiled floor, and a fountain. Willey, on the other hand, thought largely in terms of rock gardens. They both thoroughly enjoyed these inspections of the terrain, which they conducted on an average twice a month.

'Water, that is the important thing,' said Willey, nodding his head sagely. 'We mustn't forget about the water.'

'I can just see you,' Olivia said, 'in your old things, watering the garden. In your old hat.'

He glanced at her smiling, then looked away again, disturbed by the depth of love in her eyes. He knew of old this way of hers of isolating him in particular images, to stay her love on: watering the garden, marking papers by the fire, playing with the children. There was something curiously youthful, immature really, about these projections, but they served her need – since she lacked skill at expressing love directly – and she held to them with a tenacity that Willey found both moving and amusing. It occurred to him that this might be an appropriate time to tell her about Kennedy's phone call. 'By the way,' he said casually, 'you remember that fellow they sent to me a few weeks ago, Kennedy his name is, they sent him to me to be fixed up. . . ?'

'Yes, I remember. They have a cheek . . .'

'Yes, well, he rang me up last night at the institute. Wanted to know if I was free tomorrow evening to meet Eleni Polimenou.'

'The actress? But I didn't know she ever came to Greece. She lives in America.'

'She's in Athens now, it seems. Kennedy said on the phone that he had spoken to her about me, and she would like to meet me. I can't imagine why. It seems he's been helping her with some play that she's appearing in.'

'Goodness,' Olivia said, 'you *are* going up in the world.'

He knew, before he turned his head, what he would see on her face, that look of assumed indifference. Nevertheless his spirits sank at the sight of it.

'You said you'd go, I suppose,' she said.

'Yes, I did.' Willey tried hard to keep his voice free from asperity. This immediate unreasoning hostility to any move on his part not including her was something he found difficult to endure in Olivia. It meant, he always thought, that she must be unhappy.

'It ought to be interesting,' he said. 'And, after all, it is not often one has a chance of meeting a celebrity.'

'She's celebrated for more than just acting,' Olivia said, with a little smile – she went in for little smiles when she was wounded.

'I daresay she is.'

'They say,' said Olivia, looking straight before her, the little smile coming and going, 'that she *pays* people to sleep with her. She must be fifty if she's a day, and, of course, when you get to that age . . .'

'I say, look out, Olivia,' said Willey urgently, but it was too late. While she had been speaking the path had narrowed further and Willey was now walking a few paces behind. What she did not appear to see, and he only at the last moment saw, was that the path took a sudden tilt downward, the steepness of which was partially concealed by the shrubs that straggled over it on either side. Olivia, rigid with grievance, was precipitated downward before she knew what was happening. She slipped, clutched wildly, and fell headlong. She lay where she had fallen, without a sound of any sort, several feet below, in a rocky and tangled declivity roughly circular in shape. Willey scrambled down after her.

'Are you hurt?' he said wildly, bending over her.

'No,' she said quietly. 'Only winded. Give me a hand up.'

Perhaps it was reaction to his fears for her safety, but the Girl Guide, matter-of-factness of this reply infuriated Willey. And when he had lifted her to her feet; regarded the pallor of her rather equine face, the eyes moist and vague, either from pain or vexation, the dishevelled hair, above all perhaps, the burrs which she had collected in her descent, which liberally adhered to the peasant skirt; when he considered these things his fury mounted until it refused any longer to be contained.

'Tell me, Olivia,' he said, 'why is it that you are so bloody clumsy?'

Her face did not change its expression, as though no further damage could be registered facially. And immediately Willey felt ashamed, ashamed of the words he had uttered and the entire unfairness of his anger. He was not able, he would never be able, to explain to Olivia his anger and his shame, the ideal of physical grace and adroitness that accompanied him on these expeditions, for ever trembling in his imagination on the verge of its adolescent incarnation, lithe legs stepping delicately and surely where poor Olivia had tumbled and rolled. . . .

Now, unable to speak, he looked about him blankly for some moments. It was a hollow where Pan might have fluted, completely secret and enclosed, tangled with vegetation, savage with seamed granite. A place that appeared for the moment menacing, as though ready to blast the intruder with myth.

'I don't like it very much down here,' Olivia said. 'I'm sensitive to atmosphere, you know.'

The rank sweetness of thyme was in Willey's nostrils, cicadas shrilled all around and the more solemn liturgies of bees resounded. Beyond this he could sense the stony silence of the hills. There was something exciting to him in the heat and seclusion of the place; he felt that any stealthy act could be cancelled on emergence, or left down here, rather, to vibrate for ever. In order to create a diversion he stepped nearer to one of the several umbrella pines in the dell, and looked closely at the burnished quills on which the sunlight seemed to dwell with particular care. 'Aren't they beautiful trees,' he said, 'really?'

Suddenly, however, he heard behind him Olivia exclaim with disgust, 'They've got some sort of pest in them!' Then he saw that the boughs higher up were clothed with great white silky balls, slung hammockwise, glinting in the sun. The nearest of them was outlined against the sky, revealing a black squirming lump of life at the centre. Thousands of caterpillars moved blindly in there, which within hours probably would break through on to their green pastures.

While he stood gazing with repugnance upward – a similar activity was taking place on all the other pines in the hollow – he became aware for the first time, in this landscape, among these trees, of a sound he had grown accustomed to in Athens itself, the sound of chipping and tapping, metal on stone, made furtive here by reason of the impossibility of tracing it to its source, and also, strangely, by the infected trees among which it was taking place. The sound of invisible construction.

'I have it down here,' Olivia said suddenly. 'Please get me out.'

From some perversity which he did not analyse, Willey made no immediate reply to this. He was still looking upward at the branches of the pines. Olivia began circling the hollow, too quickly, stumbling over the rocky, uneven ground. Once she tripped and nearly fell. 'Did you hear what I said?' she demanded furiously. 'I want to get out.'

Willey removed his gaze from the caterpillars and looked across at her.

'You fool,' she said loudly. 'You fool.' Her head was lowered as though she were about to charge him. Hair had escaped from the bun at her nape and hung over her face. Her eyes strained upward through this screen, regarding him with hatred. He was astonished. Suddenly the shrilling of cicadas seemed to intensify, grew deafening. It was very hot in the hollow, the scent of thyme was almost overpowering. He had not thought Olivia could look so baleful. Why did he not reassure her? Suddenly he knew they were not house-hunting at all, that was a pretence, they were passing some time before dying. 'Good heavens, Olivia,' he said.

'*I want to get out*,' she said.

'All right,' he said quickly. 'This way we can get out, there, where the rock goes up, there are footholds. I'll go first and you follow.'

Slowly, slipping, clambering, clutching at tree roots and jutting rocks, they were able to emerge. They discovered a faint track that led further round the hillside, and followed this. For several minutes they walked on in silence. The path improved steadily. Then Willey said, 'We must have taken the wrong path, some-how. Before, I mean. The proper path couldn't possibly lead into that hollow, could it?'

After a very long pause Olivia said in her normal tones, 'Well, I think it's very dangerous, especially for old people, don't you?'

'Extremely so,' he said promptly.

'The municipality ought to do something about it,' Olivia said.

He nodded. Something happened down there, all the same, he thought. Something quite important in its way, to be folded into their lives, just as the declivity itself, now lost behind them, was enfolded in these violated, doomed hills. For those few minutes they had lapsed, they had failed to accord to each other the habitual, the human indulgence. Such a thing must never happen again, he told himself. 'I don't think,' he said, 'that I'd care for a house on this side all that much, you know. Rather exposed and in the winter . . .'

'Yes,' she said. 'It's so far from the sea, too. Say what you like, the sea is an important consideration.'

'Perhaps Old Faleron would be a good place to look,' he said. 'Of course, we'd have to have a car.'

They passed through a screen of trees to emerge, amazingly, upon a surfaced and sedate strip of road, up there, miles from anywhere, laid out dead straight, with concrete lamp-posts and a neat roundabout, running for a few hundred yards only, beginning and ending in the wilderness of the hills. The sounds of building grew more marked, echoing all around them.

'You'd need a helicopter to use this road,' Willey said. 'Quite unrealistic.'

Now they began to see houses, set behind trees, sugary white in the sunshine, granulated and blinding. Glimpses of paved courts and terraces, puny lemon trees in pots. Here and there the blue gleam of tiled swimming pools.

'There are people living here already,' Willey said. 'There must be another road somewhere. . . . By the way, if you don't want me to go tomorrow night, I'll find an excuse . . .'

'Oh, no, you must go,' Olivia said. 'It might lead to something quite important. Call in on your way home, if you like.'

'Of course,' he said, 'I was intending to do that.'

8

'Simpson will be all right. I keep telling you,' Kennedy said patiently, 'that Simpson will be all right.'

'He's more delicately balanced,' Thorne said, 'than you or I. That's the artist in him.'

'It's the brandy in him, I should say.'

They were sitting in Thorne's room having tea and biscuits. Thorne had made the tea. He was punctilious about this, warming the pot carefully beforehand, using freshly boiled water, which he poured on to the tea from a certain height. He had even acquired from somewhere a red woollen tea-cosy. Thorne's room was an oasis of luxury and grace in Kitty's rather sparse establishment. He had prints of English landscape paintings on the walls, a copper vase with carnations in it, even a bright red lambswool rug on the floor. And when he was bustling about in the room, Kennedy had remarked, he had an air of purpose and contentment that was not evident at other times.

'You don't understand Simpson, I'm afraid,' he said now, creasing his pale forehead, stirring his tea.

'No, I suppose not.'

'He comes in here sometimes and pours his heart out,' Thorne said.

'I expect he does. Any news of the easel, by the way?'

Thorne's air immediately became more consequential. 'They have given him a deadline,' he said. 'Within two weeks he should have either the easel or the money.'

'Well, that's good news.'

'Ye-es . . . He's not short for the moment. He got some money by selling his blood.'

'By doing what?'

'Selling his blood. At the hospital. He got three hundred drachmas for it.'

'I should think Simpson's would be mostly alcohol.'

'They took it anyway.'

'By the way,' Kennedy said, 'can I borrow another shirt? I've got to meet a girl this evening, and mine are all to pot.'

'Yes, all right.'

'And would you mind throwing in a tie with it? I haven't a great range of ties.'

'Yes,' Thorne said, 'you can borrow a tie.' He looked somewhat critically at Kennedy. 'That suit is very crumpled,' he said. 'And don't you find it hot, in this weather?'

'I'll be frank with you,' Kennedy said, 'old boy. The reason I'm always in this suit is because it is the only suit I have. I allowed myself to get a bit down on clothes in London. My wardrobe needs replenishing, as you might say. I can't wear the trousers without the jacket because the trousers come up high. Quite a bit higher than the waist, actually.' He unbuttoned the jacket and opened it to show Thorne. The trousers did indeed rise considerably towards the armpit. 'I can't lower the braces, you see,' Kennedy said. 'It would make the trousers altogether too baggy round the seat and crutch. There is nothing for it but to keep the jacket buttoned the whole time.'

'H'm, yes,' said Thorne. 'Well, it's no good my offering you a pair of my trousers, they wouldn't fit, and I don't suppose Simpson . . . I'll tell you what, I don't mind ironing the suit for you, if you can wait twenty minutes or so. I've got an iron that I brought from England.'

He made a very good job of the ironing, and it was a relatively resplendent Kennedy who strolled down Vassilas Sofias later that evening on his way to meet Veta. He was so conscious of his elegance that he picked a jasmine from a garden wall and stuck it in his buttonhole. And the scent of that single flower came to his nostrils intermittently throughout the evening, an element of its momentousness, marking it in his memory, during the short remainder of his life, as a time of self-surrender.

Already the purity of evening was in the sky, and the sliver of the new moon hung there, gaining in distinctness from moment to moment as the daylight faded. He was a good three-quarters of an hour early for his assignation with Veta, whom he had arranged to meet at eight o'clock at the point where Gennadion Street opens on the lower slopes of Lycavettos – the evening slopes of Lycavettos constitute one of the very few places in Athens where concourse with the opposite sex can be enjoyed in the open air. As he walked along Kennedy debated within himself whether he should spend the interval having ouzo in the square, or whether he should go on and have a look at Lycavettos itself, climb to the top perhaps, and get a view of the city. Both of these courses seemed equally attractive. In fact, the prospect of meeting Veta gave a glow to all preliminary activities whatever. He decided to go on.

Lycavettos rose above him, surmounted by its little white church, a cone of limestone lunging up in the centre of the city, the city's highest point. He began the ascent, up steps bordered on either side with huge, savage cactus. But something in the activity of climbing thus, some quality of mingled pain and aspiration, more like a memory than a present sensation, almost immediately began to oppress him. The slope grew progressively more arid; lower down, clay and soil in the rifts of the rock supported some pines, and seams of pale grass and grape hyacinths; but as he climbed higher there was only the milky green cactus and the stony outcrop. There was no sound of bird or insect. The white walls of the church above him gleamed in the darkening air. At the top, where even the cactus gave out, would be the church. A recollection of an agony on a stony hill came suddenly to Kennedy, read about, sung about in quavering unwilling unison in the days of his childhood. He stopped abruptly where the steps levelled off into a terrace. Above him the church was lit now. Darkness was descending on the city and the first stars were pricking out. Beyond the city he saw the cruel sheen of the sea. Bats had begun to flit about, low over the cactus – one of those spikes could impale a bat, he thought. He wondered if it had ever happened.

He was suddenly afflicted by feelings of loneliness and self-pity. He began to retrace his steps to the foot again and then along the flank of the hill where it descends in a long sweep, once more through pines, towards Leoforas Alexandras. He waited at the top of Gennadion Street for Veta and after a few minutes made out her form, walking quickly towards him up the street. She was a little breathless, either from the steep climb or some agitation, and at first she said nothing. They went together in silence off the road, and a little way up among the pines. Here among the trees it was very dark. They were quite concealed from anyone who might be passing in the street below.

She stood somewhat above him, her back resting against the slender trunk of a pine; he balancing rather awkwardly on the slope, with his feet planted at different levels. He could make out the pale shape of her face above him; the rest of her was lost in obscurity. She was silent for a long time, but he could hear her breathing.

'I have only a little time,' she said at last.

'It came to me just now,' he said, 'that I am quite alone in the world.'

'You have no one in England?'

'No one at all.'

'I am alone too.'

'So you save up your money, your gold pounds.'

'Yes.'

'You are saving to be married, I suppose.'

'Yes, it is for my *prika*, my dowry.'

'What will you do with it?'

'With one hundred gold pounds I could buy a piece of land. A small piece. To make a little farm.'

Her face glimmered above him. The hesitancy of her speech, the frequent pauses, gave to her words a strange sort of authority, a quality almost sibylline.

'But it's taken you three years to get fifty,' Kennedy said. The scent of his jasmine rose up to him, coupled with the heavier smell of resin from the pines. The night seemed to have opened wounds in the trees. All around him he smelled the gum of their bleeding. He succeeded in scrambling on to Veta's level. Her face was raised to his mutely. He took her in his arms, bracing himself against the hillside, feeling her firm body against his. Again the scent of the jasmine rose to him, crushed between their bodies. He looked over her head into the darkness. 'I will give you the other fifty gold pounds,' he said.

For a moment the girl said nothing and Kennedy thought she had not understood; then he felt her body stiffen and draw slightly away from him.

'*Plaît-il?*'

Kennedy looked blindly into the night beyond the trees. He said, 'If it will take you another three years to save the money, three years of being screamed at by the tribe of Logothetis, I tell you I will give you the fifty gold pounds.'

'I cannot believe,' she said.

'I mean it.'

'When will you give it?'

'In about ten days' time.'

'You are not saying this to me so that I will lie down with you?'

'No, I will give it to you whether you lie down with me or not. It's a promise.'

Suddenly he heard her breath catch sharply and then her hands were behind his neck, drawing his head down, and she kissed him on the lips. Her lips did not move in the kiss, but rested on his firmly and warmly.

'I will lie down with you, if you want,' she said.

'Yes, I want,' Kennedy said. 'Of course I want.'

'Now, tonight?'

'Yes, now.'

She took his hand and without any further speech they walked further up the hillside together, among the pines, further from the lights of the street. After a while they found a small level area, covered with pine-needles. Veta knelt here.

'I cannot believe it, still,' she said. Her voice was slow as ever, but it shook a little.

Kennedy put his hands on her shoulders and pressed her back gently. 'I mean it,' he said. 'I swear I mean it.' She was obedient to his touch, as though undergoing an operation of some sort; and he was very gentle with her, holding himself in check, but he could not help giving her some pain, because she was still a virgin.

On the wall of the taverna that faced on to the square were three birds in cages, goldfinches, all blind, as Mitsos had remarked previously. The dusk had stopped their singing, but he could hear them moving in the cages, the fluttering of wings, the occasional musical rasp of their bodies against the thin bars. The kiosk in the centre was still open, it would not close for another hour, Mitsos knew that; yellow light from inside it fell on the small, brilliant areas of colour, packets of toothpaste and razor blades, the cases of ball-point pens. From where he was standing Mitsos could see the top of the proprietor's motionless head as he sat in there, screened by his merchandise. The smell of warm stone came to him and the cooler, more austere smell of vegetation from the two stunted orange-trees in the square. Mitsos was always grateful for nightfall now; it brought George home to his house. He was watching George, at the end of his alley, sitting outside his door on a canvas chair. There was a small lamp set against the wall above George's head, by the light of which he was reading a newspaper. He was in shirt-sleeves, his bulk disposed comfortably, as he bent his head over the paper; and he had donned a pair of thin-rimmed glasses to read by. With the glasses on he looked benevolent and studious. Watching the man in his lonely, purely private activities had been a curious experience for Mitsos, pacifying yet painful too; it made him seem, as an adversary, more manageable, but less credible, as though somewhere in the intervening years the evil had been extracted like a sting, leaving only the sagging body, the disappointments, the asthma.

Nevertheless he persisted in making the association. Earlier, while it was still light enough, he had watched George watering his pansies in their neat pots along the window ledge. Seeing him there, so obviously caring for the flowers, Mitsos had been invaded by the same disbelief. The obvious wrong, the act of outrage all the years before, that was cool and reckonable, though attended with horror, so long as it could be kept firmly in the past and assessed there, like a debt. Much worse, almost unbearable now, was the very thing that had at first filled Mitsos with something like gratitude: the concurrence of their two lives, the rigid parallel lines that would go on and on for ever unless something was done to force a collision. The lines could not merge, obviously. One of them must stop then . . .

His own? He had thought of suicide several times before, even in London, before he had met George. Now it presented itself as a definite solution. Now, in the cool dark, with the man before him so inoffensive, he did not feel he would mind dying. Easily it could be done, simply, the mere providing of a breach for the outside darkness to enter him, take what was in any case an inevitable possession. . . . The man's mercy too could be cancelled, the idea of his murder in those yellow eyes fulfilled . . .

A real hatred, stronger than anything he had felt before, rose in Mitsos. The man then was still a threat to his life. He looked up at the pale stars beyond the houses. From the taverna there came suddenly the sound of a *bouzouki*, and a man's voice, raised in song: '*Pou petaxe o agori mou?*' The birds fluttered in their cages. Mitsos glanced for the last time that evening at George, still studiously inclined over his paper. This man, then, in his own person, whether he was the same or another, was still a threat to life.

It was a somewhat dazed but quite resolute Kennedy who descended from Lycavettos some time later, and made his way towards the institute, where Willey, he had calculated, would be just about finishing his teaching for the evening. It was by no means the first time that he had found himself in this position. Nearly all the radical changes in his life hitherto had been precipitated by one of two factors: either by getting drunk at an inappropriate time, or by committing some extraordinary rashness of generosity which forced him into courses of action previously only adumbrated in his mind. There were times when generous impulse flushed in him as ungovernable as violence, springing from his own delinquency, his basic contempt for the desired ends of life of the majority – competence, security, claims to respect other than the personal and inherent; contempt too for his own destiny. It was as though he indulged in these periodic acts of recklessness to add to the anarchy of the world. Underlying all this, however, was a deep, primitive conviction of the *commonness* of money, its availability to all. Like water it circulated the earth, but undammable, impossible to isolate in pools.

This sense of fluidity involved him frequently in practical difficulties. Now, for example, because of this promise to Veta

—which it would not occur to him to break — he found himself committed irrevocably, since there was no other way open to him of getting such a sum of money, to the piece of crookery that he had up till then been merely exploring. It was with a certain earnestness that he waited across the street for Willey to emerge. The next hour or so would be crucial.

He did not have long to wait. He saw Willey's thin dilatory form hesitate a moment under the light, and then break into a loping stride towards the square. He followed until they emerged on Vassiles Sofias and then, while Willey paused on the pavement waiting for the lights to change, he approached him and laid a hand familiarly on his shoulder. 'Well, well, old boy,' he said jovially. 'We meet again.'

Willey was obviously startled by the touch and the voice. He started somewhat, rearing back his small neat head, blinking rapidly. 'Oh, it's you,' he said, without smiling. 'You don't want to take me to see any more actresses, do you?'

'Ha, ha, no,' said Kennedy. 'She's an interesting woman, though, isn't she? No, what I wondered was whether you'd like a drink.'

'I was just on my way to Olivia's,' Willey said.

'A quick couple,' said Kennedy, 'on one's way to Olivia's, never did one any harm. Besides, I've got something I want to discuss with you. A little matter of business.'

'All right, then. A quick one. We could go to the "Ellenikon" on the square.'

'Just the ticket,' Kennedy said. It all depended, really, he thought, on two things: the way they ran the examination, and the extent to which Willey wanted a permanent post. Better to begin with the carrot.

The waiter came, took their order, returned with the drinks. Kennedy looked down into his ouzo reflectively. 'I think,' he said in measured tones, 'that I'm in a position to give you a helping hand in the matter of that permanency.'

'*You* are?' Willey said, incredulously. The other, he noticed, had a jasmine in his buttonhole. Also he had pineneedles and odd bits of vegetation in his thick tweed suit. His hair was as usual dishevelled and he exuded a pleasant odour which Willey finally

129

identified as resin. His round, very clear blue eyes regarded Willey steadily.

'In fact,' Kennedy said in the same deliberate tones, 'I think I can swing it for you, I think I can honestly say that I can swing it for you.'

'Oh, can you,' Willey mumbled. He had frequently regretted having confided his situation to Kennedy. Indeed he was puzzled to know what had caused him to do it. 'May I ask by what means?' he said.

Kennedy took a drink of his ouzo which left very little in the glass. 'By using,' he said, 'certain influence that I possess.'

'I see,' Willey said. He felt quite blank for a moment, then suddenly a wild irrational hope possessed him. He met the reckless candour of the other's regard. It seemed incredible that this person should have any sort of influence, with his perpetual look of having slept in his suit, but on the other hand . . . 'Are you serious?' he said.

'Serious, of course I'm serious. Guaranteed.'

'But how?' said Willey. 'What? Do you actually mean a London appointment?'

'I do.'

'But it depends on Jennings, as I think I told you.'

'True,' Kennedy said. 'True words, old boy, but Jennings is open to persuasion, isn't he? I am not on what you'd call an intimate footing with Jennings, but he doesn't strike me as a sea-green incorruptible, not at all. Anyway, I don't want to go into details just now. But I'm telling you definitely that I can do it. Word of honour. Within one week, the wheels being set in motion, Jennings will summon you to his office and with exquisite modulations, and hate in his heart, offer you a permanent post.'

'My dear fellow,' Willey said, courteously, but with much less than complete conviction, 'my dear fellow, if that were to happen, and through your good offices, I should be for ever in your debt.'

Kennedy drew a deep breath, 'No,' he said.

'I beg your pardon?'

'Not for ever.'

'What do you mean?'

'Have another drink.'

'Yes, all right. What did you mean just now?'

Kennedy paused for quite a long time before replying. Now that he had come to the hub of the matter he discovered in himself a certain reluctance to go on. It was not a scruple, in the ordinary sense: he was, he felt, offering good value to Willey. It was rather that he felt the proposition, lacking as it was in tangibility, bore down too heavily on Willey's scruples. He had not felt this at all while negotiating with the Greeks. That was a cash transaction, and cash removed outrage: spread money round a deal and you sterilised guilt. But the price he had to demand from Willey – and Kennedy set himself conscientiously to see it from the other's point of view – was a betrayal of trust, no less. It was tricky. Moreover, he was not quite sure that Willey could help him, even if he was willing to. He did not know yet how the pre-examination machinery worked.

'You are concerned, I believe,' he said slowly, 'in the diploma examinations?'

'Concerned in them? All the teaching at the institute is based on them.'

'No, I mean you have something to do in the actual conduct of the examinations?'

'Yes, I am one of the supervisors.'

'What does that mean exactly?'

'Well, there is a great number of candidates, you know, and Athens is divided into a number of examination centres. Each of these centres has a supervisor who is responsible for the way the examinations are conducted. Giving the proper instructions to candidates, seeing to the spacing of the desks, that sort of thing. He has a number of what are called invigilators to help him.'

'Yes, I see. And the examination papers, they are entrusted to you, I suppose?'

'They are, yes.'

Kennedy leaned forward. 'On the day itself?' he said.

'I'm sorry, I don't . . .'

'Are they given to you on the same day as the examination?'

'No, that would not be practicable. We have to be at our centres early in the morning and they are in various parts of the city. We collect the papers on the day before. This year the examinations

131

are on Monday and Tuesday, so I expect we shall pick up the papers on Saturday morning.'

'And keep them over the weekend?'

'Yes.'

'All the papers for the two days?'

'Yes, that's right. Look here, why are you asking me all this?'

'I'll tell you in a minute. How are the question papers held together?'

'They are in brown-paper envelopes, one for each subject.'

'How are the envelopes fastened?'

Willey looked at him with a completely expressionless face. 'They are stitched along the top,' he said, 'with some sort of very strong thread. You'd better tell me, I think,' he added, 'why you have become so interested in all this.'

'Would you care for another drink?'

'No thank you.'

'I should like to get a look at those papers,' Kennedy said.

Willey smiled. 'I daresay,' he said. 'So would a great number of the candidates, I fancy.'

'Or better still,' Kennedy said, 'I should like half an hour alone in the room where you keep the papers. 'On Saturday morning, say, as soon as possible after you return with them.'

They stared at each other for almost a minute. Willey's smile faded slowly. 'You are serious, then,' he said, in strained tones.

'Yes, quite serious.'

'But you must . . .' Suddenly Willey blushed crimson. The smile returned, but different now, painful. He lowered his eyes. 'You are actually asking me to . . . show you the papers before the examination?' he said, in very low tones.

'Not show me them, no. Oh, no. I am not asking you to do anything positive. That's, the beauty of it, from your point of view. All I want, you see, is half an hour on my own with the papers.'

Willey seemed to gather himself together. He raised his head and looked at Kennedy inimically. 'How dare you ask me to do such a thing,' he said.

'Think it over,' Kennedy said. He had been watching Willey closely and was on the whole satisfied with his reactions. That initial embarrassment had worried him, he had not understood it;

the hostility was all right, though it hadn't the warmth of moral indignation, seemed merely annoyance at being thought lacking enough in integrity to have this proposition made to him: not an emotion likely to get in the way after some pause for reflections. What he could not know was that Willey, after the first wave of shame, had been able to discover in himself no emotion whatever, and was now merely putting on a face which might be acceptable to some hypothetical observer.

'It's a genuine offer,' Kennedy said, recalling suddenly a phrase from his encyclopaedia-selling days. 'Think it over, old boy,' he repeated. 'Nothing to do for it. No risk. Wild horses wouldn't drag your name from me. And you are guaranteed a permanent post. Put it this way: if you are offered a permanent post between now and the Saturday morning when you collect the papers, if you are definitely and officially offered it between then and now, will you agree to give me half an hour alone in the room where the papers are?'

'The whole thing is absurd,' Willey said. 'How would I know it was through your agency?'

'What does that matter to you, if you get the job?'

Willey stood up. The consciousness that he had not borne himself in an appropriate way during the conversation was beginning to make him genuinely angry. He stood for a moment looking down at Kennedy, who had now, the proposition made, reassumed his characteristic sprawl of arms and legs. Once again the complete apparent candour of the other, the absence of any sign of shiftiness, defeated whatever further rebukes Willey might have been contemplating.

'I'm going now,' he said curtly. At least he would make a dignified withdrawal.

'I wouldn't say anything to Olivia about all this,' Kennedy said, smiling steadily upward. 'Women get things distorted.'

And this made Willey angrier still, because he realised, before he had gone far, that he had already decided not to say anything to Olivia about it.

9

'A Norwegian,' Simpson said. He winked at Kennedy and made a sort of growling or gargling sound, deep in his throat. 'She doesn't speak much English.' He growled again, as though this disability formed part of the girl's sexual equipment. He was washing his socks in Kennedy's hand-basin, since there wasn't one in his own room. He washed socks every day, drunk or sober, but Kennedy had never seen him actually wearing socks – it was one of several mysteries about Simpson that he had not yet plumbed.

'How did you meet her?' Kennedy said. He was getting ready to go out.

'I happened to be down at Piraeus, making enquiries about my easel, that the bloody Germans lost; they lost my easel, not the Greeks, the bloody Germans . . .'

'Yes, I know,' Kennedy said.

'She was having some trouble about collecting a trunk. I was able to help her. I am well known down there, of course, they all know me, ah, Americano . . .'

'Bit of all right is she?' Kennedy said, moving towards the door.

'Listen,' Simpson said. 'I want to tell you about the other night. This girl, this Great Dane . . .' He growled again and stamped lightly on the floor.

'I have to go out now,' Kennedy said. 'I have a private lesson.' He didn't really like leaving Simpson alone in his room but could see no help for it.

'Listen, we both had a hell of a lot to drink. I was so pissed I could hardly get my pants off. Jesus! And she just flopped on the bed and started sort of kicking about. She's big, you know, a big 'un. All I could see were these big white hams of hers.'

'Where was this, then? Not here?'

'No, her hotel. Listen, I thought she'd passed out on me, but . . .'

'I really have to go,' Kennedy said.

'What a night!' Simpson said.

'See you later, then.'

'I never thought I had it in me,' Simpson said.

'Did you get it in *her*?' said Kennedy, leering back from the door. 'That's the point, old boy.'

'Of course I wouldn't do this for just anyone, Mr Dranas,' he was saying a few minutes later. 'But I have always thought you a very deserving case. I do not like to see such industry as yours go unrewarded . . .' He spoke deliberately, keeping his head averted slightly. Practice had considerably increased the impressiveness of his delivery. At the same time his growing taste for rhetoric was making him less and less intelligible to his victims. 'But un-rewarded,' he said, 'I fear it might go.'

Mr Dranas looked at him with bright, rather doe-like eyes. Kennedy was accustomed to think of him as a shy, malleable youth. He had just taken a degree in law from the University of Athens, and was now trying to get a scholarship to go to Cambridge to study criminal law. He needed the diploma badly, as a proof of his competence in English, and this was why Kennedy had chosen him, even though he seemed poor. Play upon their fears, Kennedy had said to himself sagely.

'If I give you money, you will give me answers,' said Mr Dranas, 'that is the meaning?'

'I will give you the *questions*,' Kennedy said. 'Not the answers.'

'I have not ten thousand drachmas.'

'Well, how much have you got?'

'Question is not that, excuse me very much, Mr Kennedy. Question is, how much I give?'

'Well?' Kennedy lost some of his noble aloofness. The initiative appeared to be passing from him. He encountered Dranas' bright, diffident regard. 'Well?' he said again.

'Answer to that question,' said Dranas, with an air of mild triumph, 'is nothing at all.'

'Oh,' said Kennedy. 'In that case, there is nothing more to be said.'

'But yes, there is. Excuse me very much.'

'I'm sorry, but I don't . . .'

'I am not the first, I think?'

'What do you mean?'

'Others have agreed to pay.'

'Did I not say you were a special case?'

Mr Dranas smiled. 'Everyone is special case,' he said. 'I want to see the questions. But I don't pay. You must show me the questions for nothing. Then I not breathe a word.'

'That is ridiculous,' Kennedy said.

'If you do not give, I go to the bosses.'

'You can tell them nothing.'

'I tell them to be careful. They make a check-up.'

'My God,' Kennedy said, 'it's blackmail!' He wiped his face. 'And you a lawyer too,' he said. 'A professional man. You wouldn't find a British law graduate behaving like this.'

He had to agree, however. And later it occurred to him that this underhand behaviour of Dranas might be a blessing in disguise. He might have gone on and on, getting greedier, until the whole thing got out of hand. It was essential that the conspiracy should be kept to reasonable proportions. He already had five, not counting Dranas, and they were paying him an average of a hundred pounds each, it was enough.

He bade a cold farewell to Mr Dranas, and descending to the street again sought out a kiosk with a telephone and put a call through to Sophy, asking her to come out for a coffee. She could not come, however, she was too busy. She was on her own there this morning, she explained. Mr Jennings and Mr Robinson had both gone out to the airport to meet a person called Slingsby-Merd, a musician. An ambassador had been phoning all morning and getting ruder all the time.

'Ambassador?' Kennedy said.

'Yes, the Swedish ambassador. He asks for Mr Jennings. He makes enquiries about English conversation lessons. Someone is trying to get through now.'

'You'd better ring off then,' Kennedy said.

He at once telephoned the Swedish embassy and asked to speak to the ambassador, but he was not there. He was staying at the

Grande Bretagne, while waiting for some changes to be made in the official residence. Kennedy telephoned the hotel, and after some moments heard a voice that contrived to be both soft and irascible. '*Allo*,' the voice said.

'Am I speaking to the Swedish ambassador?' Kennedy said.

'You are, yes.'

'You are interested in English conversation I believe, sir.'

'That is so, yes.'

'When can I come to see you about it?'

'Come now. At once,' the voice said. Then there was a click and silence.

The interview was of the briefest. Kennedy rode up in the lift to the ambassador's suite, and after he had been waiting only a few minutes the ambassador himself appeared, in a black quilted smoking jacket. He was of an imposing height and bald except in the vicinity of the ears, and he had a slight but menacing cast in the left eye. His preliminary courtesies were not protracted. 'You will give me two hours a week to begin with,' he said in his soft overbearing voice. 'Conversation. In the mornings, between eight and nine.'

'That is too early,' Kennedy said, rendered immediately unco-operative by the other's authoritarian manner.

'I have a letter from Mr Jennings, your superior, in which he says I will be accommodated in the matter of times. I will read the English newspapers. I will repeat what I read. You will correct me.'

'You have it all worked out,' Kennedy said. 'Haven't you?'

'I will send a car for you. The charge for the lessons is fifty drachmas.'

'Just a minute, old boy,' Kennedy said. 'You've got it wrong. A hundred drachmas is what I charge.'

'That is not correct,' said the ambassador. 'I agreed with Mr Jennings for fifty.'

'A hundred is what I charge,' Kennedy said. He was continuing to discuss the matter purely out of perversity. Obviously there was no prospect of his giving the lessons at any price. Besides, he had bigger fish to fry now.

'We are Europeans, not Orientals,' the ambassador said.

'Quite so,' Kennedy said. 'But we are at present in Athens, which is not Europe. Local conditions must prevail.'

'I will give fifty drachmas. This was the price agreed.'

'Not by me,' Kennedy said. 'I wasn't there, old boy. Why should I teach you for fifty when I can teach Greeks for a hundred? Because you are an ambassador?'

The ambassador had gone paler. 'You are insolent,' he said. 'What did you say your name was?'

'Kennedy. Double "n" "e" – "d" – "y". You don't need conversation lessons, you need lessons in manners. You didn't even ask me to sit down. Would you like me to write the name out for you?'

'No,' said the ambassador, speaking now between his teeth. 'No, I can remember it.'

'Well, good for you,' Kennedy said, giving him a look of frank antagonism. Then he turned and walked out of the room.

In the afternoon he met Veta, as they had arranged, opposite the Byzantine museum. They had decided first to visit the monastery at Kaisariani which Kennedy had heard about from Thorne. They took a bus through the long suburb. There was half a mile to walk from the terminus to the monastery, along a white dusty road lined with eucalyptus, following the course of a river bed on their left, through the foothills of Hymettos, sage green and ochreous red, with pale distraught gleams of rock. The monastery was in a hollow formed by these hills, a shallow, fertile declivity watered by underground springs, planted with plane and poplar and mulberry. They walked between massive cypresses into the precincts of the monastery itself, past beds of enormous dahlias clotted with bees. The sound of bees was all the sound here, that and the soft gush of spring water from the mouth of the marble ram at the entrance to the church and cloisters. Veta cupped her hand below the blind ram's gushing mouth, and exclaimed at the coldness of the water. She drank some, wetting her chin and the neck of her dress. She smiled up at Kennedy, the water shining on her face, darkening the cotton of her dress. 'You take some,' she said. He shook his head, smiling, watching the huge black bees rifling the dahlias. She raised herself and came to stand beside him and he put an arm round her and pressed her against him. The monastery slept in its hill calm, all around them they felt the silence and closeness of the hills. From the slopes above them the sun cut great swathes of scent, majoram, myrtle, aromatic shrubs of all sorts. White doves fluttered across the courtyard where they were standing. Beyond the wall of the courtyard rose the cupola of the Byzantine church, the red of its stone mellowed to rose. Kennedy raised his head and inhaled deeply the essences of the afternoon. He felt the girl's flank against him and the response to this in his own loins. He thought of the money he would be getting hold of soon, and all the afternoons he could have with it.

'It's nice here,' he said. 'Isn't it?'

Later they walked together hand in hand among the artefacts of pagan, Byzantine and Frank, their palms moistening slowly in the contact with each other. No monks lived here any longer. There was no one about at all except for one incredibly decrepit attendant with a face the colour and texture of a long-neglected potato, who came creeping up on them from behind to ask if they wanted coffee. His voice was surprisingly vigorous. Very old, he said, widening his little pale eyes in their amazingly complex bed of wrinkles. *Poli paleio*. From the very earliest there had been human settlements here, because of the water.

'I wonder who keeps up the gardens,' Kennedy said in English as the attendant slithered slowly away. 'Cuts the lawns and so on. That old boy's obviously past it.'

'*Plaît-il?*'

'It doesn't matter. We can look in the church before we have our coffee.'

They passed into the dark nave and the chill of sanctity fell on their sun-warmed bodies. Now for the first time Kennedy became really aware of the past. The odour of the Middle Ages recalled for him *history*, in a way the sunlit world could not, though immeasurably older. He did not like the wall paintings at all: scenes of sins and sacrifices and martyrdoms; attenuated, fungoid bodies in grave cerements, a dankness to all this flesh as though it had lived far from the light. Bystanders who might have been apostles looked on with dark, almond eyes of sorrow. Over all, in the cupola above their heads, brooded the enormous, suffering, epicene face of Christ Pantocrator. Kennedy stood in silence, aware of his heart beating, fighting his feeling of awe.

'*J'ai froid*,' Veta said softly. Looking down he saw goose-pimples on her arms, on her living flesh. Suddenly, rather roughly, he kissed her on the side of the neck.

'Let's get out of here,' he said.

The ancient attendant brought them coffee as they sat on the low wall between the church and the Frankish colonnade. His cap was tilted forward over his narrow clay-coloured face and he had a large drop at the end of his nose. They sat for a while, watching little blue butterflies on the grass, recovering their sense of the day's potential. Then they walked up beyond the monastery a little way, into the hills. Near the source of water were poplar and cypress and almond trees but as they climbed higher the mountain reassumed it barrenness. They stopped and looked over the foothills at the way they had come, the cobalt sea, and the faint outlines of the near islands. The sight of the sea reminded them of their intention of bathing that afternoon, and they began to make their way down again. As they passed above the monastery, Kennedy touched Veta's arm and said, 'Look at that, will you?'

The attendant was sitting on a kitchen chair outside a low whitewashed stone hovel which was where he presumably lived. He was full in the sunlight. His head was lowered on his breast and his official attendant's cap tilted forward. His legs were spread wide apart. From time to time he appeared to snatch at something between his legs.

'What is he doing?' Veta asked.

They drew nearer, without disturbing the old man's concentration. Then they saw that he was catching flies, with a skill that could only be called consummate. Either there was some refuse near that attracted them, or this was a vicinity favoured for some other reason, but there was a cloud of flies round him, mostly round his legs and crutch. He was watching them carefully in their flight, not swatting them, but in his stealthy and nimble old claw, scooping them up, trapping them. They saw that every time he caught a fly he crushed it slowly to death between thumb and forefinger, watching it the whole time. Periodically during this process he uttered a hoarse, woeful sound, a kind of groan, due no doubt to his ailments. He rarely missed, and Kennedy thought he must have had a lot of practice. The whole posture of his body in fact, the legs splayed, the more malodorous parts of his person exposed to the sun, really constituted a human fly-trap. He probably does this every afternoon, Kennedy thought. When there are no customers for coffee. It was, after all, a pastime of a sort. What struck him as disagreeable was the seeming complicity of the flies themselves . . .

'Odd sort of game,' Kennedy said, in English. 'Costs nothing in fares though. No outlay on equipment either, and you don't need anyone else to play it.'

Veta looked disgusted. Her mouth which had been open while she watched the performance, closed firmly. 'So dirty, that old man,' she said, after a moment. 'His house will be dirty too, inside, I think.' The set of her square shoulders expressed repugnance.

Kennedy laughed. 'Come on,' he said, 'we must hurry; let's get down to the coast.'

They did not in fact get to the coast until after the sun had gone down. This was because they had chosen Porto Rafti as the place to go and it was much further than either of them thought, and also because they stopped at the village itself before going down to the beach, to have a meal at a taverna. While they were in there, there was a brief but very heavy shower. Kennedy drank a good deal of retsina with the meal and he bought a small bottle of cognac to take with them. When they emerged the road was wet, rain had cooled the air. Kennedy was not drunk, but elated, as they walked down the rough track that led to the beach. The light was fading rapidly now, and a ruddy moon hung just over the water. The sea glimmered to the darkening horizon, completely motionless, like a great platter. They left their bathing things on the shingle of the upper beach and walked together along the edge of the water. There was no sound from the sea or land. From the low hills behind them came the sweet summer scent of dust and pine. The hills themselves for these few minutes had a strange, charred distinctness of outline. When they returned to where they had left their things, the last of the day was gone. The moon had risen and whitened, laying a broad track of light across the sea.

'Shall we bathe now?' Kennedy said. 'Or shall we have some of this cognac?'

'Let us bathe first,' she said.

The silence and immensity of the night caused them to speak in low tones as though they were constrained by the possible presence of others, or within precincts demanding reverent observances. They changed in silence, standing a little apart from each other. Kennedy felt the cool air on his body with a sense of liberation. Near him Veta stood waiting. Her swimming suit was black of the old-fashioned voluminous sort, reaching halfway down her thighs. The moonlight shone on her thick hair and white, steady shoulders. She stood fronting him, gravely, waiting. In the moment before he moved towards her Kennedy felt something resigned, almost sacrificial in her posture. He pressed her body against his and kissed her face repeatedly, and her throat and the upper part of her breasts. Her body remained quiet and passive, neither responding nor recoiling. After some moments they walked together hand in hand to the sea and waded in. The land sloped very gradually and they walked steadily forward in silence for some time, the water – still warm from the day's sun – rising slowly over their legs and thighs. The moonlit sea, stirred by their progress, bubbled round them and they each trailed a bright phosphorescent wake.

When the water was deep enough, they parted and swam. Kennedy floated on his back gazing up at the moon, feeling the water sustaining and caressing him. The hills beyond the beach were dark and formless now, lumped together by the night, but overhead the sky seemed paler. There was a scattering of stars. Veta was some yards away, also floating, her face lifted to the sky. He could see distinctly the luminous beading of the sea round her dark form, she was for that moment like an impurer particle in a solution of silver. He swam towards her and found that the water was still shallow enough for them both to stand.

'Isn't it marvellous?' he said, reaching out towards her. 'The sea is still quite warm.'

'Yes,' she said. 'It is very good.' She regarded him steadily, head and shoulders only out of the water, her large eyes shining. What could she be thinking of? he wondered suddenly. What was behind that beautiful, heifer-like gaze? He had never, it occurred to him, discerned anything like affection for him in her regard. Only once had she kissed him of her own accord, when he had first promised her the money. Perhaps she had thoughts of startling profundity but was defeated by language. . . .

'Bry-an,' she said suddenly.

'Yes,'

'When will you give me the money?'

'In about six days' time, all things being equal,' he said.

Her face broke slowly into a smile. She leaned forward and began to fumble under the water.

'What are you doing?' he said. Veta laughed and straightened herself and he saw that she was now holding her bathing suit in her hand.

'This is nicer,' she said.

Quickly Kennedy divested himself of his own shorts, and gave them to Veta to hold. Their naked bodies came together under the water. He took the full globes of her breasts in his hands. They were buoyant, lifting in the water as though with a life of their own. She raised her head laughing, and he kissed her wet lips. Standing there in the bright waste of water, holding her against him, his hands on the outside of her thighs, he found that she was almost weightless. The kindly, conniving sea balanced her for him, set her down on to him, moved her gently to his wish. He looked into her face, on a level now with his own. Her eyes were closed, her mouth twisted into a slight grimace. Suddenly the element of brutality inherent in Kennedy's nature came to the fore; he determined to screw some expression out of her at last. He kept up the movement deliberately and in order to delay his own responses began to compose an imaginary letter to the *Geographical Magazine. Dear sir, I recently had carnal knowledge of a young woman in some five feet of water of high saline contents, in short the ocean* . . . Gently, rhythmically, abetted by the sea, he continued to move her speared and suspended body up a little, down a little. All the time he looked intently at her face. After a while she began to move her head from side to side as though in the grip of a troubled dream, and to breathe more noisily. *We found this a comfortable and convenient position.*

The degree of penetration could be easily controlled ... The movements of Veta's head had become more pronounced. She moaned lightly, then again, and again, each time on a higher note. *Moreover I, the male partner, found it quite unnecessary to adopt that crouching posture which makes the vertical position so unsatisfactory on terra firma* ... Veta suddenly flung back her head, her face worked for some moments, then she uttered a long, harsh inexpressibly pained cry. Kennedy began to hurry desperately to bring his letter to a conclusion, feeling his own spasms upon him, not much longer to be deferred ... *Furthermore the young woman uttered at the climactic moment a cry resembling that of a sea-gull, does this constitute proof of man's amphibious origins, yours sin* ... A series of deep and shuddering groans burst from him.

Later the brandy was very welcome to both of them.

In the early afternoon, having given Slingsby-Merd lunch and taken him to his hotel, Jennings returned to his office. He had barely seated himself at his desk when the phone rang. It was the Swedish ambassador. The ambassador was very angry and made no attempt to conceal this from Jennings. For some moments, in fact, Jennings was not able to understand the source of this anger, so vigorous was its expression. 'I have been out all morning, your excellency,' he said, assuming his Zen-master look. 'On official business. For that reason you were not able ...' As he listened, however, his expression changed. Insulting behaviour, lack of respect, complaints through diplomatic channels. 'Your responsibility, sir, your responsibility for the comportment of your employees ...' Jennings grew frightened. 'But what?' he said. 'Who? Excellency, I cannot understand ... But I sent no one to see you. No one. Nevertheless it is true, no one was sent. I was intending to send someone, yes, a question of finding exactly the right instructor, your request was a matter we were regarding as of utmost importance ... *Kennedy*? Did you say Kennedy? Yes, thank you, excellency, no need to spell it ... K.E.N.N.E.D.Y ... Yes, thank you, I've got it. ... He is not associated in any way with us, no, no, no official status whatsoever. He misled you, in that case, grossly. Insolent, yes, demanded one hundred drachmas an hour, yes. Excellency, please allow me to deal personally with this matter. And accept my deepest apologies for what has happened . . . Yes, yes, most definitely, I assure you. . . . What? The incident will none the less go down on your report, but won't you reconsider . . .'

The receiver at the other end was at this point replaced. Jennings' chin had commenced to tremble during the latter part of this conversation, and continued to do so for some time afterwards. He gazed vacantly at the bust of the dignitary, which the afternoon sun revealed to be in need of some dusting. Gradually anger succeeded to fright. Kennedy, of course, for the moment was out of reach. He pressed the bell on his desk. 'Please tell Mr Willey that I want to see him the moment he arrives at the institute this evening. He can set his class some written work and come immediately here to me. Immediately.'

Willey received this message as he was entering the institute and fifteen minutes later he was facing Jennings in his office. He thought Jennings was looking rather ill.

'Ah, Mr Willey,' said Jennings. His lips writhed slightly. There was a short silence. Willey was entertaining the hope that now at least Jennings was about to offer him a permanent post. It was the time of year when such decisions are made. And it must be something of importance for Jennings to have asked him to leave his class. However, there was no hint of the congratulatory in the other's expression.

'I want to ask you one question, Mr Willey,' Jennings said at last. 'Have you at any time been instrumental in securing private students for a person named Kennedy?'

'I put him in touch with one or two people who needed lessons, yes.'

'Were any of these people ambassadors?'

'Ambassadors?'

'Yes, Mr Willey, *ambassadors*. Persons accredited to foreign governments as diplomatic envoys.'

'Good heavens, no. They were quite unofficial people, students.'

'It might interest you to know that your friend Kennedy has grossly insulted the Swedish ambassador, claiming at the same time to be a person sent to him by us.'

'I am very sorry to hear that. I should hardly call him a friend.'

'It was most unwise of you to become involved with a person of his sort. You occupy a certain position here.'

'I am not involved with him. He was sent to me by Mr Robinson as a person needing some help in settling in, and so on. I found him accommodation and helped him to find one or two students. I have done as much for several newly arrived Englishmen while I have been here. In fact, if I may say so, it has become the habit to send such people to me more or less automatically. I do not complain about this, but it is hard to be blamed for what they subsequently get up to.'

'I regard it,' Jennings said, 'as your responsibility.'

The rage under which he had been labouring since this latest outrage of Kennedy's became extreme again as he considered Willey's drooping but undeferential posture. With a record such as his, the man was only there at all on sufferance. How dared he take this stand? 'Your responsibility,' he said again, and his voice, normally so deliberate, lost key suddenly.

'That is unfair,' Willey said slowly. The hope with which he had entered the room was all gone now, leaving a sort of void within him.

Jennings placed his fingertips together. 'I do not know if I have ever pointed this out to you before, Mr Willey,' he said, 'but our position here is a delicate one. It calls indeed for something of the qualities of an, ah, diplomat. We are representing our country abroad, Mr Willey, in our persons England is being judged. It is, to use a rather distasteful modern term, our *image* that we must be concerned with. Now I know that you are anxious to be taken on our permanent staff here, and I have been wanting for some time to speak to you about this. There are no complaints about your teaching ability, of course, but as I say, it is not purely a teaching matter. And I have to tell you that as regards what one might call the *representative* nature of such a post I could not find in my conscience to make a recommendation in our case. No, I am afraid I cannot recommend you.'

'I see,' Willey said. He thought how grotesque it was that the person before him, distinguished neither in character nor intellect, should have this power over his life and happiness. How could it have happened? There must be something wrong, he could not help thinking, with the processes of society that conferred power on such a person. He became aware that Jennings was regarding him intently through the thick glasses, and found sufficient resolution to keep his head up and say steadily, 'That is for you to decide of course, Mr Jennings, but I think I have the right to ask you whether you are basing your decision on anything Mr Kennedy has done.'

But of course he ought to have known that the other would not fall for that. Jennings made a gesture with his plump white hands and said suavely, 'Oh no, not at all. I have had this opinion for some considerable time.'

'You'd better start looking for another locally employed teacher,' Willey said. 'I shan't be available next term.'

'Don't be too hasty,' Jennings said smoothly. 'You might find it difficult to obtain a post anywhere else. Certainly you would not find one in Athens. Think carefully, Mr Willey. Oh, by the way,' he added, as Willey was turning to go, 'I should like your friend Kennedy's address.'

As Willey emerged on to the street he saw that the sky was overcast. Before he could reach the institute he was caught in a brief but heavy downpour of rain, from which he had to take shelter in a doorway.

'Everything we fought for,' said George, who had been drunk when Mitsos entered and was drunker now. 'Everything was taken from us, and at the time when it was in our grasp.'

Mitsos nodded, looking over George's lowered head at the long row of barrels down the near wall, the rough tables with their checked oilcloth covers. This was the *taverna* neighbouring George's house. It was the first time Mitsos had been inside it; the other had been so long in there that he had grown anxious finally and entered, to find him alone at a table, not eating, but drinking steadily, half-kilos of *kokinelli*. 'Have some more wine,' Mitsos said. '*Akoma ligo crasi*,' he called into the dimness at the far end of the room, and the answering '*Amesos*' came back immediately. George raised his head and looked squarely at Mitsos with an expression difficult to read, at once confidential, mournful and slightly derisive. He had shown no surprise at Mitsos' appearance, perhaps because of the drink; also, possibly for the same reason, he had been easily led into speaking of politics, the troubles of the past.

'The Government ran away,' he said, in his wheezing, laborious voice. 'It was not a people's government. The king ran away also, as he has done before. Who were those people, getting fat in Cairo, calling themselves the Greek Government? Did we fight the Germans for *them*? Here Greeks died. They died.' Suddenly he slammed both fists on the table. '*Pote tha ta feris?*' he called, his voice straining with sudden savagery. 'When will you bring the wine, today or tomorrow?'

'*Amesos*,' came again the answering shout, and the waiter came padding towards them, carrying the measures of wine.

George drank deeply. 'That was not a government,' he said.

'Nevertheless,' Mitsos said, drinking a little of his wine, 'that was the only official government at the time of liberation. What other government was there?'

'You were not born then,' George said. 'What do you know? There was the will of the people.'

'I was twelve years old then,' Mitsos said.

George shifted his bulk in the chair. 'A child,' he said. 'I had friends who died, I tell you.' He looked enraged suddenly, as though Mitsos were disputing his statement. 'I am not lying,' he said, with sudden clarity, and again his fists came down on the table.

'My parents died during that time,' Mitsos said softly, looking into the other's eyes, which had grown wet with his vehemence. 'My father was murdered, here in Athens. By Greeks, not Germans, Greeks from Epirus.'

The moist eyes held his for a moment, then slipped away. George looked down at his glass as though in concentration.

'I mention this,' Mitsos said, removing his hands, which had begun to tremble, from the table, 'I mention this to show that not only those old enough to fight suffered losses.'

The other drank again. He was blinking his eyes repeatedly, as though confused about something.

'Think of it, *paidi mou*,' he said. 'Greeks shot down by Greeks in the streets of Athens, shot in the moment of victory by those who had been police for the Germans. Papandreou and his rabble approving, back, from their bolthole in Egypt.' He opened his eyes wide at the memory of this senselessness. 'No one could deny,' he said, 'what we had done. Even the Right had to admit the contribution we had made. But after that it did not pay to have been in the Resistance, the collaborators became the respectable ones, even those who had formed the security battalions, worked directly against the Resistance. They were given the jobs, the honours. We dared not speak. And even now . . .'

'As I have understood,' Mitsos said carefully, 'the security battalions were recruited on a voluntary basis and there was no shortage of volunteers, because ordinary decent people were disgusted by the excesses of the guerillas. . . . In any case, all that is of no real interest to me. It is too abstract, too public. You suppose yourself to have suffered. I lost both my father and my mother at that time. Neither of them was yet forty years old. They were murdered, both of them, by Greeks from Epirus.'

'From Epirus?' the other said. 'Then your father was . . .'

'My father was a soldier,' Mitsos said quickly. 'Our house was in Charitos Street, number thirty-two. Now a clinic for maternity cases.'

'Maternity cases?' George said, as though incredulous.

Mitsos attempted to smile, but his face stiffened as he looked into the other's eyes which had widened and stared back at him now with something like curiosity or wonder, an expression which lasted a second or two only, before the eyes were lowered again to the tumbler of wine on the table before him.

George expelled a long, slow breath. 'Charitos Street I do not know,' he said, but almost immediately looked up again with the same wide stare.

Mitsos clasped his hands together under the table in an effort to stay their violent trembling. He could no longer look into the face before him, which in its heaviness seemed asserting already the inexorable gravity of decay, escaping from the bones that held it together, while the eyes above presided at this disintegration, wide open and staring, the eyes of a sick animal, neither defiant nor resigned. . . . The sting had been withdrawn, nothing awaited

George, no shining evil before he died, but poverty, sickness and slow deterioration. . . .

Not the uselessness of any present vengeance on the man had distressed Mitsos so profoundly however: he had been taken unawares by a sort of hideously self-abasing tenderness for George, a tenderness that had inclined him in the first moments of the other's dissembling, to reach up and touch with his trembling fingers the other's face, his eyelids, his hair; part of the reason for thus clasping and concealing his hands had been to prevent even now the perpetration of such a monstrous caress. For of course there was something he had forgotten, when he considered the intolerable parallel of their two lives: the line could be tangled together by love; and something abject and yielding in him responded helplessly to this suggestion, to the power over his life which this man or another, in a body younger and more brutal, had established all the years before. Not the man's guilt but his own appalling subjection was confirmed, it was this he had been delaying, holding at bay . . .

'No,' said George in the manner of one who has considered. 'I cannot say that I know Charitos Street.'

'Kolonaki,' Mitsos said dully. 'Parallel with Patriarchou Joachim, higher up.' He experienced a sensation of nausea. After some moments more he stood up. With a terrible effort he infused his tone with nonchalance. 'I must be going, now,' he said. The big man looked up, nodded his head slowly without speaking.

Mitsos walked blindly out of the taverna, into the street. In his distress he walked for a long time without noticing his direction. When he began once again to take in his surroundings he found himself close to the northern flank of the Acropolis. He stood still, looking closely at a great swathe of convolvulus covering the entire side of one of the small houses with which the narrow, steeply sloping street was lined. The blue scentless bells of the convolvulus were out in great profusion. A group of children squabbling on the steps of the house opposite became silent when he stopped and looked at him curiously. Then they again began their wrangling, but now in changed voices, including him in their awareness. A cat recumbent on a low wall moved its ears and tail.

All this time the sky had been darkening and suddenly while he stood there, not knowing what to do or where to go, it began to rain, large isolated drops at first, spattering the dust with dark stains, exciting the children to shrill celebrations, putting flight to the cat, causing the large blue flowers to tremble; increasing to a steady drumming roar, rattling on cobbles and tiled roofs. Mitsos stood still, raising his face to the rain, gasping a little at the faintly pricking coldness of the drops. Water ran into the corners of his mouth, beat on his eyelids. He sensed it falling everywhere, indiscriminately on the white city, flooding the gutters, swirling in the declivities of the street.

The rain did not last long but after it everything was changed. There came to Mitsos as he stood there, drenched now to the skin, the abrupt carrying phrases of a bird's song. There was a quality almost hallucinatory in the light, a sort of violence. Blue mists hung over Hymettos. The air was warm and resinous. The scent of pine and aromatic shrub washed over in waves from the Hill of the Muses and the wooded stretches at the foot of the Acropolis. Because of this shower little weeds would well up out of the stony earth, and seep into corners, a tide of green; and flowers would be revived in the cracks of the rocks. Mitsos felt all this is happening, in all the pockets of earth in the city, simultaneously.

A man with a large basket of carnations on his shoulder entered the street at its upper end and came slowly down towards Mitsos looking from side to side at the windows of the houses. He was forced proud by his burden, deep red and shining white carnations, wet from the rain. He seemed to walk in the protection of their scent. This scent, cool and sweet, very penetrating in the rinsed air, superimposed like a pale wash over the thicker odours of revived vegetation, was always to be associated for Mitsos with the memory of this rain, the seeping green he had imagined in its wake, and the knowledge which came to him now as something revealed, not reached as a conclusion, that the man he had just been talking to must be put for ever beyond the hope of such renewals.

10

The note was delivered by hand of Nikos the porter to Kennedy personally, informing him that Mr Jennings would like to see him at his earliest convenience. It was a curt note, but not, on the surface, threatening. Kennedy was in an accommodating mood when he presented himself at Jennings' office. He winked at Sophy knowingly on his way up. He had purchased recently, as a first step towards the new, leisured, cosmopolitan Kennedy he hoped to be before long, a stiff straw hat with a round crown and a bright green band. Although aware that it did not quite go with the tweed suit, he wore it constantly. He removed it now, courteously, when he entered Jennings' office.

He was surprised and angered by the upbraiding tone which Jennings assumed right from the start. For Jennings had determined in advance to be scathing.

'How dared you, *you*,' Jennings demanded with icy but undistorted modulations, 'pass yourself off as coming from our organisation?' He began at Kennedy's dusty shoes and worked his gaze up slowly, pausing with a marked derogatory intention at the straw hat in the other's hands. 'In a court of law that would be called false pretences. The ambassador takes a very serious view of it. I take a very serious view of it myself. We are considering what further steps to take in the matter. The ambassador, I am at liberty to say, is furious. This could have serious repercussions.'

Kennedy stared at Jennings for some moments before replying. 'Don't try to make an international incident out of it,' he said at last. 'The ambassador is annoyed because he is mean old bird and he doesn't want to pay a fair rate for lessons. You should never have agreed to fifty in the first place; you only did it because he is an important person. That is *creeping*, Mr Jennings. And I didn't tell him I came from you. He might have assumed it, of course.'

'You will go to the ambassador immediately and apologise.'

'You must be joking,' Kennedy said.

'I shall take this matter further. From whom did you obtain this information? It was from Mr Willey, wasn't it?' It had not occurred to Jennings to suspect his clerk, whom he regarded as simply a vehicle for telephone messages.

'Missed again,' Kennedy said. 'I hardly know him.'

'Very well,' Jennings said threatening. 'Very well.' He looked fixedly at Kennedy for a little while. He was at something of a loss as to how he should proceed. He had expected to reduce Kennedy quite quickly to a sort of loutish shiftiness and unease, but this had not happened, despite the authority of his office and the other's complete lack of official status. It was becoming clear that this insolent and unrepentant fellow cared nothing for official status. 'It's no good talking to you about the spirit of service, I suppose,' he said. 'Has it occurred to you that we have a very special responsibility here? It is not too much to say that we represent our country. England is judged through *us*, Mr Kennedy. It is, to use a rather distasteful modern term . . .'

'Just what do *you* know about England, old boy?' Kennedy said. 'I don't suppose you have spent a year there in the last ten. The English are in England, getting on with it. In England you would be some sort of schoolmaster. Your suits would get shiny and you wouldn't have a chauffeur and you wouldn't give cocktail parties. I was selling encyclopaedias in England, from door to door. We are both here because we want to be more comfortable, that's the long and short of it. So don't give me all this stuff about the white man's burden, it's a lot of cock and you know it.' He was conscious, as he regarded Jennings' pale and shocked impassivity, of a certain warmth of anger. Hypocrisy directed towards an honestly acquisitive end, like money or goods or getting to bed with someone, he did not mind at all, in fact its fusion with sincerity in the world pleased him, confirmed his inarticulate but deep-rooted belief that the world was moral nonsense anyway. But this sort of pretentiousness, these glib references to service and responsibility, he had always hated and despised; it was the rhetoric of authority cornered, powerless for the moment to punish or coerce. He felt an impulse to seize Jennings by his lapels and shake him violently back and forth.

Something of this desire may have showed in his eyes, for Jennings said somewhat huskily, 'If that is your attitude, Mr Kennedy, I will not detain you any longer. I assure you you will hear more of this matter. You have not heard the last of it by any means.'

Kennedy replaced his hat at a jaunty angle. 'You can get stuffed,' he said.

In the passage he met Mr Robinson, the assistant director, who was just coming out of his office.

'Hello there,' Kennedy said. 'How goes it?'

Instead of replying Mr Robinson narrowed his eyes and began to nod his head up and down slowly at Kennedy. He kept this up for some time.

'Are you feeling all right?' Kennedy said, rather pugnaciously.

'Gilligan, eh?' said Mr Robinson at last, with preternatural shrewdness, not ceasing to nod.

'My name is *Kennedy*,' Kennedy said.

'He doesn't exist,' Mr Robinson said. 'There is no such person.' He regarded Kennedy now with a sort of triumphant sagacity, yet at the same time warily, as though he had applied a possibly dangerous stimulus to some unpredictable animal.

Kennedy stared at him a moment in surprise, then shrugged slightly. 'I should take things easy, if I were you,' he said, as he proceeded down the passage. 'That old sod's been giving you too much to do.'

Left alone in the office, Jennings pondered for some time in complete silence and immobility, his white fingers interlocked over his stomach. Then he found a number in his desk directory and made a phone call. Speaking in fluent Greek he asked for a certain lieutenant of police. In reply to rapid questions, he gave his name, which was known there, and various details about the man Kennedy. 'Yes,' he said. 'Completely without official backing. Entered the country on a tourist visa, presumably. No, no permit to work. In the interests of the economy . . . Felt it my duty . . .'

Kennedy meanwhile found a seat in the shade in the little square below Jennings' office, and spent some time meditating on his situation and prospects. They were on the whole, he thought, very good. He had not much ready cash left – Veta was costing him quite a lot – but it was only four days now to the exams, and then he would start collecting. He had to provide the questions for six people, five of whom were paying him an average of nine thousand drachmas each. The sixth, the dishonourable criminologist Dranas, would have to be given the questions for nothing, since he could not risk a tightening of security precautions before the exam. That made forty-five thousand drachmas, about five hundred and sixty pounds. Fifty gold pounds to Veta – about one hundred and fifty sterling – and he would still have over four hundred pounds left for himself. It was a pretty good return, he felt, for no capital outlay, very little work, and no risk either, to speak of. Those to whom he sold the papers were not likely to tell anyone, whether they succeeded in the examination or not. In any case he would not be in Athens when the results came out. He had decided to take his money to Beirut and spend the next few months there.

He tilted the straw hat far back on his head and mopped his face with his handkerchief. He would find himself an Arab bit. He would buy himself a summer suit of stone-coloured terylene and crocodile-skin shoes and cuff-links, and several shirts. . . . He would get all his shaves in barbers' shops. . . . On the cool terraces of hotels he would drink gin-and-tonic. . . . It was really a foolproof plan. Willey, it was true, had not agreed yet, but Kennedy felt sure that he would. And even if he didn't, questions that would look genuine could quite easily be devised. In that case he would have to make himself scarce before they saw the genuine examination papers. They could not denounce him because they had themselves connived at a fraud. Of course they might demand to see a copy of the original before paying, but he would think of some way of getting round that when the time came. . . . Kennedy yawned pleasurably and got up. He gave a final benevolent gaze round the square, and directed his steps homeward.

When he got back to his room he found Simpson there, in his baseball cap, painting on the table. He was using water-colours on a sheet of cartridge paper pinned to the table with drawing pins.

'What are you doing?' Kennedy asked, approaching the table.

'Greek island,' Simpson, said without looking up. 'Met an American who wants water-colours of Greek islands, originals.'

'Why are you doing it in my room?'

'There's no table in mine.'

Looking over his shoulder Kennedy saw multicoloured striations denoting hills, sea, sky, a few fishing boats drawn up on the shore. The clouds, he noted, were neat plump clouds precisely delimited, not Greek clouds at all. Simpson had simply painted blue sky around them.

'I said I'd do several islands and he could take his pick,' Simpson said. He put a long squiggle of green on the sea. 'I've done Hydra,' he said, 'and I've done Poros. What other Greek islands are there, for Christ's sake?'

'Crete,' Kennedy said. 'There's Crete, and Rhodes.'

'I'll call this one Crete, then,' Simpson said. He took a Biro out of his pocket and wrote 'Crete' in one corner of the painting, adding his name and the date.

'Rhodes, the next one,' Simpson said, beginning to take out the drawing pins.

At this moment the doorbell rang. When he opened the door Kennedy saw before him a slender, elegant man in a chocolate-brown suit, who said quietly in excellent English, 'Have I the pleasure of speaking to Mr Kennedy?'

'You have indeed,' Kennedy said, beaming at this person.

'I am from the police,' the man said. 'From the Aliens Department. My name is Canelopoulos. I should like to speak with you for some minutes.'

'Certainly,' Kennedy said, his smile vanishing rapidly. 'Will you come in?'

'No thank you.' The elegant man, who had a shiny chestnut-coloured gaze, appeared to meditate a moment. Then he said, 'I have a report on good authority that you are working in Greece, for remunerations, without a *permis de travail*. Is it true?'

Kennedy thought quickly. If he denied it, and they knew, he might let himself in for more trouble. Perhaps he had been watched, seen entering and leaving certain houses. 'I have done a little private teaching,' he said. 'I did not know a permit was required for this.'

'For any work undertaken for payment in Greece by a foreigner a permit is necessary.'

'I see. I am sorry. It will not happen again.'

'No, no,' the man said quickly. 'I'm afraid that is not sufficient. By taking payment you have contravened the regulations. You have not fulfilled the terms on which you were permitted entry as a tourist. You have become, in short, Mr Kennedy, *persona non grata*. We require you, therefore, to leave Greece within forty-eight hours. Failure to comply might lead to your arrest.'

Kennedy gaped at him for a moment. 'Forty-eight hours,' He said. 'But that is . . . Can you not give me a few days longer than that?'

'Impossible, I'm afraid,' the policeman said, withdrawing without haste. 'It is statutory. Good day, Mr Kennedy and *kalo taxidi*.'

'Goodbye now,' Kennedy said, and blankly watched the policeman's narrow head receding down the stairs. The perspiration elicited by this precise ultimatum cooled on him slowly. He knew who must have informed on him. It could be no one but Jennings. But what was he to do now? Unthinkable to quit Greece now, within a few days of the dividends. Could he perhaps nip up to Yugoslavia, get his passport stamped, nip back again as a tourist? Would that be acceptable, would it be legal? He had not now, in any case, enough money for such a trip, unless he hitch-hiked, but that was too chancy. Sophy perhaps could lend him the fare, or Willey. . . . If he stayed, would he have time to devise an examination paper, collect his money, all within forty-eight hours? They would sense something fishy in such a change of plan, they would not believe he could have obtained the paper so far in advance. He must get a few days' grace, but how? He was still, he realised, wearing his straw hat, completely dressed therefore for the street. A drink would be a great help. He closed the door softly behind him, leaving Simpson still furiously painting and muttering to himself the names of islands.

He was making for Voukourestiou Street, and a bar he knew. His mind was full of his trouble, so that he did not recognise the person coming towards him until the person had almost passed. Then he saw it was the slightly built and rather intense young

Greek he had first met on the boat. What was his name again? The fellow would have passed him without a second glance. Perhaps it was the hat that made him difficult to recognise?

'Well, hallo there,' said Kennedy, obtruding himself into the other's path. 'How goes it?'

The Greek started violently at Kennedy's greeting and stood for some moments speechless. Kennedy thought he looked distinctly ill. His eyes glittered feverishly, there were dark pouches below them as of sleeplessness or dissipation. Been beating it up, Kennedy thought. Too much shagging perhaps. Or hitting the old ouzo.

'You *said* Athens was a village,' he remarked. 'And that we should be sure to meet.' For some reason he had remembered this dictum, even though he had forgotten the other's name. 'What was your name again?' he said.

'Mitsos,' the other said, looking beyond Kennedy as though seeking a way of escape.

'I don't mean your *surname*,' Kennedy said. 'Of course I remembered *that*. No, I meant your first name.'

'Stavros.'

'Stavros, of course. Would you care to join me for a drink?'

'No, not now, thank you.' Mitsos continued to look over Kennedy's shoulder. The other's large body blocked his way. He felt completely exhausted, unable for the moment to mobilise himself to get past this perpetually inopportune person, with his broad and hateful smile, who it seemed had been accosting him all his life. The knife he had bought some half-hour ago, still in its wrapping of white tissue paper, was under his jacket, clamped against his side by his left arm, the handle under his armpit. He had had considerable difficulty in the choice of weapon, not having understood previously how specialised an activity killing a human being is, requiring tools not normally to hand. The only thing at all possible that he could find in his cousin's house was a light, narrow-headed hammer of the sort that is used for putting in tacks. It would have needed repeated blows with that, and he knew himself to be without the strength or the resolution to peck the man to death so, the skull softening, blood in the hair roots, the brain still labouring in its liquids beneath. No, a knife was the thing, a knife got at the vitals without brutality.

All this he had pondered over carefully, thoroughly and with a half-irritable sense of unreality, as though this nicety as to means, by its prolongation, kept him from the only meaningful thing: the extinction of the life in George. He had almost bought a scout knife, vaguely associated in his mind with practical, outdoors efficiency, but rejected this at the last moment because of a superstitious dread of the hilt – the hilt might arrest the point just short of the man's life. Finally he had bought, second-hand from a small shop in the Plaka, a butcher's knife with a long perfectly straight blade, a flat wooden handle and no hilt at all. It was this he held now rigidly pressed against his body.

'Not even a quick one?' Kennedy said.

'I beg your pardon?'

'Haven't you got time even for a quick one?'

'No, I'm afraid not. Thank you very much.'

'Don't mention it, old boy,' Kennedy said. 'By the way, I have to go to Yugoslavia quite unexpectedly – a business trip, actually, and I'm a bit short of the ready just for the moment. Of course, there are plenty of people I can call on – you've seen some of my testimonials I believe – but they are in England you see, and it all takes time. What I was wondering was whether you could lend me a few pounds . . .'

'I'm sorry,' Mitsos said. Gathering himself together he sidestepped and got round Kennedy on the outside of the pavement.

'To tide me over,' Kennedy said, but Mitsos was by this time several yards away and going fast. Kennedy gazed after him resentfully. It was not the behaviour of a gentleman, as he understood it, to bolt at the request of a loan. This fellow seemed prone to unceremonious departures. He remembered the last time, when Mitsos had just got up from the table without a word and disappeared. Before on the boat, he had refused to lend a fellow traveller a pound or two, refused to refer to the Bishop of Jarrow, refused even to part with his telephone number. . . . Next time they met, Kennedy promised himself, he would point out to Mitsos the error of his ways. He had known, however, all along, that he couldn't risk the Yugoslavia business, couldn't risk being refused re-entry just when the examinations were about to start. Then his chance would be gone for ever. Meanwhile, however, time was passing. What on earth was he going to do? Suddenly, while he still stood there, the solution came to him with a beautiful fullness and radiance. Eleni Polimenou. If she could swing it for Willey, maybe she could swing it for him. A package deal. She was the only one who could help him now. He must see her immediately. There was no time for a drink.

It had been Mitsos' intention, on returning to the house at Kiffisia, to go straight up to his room and hide the knife somewhere. But at the head of the stairs he came face to face with his cousin Alexei, who, dressed in a bathrobe of white towelling, had been just about to descend.

'Come and have a drink,' Alexei said. 'Why do I see so little of you? You have everything you need here?'

'Oh yes,' Mitsos said. 'Everything.' He was conscious of the same exhaustion, the same lack of volition, that he had experienced with Kennedy. It was as though he could only keep up his momentum in the absence of human contacts. He attempted very slowly to edge past Alexei and get along the passage to his own room, but Alexei put a hand on his shoulder.

'Come and have a drink,' he said again. 'We have not talked together for a long time.'

Mitsos suffered himself to be guided downstairs again, into the *salon*, where he sat in an armchair, the knife still held uncomfortably against his side, while Alexei busied himself pouring drinks.

'*Paidi mou*,' Alexei said, smiling across at him. How ill Stavros looked. '*Ti nea?*' 'What have you been doing?'

'Very little,' Mitsos said, achieving a smile.

'Ah so you say,' Alexei nodded knowingly. 'So you say. You are one of the quiet ones. In my opinion no girl is worth suffering for.'

Mitsos regarded him in silence.

'Listen,' Alexei said, 'why don't you and I have a night out, one of these nights? *En garçon*, eh? How would you like that?'

'Very much,' Mitsos said politely.

'We could go down to Piraeus, have a good time.' Alexei closed his left eye. 'I know my way around down there. Not a word to Kikki, though.'

'Of course not.' But what could I say to Kikki? he thought. Why should I speak to Kikki? He sat rigid in the armchair.

'Women do not understand these things,' Alexei said. 'Man is a hunter, that is an opinion I have come to, he is not by nature monogamous. . . .'

Mitsos ceased to make the effort to understand what Alexei was saying. He smiled faintly, glanced once more at Alexei's face, then helplessly lowered his gaze to where, in the other's body, below the white towelling, the heart might approximately be.

By impressing on him the urgency of the matter, Kennedy got Willey reluctantly – since the afternoons, sandwiched between two sessions of teaching, were precious to him – to agree to a meeting in the English library. Here they stood together before the shelves marked 'Fine Arts' and conversed in low tones. The shelves were eight or nine feet high and so it was not possible to see people not in the same lane, but occasional snatches of conversation came to them.

'Have you thought about what I said?' Kennedy enquired very softly.

'I have, yes,' Willey answered in equally muted tones. It had been from his point of view a mistake, he immediately felt, to meet here. Discussing in this furtive manner Kennedy's proposal restricted him from the start to a conspiratorial rôle. Of course he was going to agree, he knew that: Jennings' abrupt dismissal of his hopes had helped Kennedy more than he would ever know – had it not been for that, he would almost certainly have gone on hoping until the time for action had passed. Yes, he was going to agree, but regretted that there was no scope, when the conversation was conducted at a volume little louder than a whisper, for indicating his reservations in the matter, his distaste. Had Kennedy, he wondered, thought of this when arranging the meeting? Probably not. As usual the other's round blue eyes, with their reckless fixity of gaze, gave him no clue.

'Well, what's the answer, old boy?' Kennedy muttered. 'Is it yes or no?'

At this moment they heard from beyond the partition a resonant voice with a slight lisp, saying, 'Simply *huge* anemones, you've no idea.' Kennedy and Willey became silent and still, looking closely at each other, while the voice went on at the same volume. 'Along the new national road, yes, then off right towards Kalamos, that's the Eubeia side, you know, past the road to Lake Marathon, then we went up to this little place called Polidendron, the apricots and almonds were in first flower, so pure, you know, quite beautiful, there was still snow along the sides of the road. . . .'

'I wonder who that can be,' Willey whispered.

'No bloody idea. Well, is it a go or isn't it?'

Willey still hesitated, experiencing some faint return of that embarrassment that had filled him when Kennedy had first made his proposition, a sort of shame for them both, trapped in this situation. Some time after that talk of theirs, he had recalled an occasion in his childhood when he had invited a friend to come and see his stamp collection. It was a friendship of vivid but shallow growth, only some weeks old. The other boy, whose name was Alan, had gone through the album with many expressions of admiration most pleasing to Willey. Only at the end had Willey seen his friend's hand conveying something to his top jacket pocket and investigating found some thirty of his most precious stamps there. . . . Willey was never to forget the shame that had filled him at the moment of detection, a sort of anguish that had brought him near to tears. . . . But Kennedy would never feel like that, he reflected, looking into the other's waiting face; never mourn his own nature or another's. What was there in that face though, that made one feel safe, condoned? Perhaps it was difference, merely. 'Did I understand you to say,' he whispered, 'that I should not be asked to do anything until after I have been promised a permanent post?'

'That's it, old boy, not a thing. And after that not much. Only to give me access, as the saying is. You agree then?'

'Yes,' said Willey, 'I agree.'

The voice beyond the partition was raised again, abruptly: 'The sea was an absolute peacock blue, and we could see across to Eubea, snow on the peaks, and then we went down to Amphiarion, and there were these huge red anemones among the ruins . . .' Willey and Kennedy stood with their faces not a foot apart, Willey's quite serious, Kennedy's beaming widely.

'Here's my hand on it,' Kennedy said. They shook hands briefly.

'Now then,' Kennedy said. 'Let's see. I want to know this first, when are the envelopes with the questions in officially opened?'

'In the presence of the students, some minutes before the examination begins, by the respective supervisors.'

'You'll be opening one complete lot yourself then?'

'I expect so, yes, certainly.'

'Good, then if I sew the thing up again, it won't matter if I make a crude job of it, because you will be the only one handling that particular batch.'

'That is so, yes.'

'All right then. Now do they put in extra copies or only the exact number?'

'They have always up to now put in several extra copies, in case of emergencies.'

'Are they accounted for at the end?'

'No, the students are allowed to keep the question papers if they want to.'

'We're in the clear then. I can take one copy of each, one single copy, without anyone missing it afterwards.'

'As far as I can see, yes.'

'But that's marvellous,' Kennedy said. In his exhilaration his voice rose. 'It couldn't be better,' he said.

'Sh!' Willey said.

In the silence that fell between them they now heard another voice, an upper-class voice of conscious competence, thickened however, and curdled at this moment by a sort of coy appreciativeness. '*The Towers of Trebizond*,' this voice said. 'A *delicious* book, have you read it? Yes, Rose Macaulay. You know? She travels about Turkey on this *camel*. Yes, yes, a perfectly delightful account of . . .'

'That's Robinson, the assistant director,' Willey said. 'I'd know that voice anywhere,' he added, with an involuntary grimace of disgust. 'He always uses it for showing people around. It's his cultured-but-lively voice. These people have hyphenated attitudes, you know. Crazy-but-nice, that's another favourite.' He and Kennedy exchanged a look of complete sympathy and understanding, similar to the one they had shared over Mackintosh. Willey felt suddenly warm and affectionate towards his fellow conspirator. He was a crook, of course; lacking no doubt in some of the qualities essential if mankind was to progress; but he would never, one felt sure, go in for this awful glibness, he would never call a book *delicious*. *Willey's puritan soul shuddered. It had always seemed a wet-lipped word to him, and applied to a book . . .*

'I think Robinson *is* crazy,' Kennedy said.

Beyond the partitions Robinson was chuckling. 'All about people writing their Turkey books,' he said. 'You know?' A female voice, presumably belonging to one of the visitors, said earnestly, 'But it's a book embodying a *quest*, really, isn't it? It's a religious book, basically.'

'Why do you say that?' Willey asked.

'I met him this morning and he gave me a nasty look and called me by another name. Then when I told him who I was he said there was no such person.'

'What name did he call you by?'

'Some Irish-sounding name. Mulligan, something like that. No. Gilligan, that was it.'

'He asked me once if I'd ever heard of a poet, a contemporary poet, called Gilligan. I said I hadn't.'

Kennedy broke suddenly into a loud laugh. The voices beyond ceased abruptly. 'So that's it,' he said. 'I always had a bad memory for names.'

'What's the matter?' Willey said.

'Never mind.' Kennedy was still laughing. 'Let's get out of here. You'd better go first, we don't want to be seen together too much, do we? You won't regret this, old boy, I promise you.'

Later that afternoon Jennings had a visitor. He had been sitting quite motionless for at least an hour, lost in contemplation of the English verbs of utterance, particularly the four central aspects: 'say', 'tell', 'talk' and 'speak', when Eleni Polimenou was announced.

'This is indeed a pleasure,' he said, coming right round in front of his desk, bowing his head, and rubbing his hands together.

Eleni Polimenou in a large green hat stood magnificently in the centre of the carpet, smiling, or rather stretching her lips, at him. 'Good afternoon, Jennings,' she said. 'This, then, is your *sanctum*.' Something in the tone caused Jennings to recall the biscuit crumbs scattered on his desk, wonder if possibly there was a closeness, a fustiness in the room, scholarly of course, but none the less perhaps oppressive to people of a less bookish turn.

'Yes, yes,' he said. 'You see here the scene of my labours. This is where I spend my days, alas.' He separated his hands and held them palm upwards in the gesture of humility he had learned during his stay in Japan. The quality of the actress's smile did not change. Jennings after a brief pause cleared his throat. 'Won't you sit down?' he said, indicating one of the brown leather armchairs. She surveyed the chair for some moments then sat gracefully on one of its arms, crossing her legs and bringing out from her large handbag a black cigarette holder. Jennings remembered suddenly the lacquered box in one of the drawers of his desk, in which had reposed for as long as he could recall the greater part of fifty cigarettes. 'Cigarette?' he said. He went rapidly back behind his desk. After opening and closing several drawers he found the box. 'Cigarette?' he said, bustling forward again.

'Ah, English cigarettes,' Eleni Polimenou said graciously. But Jennings did not smoke himself and it did not often occur to him to offer them, and the box had been there a long time, so that when she selected one of the cigarettes most of the tobacco, by now reduced to dust, fell out of one end before she could fit the other into the holder. 'Never mind, it is of no importance,' she said, with the same direct and rather ferocious smile, in reply to Jennings' exclamations of distress. She brought a small silver case from her handbag and took out a cigarette.

'I am glad of this opportunity, dear lady,' Jennings said, 'of expressing my admiration for your performances, an admiration which . . .'

'Thank you, thank you,' Miss Polimenou said.

'It is not too much to say that . . .'

'You are too kind.'

'An ornament,' Jennings said, rolling his head slightly as though to dodge further interruptions or disclaimers, 'if I may be permitted to observe, not only to the Greek stage, but to the theatre in our days, and I venture to think . . .'

'I came to thank you, Jennings, for your most kind and invaluable help to me,' Miss Polimenou said, expelling smoke.

Jennings hurried to place an ashtray on the arm of the chair beside her. 'My help?' he said. 'My help, dear lady?'

'Yes, this excellent young man Kennedy whom you sent to me, when I am sure you could ill-afford to spare him. A very gifted teacher.'

There was a prolonged pause during which Jennings looked fixedly at the bust of the dignitary. 'Kennedy, yes,' he said at last. 'We regard him as promising, promising.'

'If you had not so promptly sent him I could not have been ready for the play. Believe me, Jennings, I am grateful. And with Eleni Polimenou gratitude is not silent.'

'It really is too kind of you,' Jennings said. 'I have done so little to deserve . . .'

'But no, you have done much. And now this poor Kennedy, he has some little misunderstanding with the police, he tells me. Something to do with the *permis de travail*. "Why, don't be a silly boy," I told him – he was upset, you know – "Mr Jennings will take care of it," I said.'

Jennings said nothing for the moment, merely fingered the lobe of his left ear with a rather abstracted air. Then he said, 'I do not think I can intervene in a police matter, much as I should like . . .'

'I intend,' Eleni Polimenou said, with great sweetness, 'when I am in London, to insist that your name appears in the acknowledgments. And of course I shall be calling at the headquarters of your organisation, to tell them of the valuable part you are playing in Greece. I shall say that I perceive here an example of what is talked about often but practised rarely, and that is international co-operation in the arts. Mr Kennedy wishes not to be mentioned, he is only concerned to clear up this trouble of his, and, besides, it is the head, the organising brain, which in cases like this should take the credit.'

'Dear lady,' Jennings said. On his face had appeared a visionary gleam. *This* would be something to show those people in London, who had the power to move him about the globe as though he were no more than a coloured flag on a map, that he was no mere itinerant pedagogue but really what one might call the permanent cultural attaché in Athens. He was getting too old now for radical changes. He liked Athens, the climate was excellent, it was handy for home leaves. He knew the language, had a circle of friends here, people who shared his interest in Structures. His five years was nearly up, he had applied for an extension of course, but at this very moment some upstart in London might be saying to some other upstart, 'Let's send old Jennings to Bahrein next, shall we?' or Libya, or Rawalpindi. With whom would he discuss Structures in Rawalpindi? Another three years and he could claim to be regarded as an expert on Greek affairs; a kind of Cultural Ambassador Extraordinary, indispensable, untransferable, consulted by foreign powers. . . . 'Dear lady,' he said again, and his face looked suddenly years younger. 'That would be too kind.'

'It is your due,' she said, with a glance of irrepressible curiosity at his rejuvenated aspect. 'There is one thing, however, that you can do for me if you wish,' she added.

'Yours to command,' Jennings said instantly, making his well-known gesture of abasement.

'It concerns another employee of yours, a young man named Willey. I have discovered by a strange coincidence that he is the nephew of an old friend of mine, a school friend from years ago . . .'

She smiled at Jennings, who fluttered his fingers in remonstrance, and said, 'Oh no, no . . .'

'Yes, I am old, Jennings, now. Still, this young man, I want to do something for him, for the sake of the old friendship. All he seems to want is that his position here should be made permanent. An unromantic fellow, to seek first security, but we cannot change others. So I ask you, if you will, to do that for him.'

'H'm, yes,' Jennings said. His radiance had flickered during this speech, but not gone out entirely. Certainly it would be galling to have to retract his words so soon. He thought for a moment, with deep malignancy, of Willey: lanky, undeferential, perverted. A man who had committed indecent assault. A man, moreover, very useful in his present dependent position. Still, he reflected, Mackintosh could take over those functions. Mackintosh had been taking too much on himself recently, proffering suggestions that should rightly have emanated from him, Jennings. A year or two of proof-reading would do Mackintosh no harm. Then there was the oaf Kennedy. The only way to avoid being thought a complete fool by the police would be to insist on Kennedy's value to the establishment, clamour as it were to be regarded as that disgraceful person's guarantor. . . . For a moment he wavered. Then he pictured himself in some makeshift hut, in Afghanistan perhaps, unable to concentrate on Structures for fear of the Pathan, wielding a fly-swatter all day long, grit in his biscuits . . . He allowed a deep sigh to escape him. 'I will see to it,' he said.

11

The Saturday immediately preceding the examinations was a very busy day for Kennedy. At ten o'clock he was entering Willey's room; the latter had given him a key and left the room vacant by previous arrangement – in fact he had taken Olivia on another house-hunting trip. The question papers were on the table where Willey had left them, in thick brown-paper envelopes cross-stitched along the top with thin but strong white thread. Kennedy had come provided with a razor blade, a needle and some white cotton thread. It did not take him long to open the envelopes, the one marked 'Translation' and the other 'Composition', and abstract from each a single question paper. Sewing up the envelopes took longer, but by half past ten he was finished. They did not look quite the same – the original stitching had been done by machine – but they would do; no one but Willey would be handling them anyway. Locking the door carefully behind him he made his way as quickly as he could back to Kitty's, where the real labour still awaited him: he had to make six copies in longhand of each paper, and one of the translation passages was in Greek, which made things even more difficult.

It took him the best part of four hours to complete the copying. It could not be rushed as his clients would naturally insist on legibility. However, it was finished in the end. He had a quick salami sandwich and a glass of beer at a nearby bar. Then he began on his rounds. He had notified all the people concerned of the probable time of his arrival, so that not much time should be spent over each transaction. Ten minutes at each house, he had calculated; to demonstrate the authenticity of the papers, hand them over, collect the cash, utter a little homily he had prepared in advance, round it off with some appropriate general sentiments, and depart. Altogether a miracle of planning, he told himself as he set off. His straw hat was set at a severe and business-like angle.

Since Mr Logothetis had given him the idea in the first place, it had seemed to Kennedy only fitting to begin with him. Also, the Logothetis apartment was nearest. To his disappointment Veta did not come in answer to his ring, nor did she appear at all during his visit. He was conducted on this occasion not into the *salon*, but into a small room containing bookshelves and a filing cabinet and safe, and a large desk behind which sat Mr Logothetis, dressed in the same way, smiling in the same way. Before him on the desk, and immediately securing Kennedy's whole attention, was a bottle of Scotch, two glasses, a soda-syphon and a large white envelope slightly bulging.

'Ah, Mr Kennedy,' Mr Logothetis said, rising to shake hands. 'I hope I find you well?'

'You do, yes,' Kennedy said. He had bought a newspaper to serve as a holder, inside it reposed the papers, copies and originals. 'Here it is,' he said, patting the newspaper. 'As per ordered.'

'So your friend was able to oblige you?'

'He was, yes.' Kennedy handed over first the two originals, allowed Mr Logothetis to glance through them, and then took out the longhand copies. 'They are exact copies, as you see,' he said.

'Yes, yes.' Mr Logothetis had put on a pair of horn-rimmed glasses, and now compared the passages carefully for some minutes. During the silence Kennedy began quite uncontrollably to sweat. Mr Logothetis looked up finally, smiling. 'I congratulate you,' he said.

'I want the originals back, if you don't mind,' Kennedy said.

'Yes, of course. Now if I had what they call a photographic memory, I shouldn't need to pay you at all, ha, ha, eh, Mr Kennedy?'

'No, ha, ha,' Kennedy said, taking out his handkerchief.

Mr Logothetis took the envelope from the desk and handed it to Kennedy. 'There are ten thousand drachmas there,' he said. 'For your friend.'

'Thank you,' Kennedy said. 'Do you mind if I check?' Rapidly he thumbed through the large, muddy-coloured notes. Ten of them, each worth about twelve pounds. Now that he was actually touching the money an almost incredulous delight possessed him. 'All present and correct,' he said, striving to keep his self-possession.

'And now,' Mr Logothetis said, 'a drink on it. You don't take anything with your whisky, as I remember.'

'No, that's right, nothing.'

Mr Logothetis poured out a full, indeed a brimming, glass for Kennedy, putting much less in his own and filling it with soda.

'To absent friends,' said Mr Logothetis, with the suspicion of a wink.

'Happy landings,' Kennedy said, taking a swallow of his vast drink. The other's harping on friendship verged on the offensive, but he was too pleased with the smoothness of the transaction to care much about this now. It was time for his speech. 'By the way,' he said, 'it would be most unwise of your daughter to take any written material into the examination with her. They are most particular about this, and they would disqualify her at once if it were discovered. She must memorise the answers beforehand.'

'My dear Mr Kennedy, of course.'

'It wouldn't affect me, particularly, you know,' Kennedy said laughingly. 'I've been paid. But it might mean you had wasted your money.'

'Ha, ha, yes, quite so.'

'Also, the less said about this the better, as I'm sure you realise. Discretion is the better part of valour, Mr Logothetis. Warn your daughter against any sort of gloating before or after the examination. Some envious little friend of hers would be sure to report it.'

'We shall maintain a silence of the grave.'

'It only remains for me,' Kennedy said, passing easily to the general sentiments part of the business, 'to wish your daughter every success, in the examination, and in life as a whole.' It occurred to him suddenly that he was falling behind his schedule. He must have been here twenty minutes at least. He finished his whisky in a series of quick gulps. 'Goodbye, then,' he said. 'And all the very best.'

Going down in the lift, he felt dizzy. He regarded his exultant face in the wall mirror. I drank that whisky too fast, he thought.

He took the money out of the envelope, folded it neatly and put it in his hip pocket.

A person called Courcoulakos, who lived in Sina Street, was the next client on his list, a tall spare man with a brigand moustache, who owned an asbestos factory and whose twenty-year-old son, an elegant and vivacious youth, had the distinction of having already failed the examination four times. This man's English was rudimentary and he took much longer to satisfy himself that the copies were genuine. When he was so satisfied, however, he became very expansive, gave Kennedy his money in another large white envelope, patted him on the back.

Kennedy rose to his feet. He was still worried about his schedule. 'I must be pressing on,' he said. 'By the way, it would be most unwise . . .'

'No go yet,' Mr Courcoulakos said. He disappeared for a few moments then returned with a large tumbler of amber-coloured fluid. '*Sigeia*,' he said. He did not seem to be drinking anything himself.

'Cheers!' Kennedy said. It was rum, he decided, slightly diluted with something or other. 'And tell him,' he said rather later, 'not to take anything with him into the examination room, they'll have him out of it quicker than that, you can say what you like about the British, but they've got their standards. They've got their standards. I wouldn't like to see you wasting your money. There's some I wouldn't mind seeing wasting their money, but I don't count you among that number, no. . . .'

'*Efcharisto*,' said Mr Courcoulakos, who seemed to be getting the gist. '*Sigeia!*' he said again.

'And the same to you,' Kennedy said. He squinted at his glass. There was still quite a lot left in it. How long had he been here now? Half an hour? His sense of time was getting blurred.

'Reconsidered my position and yours,' Jennings said. 'Your valuable work through the years . . .' The late afternoon sun slanted through the window, glittered on Jennings' glasses, mellowed the marble sneer of the dignitary. Golden motes swirled slowly. 'Allow me to congratulate you,' Jennings enunciated, averting his head. 'Let us hope for a fruitful collaboration in the years ahead . . .' And so it had been borne in upon Willey that he was being offered a permanent post, permanent, pensionable, carrying annual increments. He had emerged at last, stony-faced, jubilant but frightened too, because his deprivations had constituted a way of life, after all, and now everything was changed, Olivia awaited him, and the rock garden. . . .

Mitsos waited until Kikki and Alexei had gone to bed, then went quietly down and took Alexei's Home Doctor book from the shelf. There was a diagram of the male anatomy on it, in colour, showing the skeletonic structure and the organs beneath. The heart had tentacles of veins, like an octopus. Below the rib cage the knife would have to enter, an upward thrust. He practised upward thrusts some time before the mirror, trying to fight the tendency to close his eyes at the last moment. At about half past four he replaced the book, wrapped the knife loosely in a table napkin, put it inside his jacket with the point tucked into the top of his trousers, and left the house quietly.

'No, no, not in that way,' Mr Andronakis said. '*Aspro kato*.'
   'What the hell does that mean?' Kennedy said. This was his fourth visit, he had no idea what time it was, and didn't care any longer. His hat was on the back of his head, and the top button of his shirt had come off. His hip pocket bulged with money.
   '*Aspro kato* means white bottom,' Mr Andronakis said.
   'In that case I'm all for it,' said Kennedy, whose behaviour was steadily deteriorating. 'But what has it got to do with ouzo, that is the point at issue, that is the point I am trying to get over to you. This is ouzo, isn't it? *Ouzo*.'
   '*Malista*.'
   'Well then,' Kennedy said. 'Well then.' Behind them on the balcony the eccentric canary broke suddenly into fervent song.
   'Sing, sing for Mr Kennedy,' said Andronakis. 'No, you not understand. When we are drinking ouzo and I say *aspro kato*, you must drink all at one time, not putting glass two, three times or more to your face.'
   'Right,' said Kennedy. '*Aspro kato* then.' He drank the remaining ouzo in his glass.

'No, no,' Mr Andronakis said. 'We must do it again. The glasses must be full up.'

'*Jesus*,' Kennedy said. 'Listen,' he said slowly and carefully, 'don't take any papers into the examination or you will be disqualified.'

'What means "disqualified"?'

Kennedy passed his tongue over his lips. 'You will be out on your arse,' he said. 'You will be given the old boot. Keep it all up here, Mr Andronakis.' He tapped his right temple with a forefinger, then paused for a moment, looking solemnly at Andronakis, trying to remember the things that remained to be said. 'Don't tell a bloody soul,' he said, 'and it only remains for me to wish . . .'

'Understood perfect,' Mr Andronakis said. 'The future is forward. *Aspro kato.*'

'*Aspro kato.*'

From this point onwards the afternoon became disorderly, fragmented; his joy was constant, however, his sense of the growing bulge of drachmas at his hip. In the street, clutching his newspaper and the few remaining question papers that were folded inside it, he swayed a little, and sang 'Speed Bonny Boat' quietly to himself. Attempting to find a short cut to Pattission Street where his fifth client lived, he lost himself among narrow cobbled streets. At one point he fell full length, his hat rolled off and his papers were scattered. He was helped to his feet and dusted down by a greengrocer and his papers were gathered up again by several competitive children, getting somewhat crumpled in the process. Thereafter he travelled by taxi. Dranas, whom he had left to last, received the most soiled and damaged copies, but did not seem to mind. He offered to make coffee, but this Kennedy refused with hauteur.

By six o'clock it was finished; the papers were all distributed; he had forty-five thousand drachmas in thousand-drachma notes in his pocket. He took a taxi back to Kitty's, knowing through his drunkenness that the events of the afternoon had changed him, magnified him, enlarged his sense of his own potential, like a first experience of love. After such a *coup* he could never be the same again. Dazzling prospects opened up before him. There was a career in it. Millions of people wanted to learn English. All over the globe they were striving to obtain certificates and diplomas, everywhere over the face of the globe there would be Cultural Centres, running examinations, following more or less the same system. He could make a packet wherever he went, from Bombay to Brisbane . . . No, not Brisbane, they spoke a sort of English there, but certainly far-flung, he told himself sagely. Certainly far-flung. Now that he knew the ropes he would be able to plan more elaborately, extend the scale of his operations. Widen his net. You are made, old boy, he told himself. Absolutely made. All tax-free too.

He did not want to be alone just now in the first flush of his success, so he went directly to Thorne's room where he found, in addition to Thorne, Simpson and an enormous smiling blonde girl. Simpson was holding a bottle of cognac, two-thirds empty. When he saw Kennedy he raised the bottle high in the air. His face was damp, and he was continuously stiffening and relaxing his upper lip, which kept his nostrils in perpetual motion. 'Compensation!' he shouted. 'I got my compensation for the easel. Six thousand drachmas, paid on the nail.'

'There really was an easel then,' Kennedy said. 'How about a drop out of that bottle?' He was somewhat put out. Simpson had not exactly stolen his thunder, since he could not make his own success public; but he did not care that they should be co-beneficiaries of the gods this evening.

Simpson said, 'I want you to meet Miss Bodilsen. Miss Inge Bodilsen.' The girl smiled at him in silence. Her eyes were ox-like, enormous. 'From Scandinavia,' Simpson said, smiling meaningfully at Kennedy.

'How do you do?' Kennedy said. He was having some difficulty in focussing. The correct thing to say came to him suddenly. 'Mr Simpson has talked a lot about you,' he said.

'Too bloody true,' Simpson said.

'Have you got any more glasses, Roland?' Kennedy said to Thorne. 'Why don't you get one for yourself? It's quite an occasion, Simpson getting his money.'

'You look as though you'd had a few already,' Thorne said. 'Your suit is all dusty, too. All right,' he added surprisingly, 'I *will* have a drink.' He got the glasses and Simpson filled them up, which left the bottle nearly empty.

'Don't worry,' Simpson said, 'I have two more bottles.'

'Are you staying in Greece for long?' Kennedy said to Miss Bodilsen, with a glazed courtliness of manner.

Miss Bodilsen smiled once more. She had very strong white teeth. 'Thank you very much,' she said. 'All here very good peoples.'

'Have another drink, Roland,' Kennedy said, giving her up abruptly. 'I'm bloody well going to.'

'Yes,' Thorne said. 'I *will* have another.' His face was quite flushed. He approached Kennedy and said in low tones, 'Do you think she's suitable? He's going to Denmark with her, now that he's got his money. I knew he'd go, of course, I mean I knew he'd go away. He doesn't seem to me to *respect* her at all. Surely there must be *respect*.'

'Good God, I don't know,' Kennedy said. 'Do you think she respects *him*? Look at him now.' Simpson had begun to execute a sort of rubbery Charleston. 'Simpson will end up in the gutter anyway,' Kennedy said. 'He might as well get as much as he can now.'

Thorne looked affronted. 'That's my tie you're wearing, by the way,' he said coldly.

Kennedy broke into loud laughter. 'So it is,' he said. He raised his hand to his neck with a wide clumsy gesture and pulled the tie loose. He had a sudden dazed realisation, the first time his new wealth had taken concrete form in his mind, of the rows of resplendent ties he could afford to buy now. 'Here you are,' he said, and looped the tie round Thorne's neck.

'I say, steady on!' Thorne said. 'You don't care, do you?'

At this moment the bell rang and when Thorne opened the door there was Willey. He hovered at the threshold a few moments blinking somewhat affrightedly at the cavorting Simpson who had now begun to sing 'Beautiful, Beautiful Copenhagen', using the empty brandy bottle in an obscene phallic way behind Miss Bodilsen's back. 'You weren't in your room,' he said to Kennedy, 'and I heard these voices. . . . Can I have a word with you?'

'Come in, come in,' shouted Kennedy. 'My comrade-in-arms,' he said to Miss Bodilsen, who smiled and said: 'Thank you very much.'

'Everything went off all right then?' Willey muttered to Kennedy.

'Like a bloody dream. Any developments your end?'

'Yes,' Willey said. 'I signed the contract this afternoon.' He looked into the other's sweating face, fixed now in a broad ecstatic smile, and thought how strange it was that there should be anything like complicity between himself and this person.

'Congratulations, old boy,' Kennedy said. 'You let me get at the papers before any definite offer was made to you. I'll never forget that.'

'That's all right.' Once he had agreed it had ceased to matter whether he got anything in return. Useless to tell Kennedy that, of course.

'My friend Willey,' Kennedy said loudly to everyone in the room, 'has just had a bit of good luck, I mean a bit of good news. He has made an upward step in his career. I think we should congratulate him in the traditional way.' He stood for a moment looking bemusedly round the room, shirt-front gaping widely open, fair hair falling into his eyes. Then in a slow and raucous voice he began to sing 'For He's a Jolly Good Fellow'. Simpson, abandoning his by-play with the bottle, joined in almost immediately and after a few moments Thorne too, in a surprisingly tuneful tenor. The three men sang loudly but with serious expressions, looking steadily at Willey; and the elemental affirmation of the chorus gave them all for the moment a sort of sincerity, which Willey found unexpectedly moving.

He was attempting to sustain his smile of acknowledgment, and they were entering on the chorus for the third time, when a sharp knock was heard on the door, and a moment later the door was opened and Kitty's fleshy but nobly curving nose appeared, and her Byzantine eyes, filled now with accusatory fire. What was the reason, she wanted to know of Mr Thorne, for all this *tapage*? She had always thought of the English as a people *sérieux*. Now other guests were complaining. And in Mr Thorne's room too, he who had always comported himself so well in the past. . . . Kitty's abundant form quivered, beneath the pink flannel, with the agitation of her feelings.

'We were just having a little drink,' Kennedy said. He adjusted his shirt hastily and did his best to reduce his smile to sober dimensions. He liked Kitty. Her perpetual quest for propriety appealed for some reason to his imagination. He had an idea she might have whored it a bit in the past. 'We were celebrating the good fortune of our friend here,' he said. 'He has obtained a *bonne situation* in Athens. He is a *professeur*.'

'Ah,' Kitty said, mollified immediately by this presence of a professional man in her house. A certain calm descended on her flesh. '*Soyez le bienvenu*,' she said. 'I was myself at the French School in Constantinople. *Chez les soeurs*, you understand.'

'As a matter of fact,' Kennedy said, 'we were just on the point of inviting you to join us in a drink. *Sans façon*, you know.'

'It is not with me a *habitude*,' Kitty said, 'but on this special occasion . . .' She smiled richly at Willey.

'When I was young,' she said, halfway through her second glass, 'I had a voice *très forte*. When I sang I could clearly be heard at great distances. Even now . . .' She raised her head and sang *mi – mi – mi* in a somewhat clotted but still powerful contralto. 'You see?' she said. '*Ça pénètre, n'est ce pas?*'

'It does indeed,' said Willey, in whom the cognac was effecting a perceptible thaw of reserve. 'An extremely powerful voice,' he said, to no one in particular.

Thereafter they passed on to other things, but as she was coming to the end of her third glass Kitty reverted to the topic. 'This gift,' she said, 'was of use to me during the war. I was returning to Greece on a passenger ship when we were attacked near Rhodos by Italian planes. I saw the first plane diving towards us, monsieur. I knew he was about to release his bombs. I lifted my head and sang up to the aeroplane in the sky.' Kitty raised her head and flung wide her arms in a gesture of supplication. Sounds of astounding volume broke from her open mouth: '*Perche, perche, signore? Siamo Italiani, Italiani!*' In the hush that followed she looked from face to face, her bosom heaving slightly. 'They heard and believed, those pilots,' she said. 'The planes departed. The lives of all were saved.'

'That is amazing, truly amazing,' Willey said.

Kennedy frowned at Simpson, who had begun obscenely wielding the bottle again, unnoticed as yet by Kitty. 'There's one thing I would like to know,' he said. 'And that is, why was the man who had my room given the boot? Why was he given notice, I mean? What did he *do*?'

Kitty paused a long time before replying to this. She finished the rest of the brandy in her glass. 'It is a painful topic,' she said at last. Then she seemed to come to a decision. She drew closer to Kennedy and said in a rapid whisper, '*Le scélérat, il a pissé au dessus du balcon.*'

'Good God!' Kennedy said. 'In full view?'

'Ah, no, moniseur, there is the baseness of it. He stood within his room and from there he directed his *sale urine*. Over the top. And an acquaintance of mine, an elderly lady who makes lampshades, who was passing at the time, had her head wetted by it.' The recollection of this horror had given Kitty the trembles again. 'Of course,' she said, 'I gave him notice *sur le champ*.'

'I should think so,' Kennedy said, with a soothing intention, but Kitty had distressed herself, and after a few moments took leave of them.

Willey followed soon after. 'Olivia is expecting me,' he said.

'The best of British luck!' Kennedy called after him, 'to you and yours.'

Outside it was very dark. Willey decided to walk back, to clear his head. The brandy and the noise had given him an illusion of solidarity with those people, but this rapidly faded as he walked. He thought again of the chorus they had sung for him. Quite ridiculous, of course, but at the time ... Very primitive thing, altogether, singing. He remembered student songs full of ingenious anatomical reference, and other, jollier songs of remote camping holidays. All sexual, of course – young men reminding one another of their intention to undo the whole female population. Only the young could sing in just that way, before they had understood how few women they were ever going to have, when reciprocity could still be taken for granted, and the permanence of their own desires. ... Young girls too did not know their limits, that was what made them so touching, so poignant. There was a time in a young girl's life when she felt herself to have a complete licence. Merely by moving her limbs they assaulted the senses, knowingly, innocently ... inviting what was still unimaginable.... Once, one Easter, when he had already been teaching some years, he had gone on a solitary walking tour through the Quantock Hills. He had come into the outskirts of Taunton in the early evening, a golden evening, the first really warm weather of the year. His memory had not retained the sense of any buildings, only a long straight avenue planted on either side with some sort of miniature trees with slender, pointed leaves, rowan trees perhaps. A light breeze stirred the narrow leaves continuously and at intervals along the avenue, like something precious and ephemeral brought out by the sudden warmth, groups of young girls, talking and laughing. No buildings, no traffic, no other sound. Only the long avenue, dead straight, the trembling leaves, the clusters of girls like flowers on the pavement, in light cotton dresses, summer dresses, for the first time in the year probably, and not yet accustomed to this thin covering, after the coddling wools of winter.... And just as the leaves on the trees were in constant agitation, the girls themselves were never still, they were chattering and laughing, they were looking at themselves, raising arms or legs to be inspected, sometimes revolving their bodies quickly, causing their skirts to swirl briefly and subside, occasionally clutching themselves in a sort of embrace as though in self-protection against the mild air, the sunshine, the promise of the spring. Helplessly, helplessly, in every movement and gesture they invited some violation....

Willey, as though looking down a long tunnel at some framed image at the other end, saw again the trees, the sunshine the laughing groups. He had passed by awkward, ungainly in his heavy walking shoes, of no account to them, containing his impure admiration; and the avenue had closed behind him like a track in water or sand, impossible to find again, except in memory.... Quite suddenly, as he walked steadily on through the darkness, Willey felt his eyes filling with tears.

'Did you hear that?' Kennedy said to Simpson. 'He pissed right over the balcony railing. Standing inside the room. It must be a good four feet. And then he'd have to clear the railing too. I wish I'd known him.'

'I think it's disgusting,' Thorne said.

'That's as may be,' Kennedy said. The look of ecstasy had returned to his face. 'I'm going out now,' he added. 'I have to see a man about a dog.' He recovered the straw hat which had fallen to the floor and been somewhat trampled during Simpson's dance.

He met Veta, as he had arranged, at the corner of Lysistratus Street. On the way there he found himself inclined to stagger, as much from fatigue as drunkenness: it had been an exciting day and he had eaten little. He had planned to take Veta into the Plaka. They would have supper at a *taverna*, during which, at an appropriate moment, and with a few well-chosen words he would hand over the drachmas.

'*Ça va?*' Veta said. She was chewing again.

'*Ça* bloody *va* all right,' Kennedy said.

They walked down Lysistratus Street, Kennedy steadying himself by putting an arm over Veta's shoulder.

'I am going to give you that money tonight,' he said. 'You will see that Kennedy is a man of his word.' He took a pace away from her and attempted to tap himself on the chest, but staggered badly. Veta took his arm and held him steady. She was very strong. She looked for a moment, intently, at where his breast pocket would be, below the hairy tweed.

'How do you like my hat, by the way?' Kennedy said.

'Please, Bry-an,' she said, 'give me the money now.'

'Oh no,' he said. 'First things first. Let's do the thing properly.' He was determined to have his little ceremony. 'I'm going to buy a couple of suits,' he said. 'First thing in the morning.'

'It is with you, the money?'

'Oh yes.'

She looked sideways at him for a long moment, as though trying again to gauge something about him, the degree of his drunkenness or his veracity. Then her substantial shoulders moved in a slight shrug. 'Very well,' she said. She continued to support him into the narrower and darker streets of the Plaka.

Mitsos waited at the corner of the square. The knife was inside his jacket, pressed against his side. It was half past nine. He had been standing there for two hours. He had watched George watering his flowers, watched him settle down with his newspaper, seen the kiosk shuttered and locked. Several people had passed through the square, most of them entering the *taverna*, but it was very dark where he was standing and he did not think he had been noticed. Certainly no one could have seen his face. He had about twenty minutes left if he was going to kill George this evening – the other was very regular in his domestic habits in spite of his variable days, and always went indoors a few minutes before ten, usually remaining there, but occasionally re-emerging and making his way to a brighter and more populous square, where he sat in a certain café playing *tric-trac* for a couple of hours. Mitsos had no thoughts except an awareness of the evening – the coolness, the dark, his own body motionless there, waiting; not lonely, no longer lonely, because his intention allied him with all the things that waited for night with purpose . . .

George had abandoned his belt tonight and was wearing narrow red braces. Even at this distance it could be seen how grateful his corpulence was for the coolness. Ten minutes or so. Suddenly Mitsos knew that he was going to do it tonight. He reviewed in these moments the long illness his life had been since he had first seen George in the Cathedral Square. The sight of that face had stricken him. Diseased thus, as though seeking medicaments, he had followed this man about the city, for how long now? Past monuments, through streets and squares that repeated themselves, were always the same squares and monuments and streets, one scene endlessly reiterated against which George, the carrier, stood or walked and he, plague-spotted, watched and followed. Tonight would begin his convalescence, restore the city's multiplicity. He slipped his hand inside his jacket, rested it on the handle of the knife. He felt no doubt, as though the responsibility for the decision was not his, but someone's much wiser. At the last moment it occurred to him to wonder briefly whether George was really the same man, but of course that didn't matter now. . . . He took a few steps forward, passed under the light at the corner of the square, entered the alley.

And as he did so a voice from somewhere in the darkness

behind him, quite close, an English voice, a voice he knew, shouted, 'Hey there, old boy, a word in your ear.' He saw George look up from his paper, raise his spectacles over his eyes to peer down the alley. He wheeled, passed once more under the light, which there was no avoiding and walked quickly away into the darkness at the side of the square.

'No you don't!' Kennedy shouted. 'Oh no you don't!'

If it had not been for the altercation over the rose Kennedy and Veta would have passed some minutes earlier and then Mitsos, still standing in the dark, would not have been seen. They had been walking quite at random through the streets, looking for a promising restaurant. Gradually, imperceptibly, they had found themselves in a less-frequented district, where the streets were darker and narrower, passers-by rare. A gypsy girl had stopped them, holding out a white rose. Ten drachmas she wanted for it. A rose is a thing beyond price, she had contrived to suggest merely by the gesture of offering it, and besides to lovers money shouldn't matter. Her face worked while she cajoled them, with supplicatory yet insolent grimaces, the facial equivalent of a whine. Kennedy would have paid at once, what was ten drachmas to him now? But Veta had been outraged by the price, ten drachmas for a single rose. In the end she got it for seven, and pinned it to the front of her dress. Then they had reached this square, seen the taverna with caged birds on the wall. 'Looks a bit scruffy,' Kennedy had said. 'But I'm too hungry to care.'

And at this precise moment he had seen the Greek chap pass under the lamp at the entrance to the alley, start off down the alley, then turn and scuttle away into the dark. 'No you don't,' he said again. He plunged into the darkness. He could see Mitsos' face and his white shirt-front. By going directly across to the wall he was able to intercept Mitsos, get in his way. Even then the other would have rushed past him, but Kennedy seized his arm, forced him to stop. 'You're always trying to dodge me,' he said, breathing heavily. 'Aren't you? Did you think I was going to ask you for money again?'

'Take your hand from my arm,' Mitsos said.

'A man with my assets,' Kennedy said, keeping a tight hold on the other. 'What were you up to in the alley?'

'I was simply passing by,' Mitsos said, beginning to tremble.

'Balls,' Kennedy said thickly. 'That's a lot of balls.'

'Let me go,' Mitsos said, 'you interfering fool.' He thought of George, folding up his paper now, preparing to go indoors. Rage rose within him. He saw in the darkness the broad outline of the other's face surmounted by the hat; smelled the liquor on his breath. 'You're drunk,' he said.

This simple truth enraged Kennedy. 'Who are you calling names?' he said. 'Here, let's have a look at your face under the light.' He began tugging at Mitsos, pulling him towards the lamp at the entrance to the alley. Mitsos felt himself drawn helplessly several paces forward. Kennedy was holding the upper part of his left arm, in a painful grip that threatened at any moment to unclamp it from his body. Behind him Veta was saying something over and over in a frightened voice, but Kennedy took no notice. He was intent. Some innate brutality had been roused in him by the other's slightness, his lack of muscular power. Through the mists of drunkenness he groped for further pretexts.

'You said Athens was a *village*,' he said. 'If Athens is a bloody village, why haven't I come across Mrs Pouris, tell me that?' He pulled Mitsos closer towards the lamp. 'Tell me that,' he repeated. They were almost under the light now. Mitsos felt his arm being forced away from his side, the knife slipping down. He thrust his right hand under his jacket and grasped the handle. 'Come on, let's have a look at you,' Kennedy said, still tugging. 'And don't tell me you don't know who Mrs Pouris is, we were on the same . . .' His last sensations were over too quickly for him to register them fully. He saw Mitsos' right hand emerge, saw the gleam of metal as the blade was lowered quickly, grabbed at the other's wrist and missed, felt a sudden violent blow under his ribs. There was the intimation of a terrible, an irreparable, hurt done to him, but no pain. He clutched Mitsos a moment longer, then the night darkened and he fell down at the other's feet. He seemed to settle himself for a moment on the pavement with a slow writhing movement, as though seeking some ease for his limbs. This ceased, and he did not move again.

Mitsos stood for perhaps ten seconds looking down at the man who had taken George's place. The girl was strangely silent, but of course that was right, before such an appalling mistake no sound could possibly be uttered, there was no response in the human register. He looked at her indifferently for a moment, then back to Kennedy's body. Someone would be coming, he should go away as quickly as possible. He should take the knife and go. But he could not believe there was any urgency in this now. He felt immune. The complete accuracy of that blind blow implied an intention beyond his own. He stooped over Kennedy with the idea of taking out the knife, but one of the other's hands was curled loosely round the handle. Something helpless and childlike in the curl of those large blunt fingers which would never grasp again suddenly horrified Mitsos. This was clay now, however marvellously moulded. He straightened himself quickly and turned and walked away into the darkness, walking faster and faster, but without purpose, for, of course, he had nowhere to go now, nothing to do.

Veta watched him walk away. In spite of her shock and terror, a certain process of reasoning was going on in her mind. Watching that writhe on the pavement, and the stillness after it, she had known that Kennedy was dead, and the knowledge had kept her silent. Soon someone would come and find Bry-an lying there. They would get the police, and she would say what had happened, and perhaps they would catch the man. In that case, all Bry-an's things would be taken and sent to England to his nearest relative. She would get nothing. But there was this promise he had made to her, which no one would ever believe. He had promised her fifty gold pounds. Nothing else much in their brief acquaintance mattered. Her virginity any doctor could restore for a hundred drachmas, sew up the hymen, so that her husband could shed a little blood, be satisfied. But fifty gold pounds would take years to get. And she would soon be twenty-one. . . .

Kennedy lay on his back, legs splayed out in an attitude of dreadful ease. His eyes were not open but not completely closed either, the lamplight elicited a gleam from below the lids. One hand rested loosely round the protruding handle of the blade, the other was outstretched, palm upwards. Several feet away the straw hat had come to rest, upturned on the pavement, as though inviting contributions while its owner slept.

Veta came to the only possible conclusion. Her eyes were dry now. She leaned over him very carefully, slipped her hand inside the jacket and took out the wallet. She felt its bulkiness in her palm. She had intended to count it out, the sum due to her, but now that she was actually holding the wallet a panic filled her to get away. They would say she was stealing. She lowered herself still further and kissed Kennedy on his forehead. Then she rose and began to walk rapidly back the way they had come, holding in both trembling hands Kennedy's glowing testimonials, while slowly blood from his wound welled up round the plug of the knife-handle, ran over the curve of his belly and flank and stained the outer edges of the thick bundle of notes in his hip pocket.